THE
MIND
TRAVELLERS

BOOK One: Zed & Olaria

Phillip Boas

Printed in Australia

First Printing: May 2021

Shawline Publishing Group Pty Ltd
www.shawlinepublishing.com.au

Paperback ISBN- 9781922444950

Ebook ISBN- 9781922444967

A work of Utopian Science Fiction and Fantasy.

These 5 books collectively represent a 21st century conceptual and survival allegory.

These books are dedicated to two very different people.

First to my wife, partner, lover over many decades, Madeleine, who has tolerated thousands of hours of me vanishing into my study to sit in front of a computer.

Second is to the nearly two thousand participants in my workshops and participants in individual and group therapy sessions who helped hone my skills and build many lasting and satisfying relationships.

Another Solar System, Another Planet, Life.

Imagine you are in a room.

Everyone in that room can know everything that you and all the others are thinking and feeling all the time.

Yet, everyone chooses to stay.

Might this not be, emotionally, the safest place in the world? PJB

List of Contents:

Phillip Boas

To The Reader:

Follow the adventures of Dr Zed Eko, the crew PsycHologist of the Explorer Class Spaceship, Sunstreamer. His story begins here in Book 1 of The Mind Travellers. Then, through his eyes, follow his journey in books 2 through 5. His adventures eschew duplicity, lies, deceits and subterfuge. He deals with problems directly, openly, honestly and without fear. His journey first involves two worlds. Enjoy the Mind Traveller Series and the adventures of its hero.

Phillip Boas

PROLOGUE
Moon Base One (2095)

No human ear heard the scream of the decelerating positioning rockets as they died. Deep Space Alpha Probe26 settled smoothly into moon orbit broadcasting on all Space Fleet Command primary frequencies,

"DSAP26 is home".

The little probe had travelled many thousands of light years since its launch in 2091. Its job nearly done. It found SFC's decoding frequency and began its final act, dumping the data from its maxed-out memory storage to its Moon-base parent unit. It was not a sentient unit. Consequently, it had no idea of the significance of the data it was now uploading.

Of all the DSAP's, only DSAP12 had been as successful. It had returned with data on a habitable planet in a distant galaxy. That planet now supported a colony of a million young humans. Mankind now had a second home. Forty-five minutes later, DSAP26 completed its upload and the probe fully shut down. It would probably never be used again. The data, however, was exciting. It had found another possibly habitable planet it had codenamed Omega5Z3, in a system so far unknown to Astronav, SFC's Astronomy/Navigation research unit.

Deep in the huge, domed Moon base One facility of Space Fleet Command the senior decryption staffer for the Probe project breathed a sigh of relief. Potentially habitable planets meant budget security.

She looked carefully at the two data anomalies the computers had found. The planet, although seemingly perfect in every way, lacked any sign of animal life. Odd, but not a strong negative. She made a note on the file. The other oddity was more difficult to explain. An area approximately the size of the entire North American continent was blank. Absolutely no data on it whatsoever. As if someone had wiped that part of the planet off with a magic eraser.

The decryption staffer requested a check of the probe's circuits, electronics and scanners, but no damage or malfunction of any kind showed up. So, she noted the two anomalies and passed the records to Space Fleet Central Intelligence, who, after a brief scan, passed them on to the Deep Space Exploration Unit.

Sunstreamer, SFC's newest Explorer vessel was allocated the exploration role and whilst the unusual aspects of the probe's data had been the subject of extensive speculation, most of it had been fruitless.

If, however, Omega5Z3 was what it seemed, no time should be wasted getting a human team there.

On 25 September 2096, Sunstreamer was ready to depart Moon Base One to undertake the exploration. Sunstreamer was a truly amazing craft, a perfect sphere, built to be run by a small human crew and three Quantum Computers it could travel at close to the speed of light. The Spacecraft was almost sentient. The crew were multinational, the mission had no military objectives so Sunstreamer carried no Space Weapons System, no weapons of any kind.

CHAPTER – 1
New Life

I follow orders because I feel obliged to do so. My shuttle is about to dock in the entry port of the Explorer Spacecraft Sunstreamer, presently in moon orbit. Lord knows I do not really want to be going on this mission. I have my requisite space hours for this year and for absolutely no good reason I don't want my thirty-eighth birthday to happen over a planet no one has ever seen, in a Solar system, so far away, it will take three days of travel at near light speed to get there and require us to transit 3 wormholes. So, it has to be billions of miles or light years away. I feel like a 10-year-old stamping his feet. Brilliant.

'We are docked at Sunstreamer's entry port, Dr Eko.'

It always irritates me that the damned Transit talks to me. I know where we are, I heard us connect to Sunstreamer's systems, anyway I issued its orders! My name is Zed Eko, and I am the crew Psych. And yes, I am feeling touchy today. I ought to be feeling comfortable and safe. It's true, the crew here are the cream of the Explorer group, I have been working with them for the three months of pre-mission training. The Captain John Washington is a giant of a man, experienced but gentle, solid, smart and devoted to his crew. I heft my flight bag and head through the triple shells of the circular Spacecraft, dropping my bag into its allotted space before entering the flight deck. It would automatically be delivered to my sleeping quarters.

'Reporting in Captain.'

'Welcome aboard Dr Eko.'

I was the last aboard, always; I was the least relevant to pre-flight prep. I walked to my seat, clipped my flight communication system on and blinked in the crew frequency. I Let the seat harness attach itself then turned to Raille Korzyst, my only real friend and smiled a one-sided smile which he acknowledged then I sat back in my seat and waited.

'Orbital escape point and track logged in Captain.'

Astronavigators were amongst the elite of the Space Fleet, and Tanzin Artez was one of the top two in the world. She smoothed a hand over her shoulder length red hair, quickly smoothing the fly-always back into her ponytail. She was petite and attractive and when she spoke it was quietly but with authority.

The Captain looked up at the right-hand screen down which equations and data flowed in an unbroken stream and saw the background of the screen change to a soft green, showing agreement with all of Tanzin's computations. The navigation system was set and the computers, there were three quantum computers that actually ran us, the Spaceship itself and the Energy shields that protected us from just about everything. For ease of access, they had names and Lotus was available for the exclusive use of the Astronavigator. I was not a novice, but always as we began our departure I felt the stirrings of anxiety; the slight pressure increase on my back as we departed moon orbit, and I wondered, for just a moment, would I live to feel the slight pressure decrease that would signal my safe return in 11 days.

I made a scan around the Flight Deck then settled back to await our entry into the first of three wormholes, about nine or ten hours away, after that we would be no longer able to communicate with Earth until we exited this wormhole on our return.

Time is a distorted experience in space travel. I realised the three days had passed when I heard Tanzin's voice, clear and strong.

'Orbit in 120 seconds, Captain.'

On the Holo screens the planet did not look that close but no one doubted the Astronavigator's calculations. 120 seconds meant exactly 2 minutes.

About a minute later, the deep, powerful hum of the engines lessened as the image of the planet grew on our screens. It was a beautiful blue planet, surprisingly like earth, except, in a totally unknown Solar System.

Was this planet suitable for human settlement? This was the overarching mission parameter.

The determination could actually have been made by the 3 quantum computers. Despite that, SFC (Space Fleet Command) expected the computer scans to be confirmed by 'On Planet' verification - by people! Hence the specialised eight-person crew.

The Captain spoke to Yuri, the name given to the computer set aside primarily for his and the First Officer's use. 'Immediately our orbit is stable commence a full spectrum planetary scan.'

We could see right to the planet's surface. No buildings, no animals. It looked strangely bare. Some of the greenery looked like gardens that ought to be around houses. But there was nothing. I heard Raille our Vegetation Analyst mutter, 'That's just wrong.'

Several of the crew swung round to look at him.

But the Captain had heard. 'What exactly is wrong Raille?'

When the Vegetation Analyst says something is wrong, it is likely something is wrong. But what, exactly?

'Well skipper, the vegetation says the planet is inhabited, however, the images and the data from DSAP21 say it's not. Something's wrong.'

'Raille, freeze one of the images that is disturbing you.'

His hand moved to follow the Captain's instruction when a voice came over every speaker on the Flight Deck, and it was speaking in English.

'Hello people from the Planet Earth, we are Olarians and we are currently...' she paused, 'engaged in assimilating your language. Please wait just a moment.'

Thirty seconds ticked by without any member of the crew moving or speaking a word.

'Hello again, people of Earth. We believe we have mastered sufficient of your English Language to speak with you. Does what I have said make sense?'

There was a chilling stillness on the Flight Deck. No one knew where to look and initially, no one spoke. I turned slowly to look at each member of the crew. The Captain made no effort to hide his frown. I knew that expression. The Skipper had no idea what to do next. I was not sure anyone could really have known.

Everyone was staring at the speakers. Every astronaut in history had some fantasy about alien life. Now, it seemed, Sunstreamer had hit the jackpot. I could sense the Captain's tension, saw him quickly regain his equilibrium, take a slow breath and respond in a deep voice edged with caution.

'Hello, yes we understand, my name is John Washington, Captain of this vessel, the Explorer Spacecraft Sunstreamer. Who are you? From what vessel?'

The Captain stared at the nearest speaker. Not, I thought, our Captain's most verbally astute moment. Then the Captain smiled, as if the irony in this situation had dawned upon him. His was an exploratory mission. Well, he mused, this was certainly bloody-well exploratory!

'Captain, with your permission a colleague and I will come aboard, is that acceptable?'

Every member of the crew looked at the Captain and I knew he was feeling the weight of their expectations. The Captain was ultimately responsible for everyone on this crew, and I knew he took that responsibility seriously. We were in orbit; the computers restated their first report,

<<<No sightings of anything resembling another Spaceship>>>

I could see the expression on John's face. His eyebrows were furrowed. Where the hell were these people coming from, and how could they come aboard? The Captain knew this team: some had worked previous missions with him. For the others, John and I had worked with them for three months during pre-mission preparation. We had also studied their files until each was as known as we could manage. I felt confident none of them had come this far to miss what was likely to be an unbelievable discovery, in case these people were actually from the planet below and not from another space vehicle.

'If you are able to do so, please do.'

An instant later, two figures appeared in front of the Holo screens that formed the forward area of the Flight Deck. The crew stared. Ghia, the Biometrics Officer grabbed the arms of her seat nearly hard enough to crush them and I hit the release on my safety harness and came to my feet as did the rest of the crew. No one was frozen, but neither did anyone appear to know what exactly they should do next. The logical response would have been for us to draw sidearms, that being the normal human response from military-trained personnel being surprised by unknown intruders, however, none of us was carrying sidearms on this mission and at this moment I was imagining the Captain felt somewhat pissed about that, at least if we had been armed, we could have felt in some kind of equitable relationship on the flight deck of our own spaceship.

The two, apparently a man and a woman, were dressed in beautifully coloured clothing which seemed to be alive, the patterns and colours slowly changing. They appeared to be carrying no weapons.

The smaller of the two figures, a woman, spoke in almost fluent English with a very pleasant and slightly lilting accent.

'Please allow me to introduce us. My name is Olaria and my colleague is Jald.'

The words had been spoken out loud, but I had also heard them in my head, if that makes any sense. Olaria looked to be in her thirties, as did Jald. She was in every visible way human looking. She had shoulder length straight black hair, large, greenish eyes, her ears were not fully visible but appeared much like human ears and she possessed a trim well-proportioned figure, around 5'6" tall, in fact, I found myself thinking, she could have been an attractive human woman from any street on Earth. Her skin was a pleasant, healthy tanned brown. She had small hands. Clothing aside, she could have been taken for a member of the crew.

Jald, her male companion appeared to be a similar age, height and build to me, around 5'10-11", slender but strongly built, his eyes were not a dark brown but a hazy grey-green, and his hair was longish, curly, untidy by human standards, but he too was an interesting healthy-looking man. I shook my head. This had to be a figment of my imagination. But the two stood looking at us, and if this was my imagination, then all of us were part of it.

I tried to think of an appropriate word for how I was feeling. Surreal, dreamlike, I was thinking but excited and disturbed was probably closer to how I was feeling. How could they possibly have just appeared on the Flight Deck of our orbiting spacecraft?

I watched the woman Olaria. I was pretty sure she was aware of our questions and appeared to know it was not only, how, occupying probably everyone's stunned minds.

'You could be human. You look incredibly like us!'

I smiled. Ghia, apart from being the Biometrics Officer, was also three months pregnant to Gerard the Sunstreamer's Engineering Officer and I could feel her unabashed embarrassment as soon as the words were out of her mouth. 'Good Lord.' Everyone heard her mutter under her breath, 'It seems being pregnant is playing havoc with my manners.'

Olaria and Jald, however, simply smiled. Then, Olaria, speaking slowly and a little hesitantly, out loud and telepathically!

'I think we should take that as a compliment.'

I muttered, 'We could use Carl Sagan right now.' And when the woman looked at me with a puzzled expression, I felt obliged to say; 'A writer, a very long time ago, he wrote a story about the first contact humans might have with alien beings.' I immediately felt bad about the Alien part of that, but Olaria was just looking at me and smiling.

Suddenly, in my mind, *why did you not contact us?*

I assumed it was her and if it was, I had no idea what she was talking about and the moment passed. As seconds ticked by, I became unsure she had even spoken to me.

I looked at Olaria; she was smiling. Then, as I looked at each of the crew, I became aware I was not the only one feeling warmth and friendliness. Like the smile, this seemed to be emanating from her as a physical sensation.

'I'm sorry,' John began, but Olaria held up a hand.

'Please, there is no need to apologise. I too was thinking; these people could easily be Olarians.'

Everyone laughed and the tension on the Flight Deck eased slightly, but I noticed no one was looking at anyone else. It was as though the entire crew were in a state of mild shock. As I looked around, my mind gave me one of those images of the Keystone Cops clinging to the bumper of a car going too fast around a corner, everyone at risk of being thrown off.

Discomfort was the primary emotion I could detect amongst the crew. I thought about the discussions had about Aliens in our training programs. Seriously, how could anything prepare us for this? But Olaria was speaking.

'I will try and answer the questions you are asking. We are a telepathic and telekinetic race, and we came aboard using a process you call simultaneity, we focus on a place we see, which we can do even when we are not physically present, and we simply make the jump. It is the way our brains are organised. Your computers do not see us, other life forms or buildings on the planet because three years ago a very tiny spacecraft arrived in our system, which we now assume was yours?'

John nodded. 'It did not communicate with us and we came to realise it was not actually a life form, and did not contain life forms, however, it was evidently the instrument of a sentient species. It was scanning us, collecting data, we assumed, to take back to its sentient masters or mistresses. So, because we can manage energy, we blocked its access to our living energy. Thus, it would not see us nor any other creature on our planet. It seemed a safe way to proceed, given the object did not communicate with us and we had no way of knowing what the intentions of its creators were. We also screened out the energies we used to construct our dwellings and other objects. When it left, we assumed it likely we would one day meet its makers. It would seem you, are they?' John nodded.

'That is essentially why you have been unaware of us whilst we have been studying you and learning one of your languages. We know your computers informed you we had bypassed their defensive screens and acquired your language library once you had slowed sufficiently for us to come aboard. What they did not know was who we were. We were careful to do no damage.'

The silence that followed Olaria's remarks was disturbed only by the very light hum of the Sunstreamer's powerful engines and the gentle, almost inaudibly soft hiss of the air purifiers. Olaria smiled once again at the gathered humans. For the immediate moment, our only response was silence. However, I did not think it was the silence Olaria was hearing and wondered exactly what that was. John was probably wondering, like me, and probably most of the crew, what we had got ourselves into, yet, I felt strongly, I wanted it to go on! I could feel her in my mind and imagined she might be following my thoughts.

'You are right, we are following all of your thoughts, it is who we are, Zed.'

I shook my head but knew she was still there and thought, you seem friendly, you do not appear to be violent nor threatening. I felt uncertain, it seemed to be about almost everything, so I didn't even know, at this moment, what exactly I was feeling uncertain about. The image that slid unsought from my mind was a glass of soda water, bubbles sliding quietly up to the surface, no real stillness possible. Then slowly I became aware, my disquiet was about my, our, future.

Then I realised Olaria was still speaking.

She went on. 'We are wondering how you constructed this spacecraft and how you managed to locate us in a solar system in which we know you do not live. We were fascinated with the little object you call a Probe, but this is an amazingly complicated and very much larger thing. This is but one of the many, many questions we have for you. We are feeling the need to make some plans with you about how to share information. We are not exactly sure how it would be best to do that?'

She and Jald were watching and listening, and I thought they would certainly be hearing minds in turmoil.

I looked at her and guessed that I was not alone in wondering if we were going to be able to leave here to get home.

I knew the question had not been missed by Olaria, who looked at me and frowned.

Then she and Jald were silent. 'Jald and I have been consulting with the other six members of the Council of Eight who currently manage the affairs of our world.' The crew were silent, and Olaria continued. 'Your machines are scanning our planet, apparently collecting information on many wavelengths. What exactly is it you are doing here? Are you simply looking for new life or do you have some other intention?'

John looked at me.

'We came here because our probe could see that your planet might be suitable for human life. Our planet is overburdened with people and the politicians who manage our world want to transfer people to other planets in other solar systems. I think it is in part about species survival, and in part, political ambition.' He noticed the puzzled frowns but continued on.

'So, our job, for the next five days was to scan your planet and learn enough about it in every detail so as to allow us to see if it is suitable for human habitation.'

'And if it is?' Olaria's tone was not querulous, but he felt the edges.

'We report back to Earth with our findings. If it was suitable, fleets of transports would bring humans between the ages of twenty and twenty-five to build a new world for humans here.'

Surely you can see that from our perspective this would be totally unacceptable. Why can you not solve the problems on your planet? Is it dying?'

'No'

I tried to shift my mind so that her conversation with John was playing in reverse. If the Olarians had arrived on Earth with just such a proposition. I knew, with clarity, this would be considered a hostile act and would probably lead to a war, the powers that be attempting first to extract whatever learning they could about the enemy before destroying them or driving them out into space away from Earth. I had already figured that my drive for honesty and openness was not unlike that of the Olarians, and I knew they would be clear about my thoughts. So, I imagined how I would feel if the roles were reversed. Mankind would not be seeing positives in this nor seeking friendship. Quite the contrary.

Olaria spoke quietly to all of us. 'You are scaring us, Zed. We must admit to being seriously disturbed by what you are calling your mission parameters. You need to understand that we can't in good faith allow you to proceed to treat our planet as a future home for humans from Earth. It feels like a hostile thing to do and I gather from your thoughts that if our roles were reversed, humans would be trying in clandestine ways, to learn from us before destroying us. Are we mistaken?'

Then, realising with frightening clarity that she was correct, Olaria shared her thoughts with the entire crew. Whilst we do not feel any of you to be hostile toward us, the idea that you could return home with all the information your authorities need to decide to make Olar a human habitation is totally unacceptable. To this end, our Council of which Jard and I are two members of the eight, need to inform you that we do not feel free to allow you to leave orbit here until we have worked together to build an entirely new understanding. Furthermore, we would like you to cease scanning our planet immediately.

John glanced briefly at me, then spoke to the computers.

'Yuri, (The computer to which John issued instructions) please cease all surface and environment scanning on the planet designated Omega5Z3 and change the planet's designation to Olar.'

He turned to Olaria frowning, 'Please understand, we cannot erase the scans already made. However, for the moment, whilst the computers will cease scanning on exploratory search parameters, they will automatically continue to maintain security surveillance.'

For several moments there was silence. Then Olaria spoke.

'John, I believe, with some assistance from yourselves, we could erase the memory traces your computers are maintaining of the scans.'

A feeling of deep concern crept through him. These creatures, these people—he didn't know how to think of them—had already proven conclusively they could manipulate his computer systems, the three Quantum computers had indeed informed him something had already bypassed all Sunstreamer's defences and read specifically the language library at extreme high speed, then left. What she was saying was probably true. I could see that the consequences of the Olarians engaging with the computer systems sent fear through every fibre of John's being, he knew we could lose our ability to navigate home.

John's voice took on a new timbre. His position now unmistakable.

'At this stage in our relationship I do not want to do that.'

He was clear with her and for the first time she turned to him, seemed to recognise his need for some control of his spaceship and appeared to decide not to interfere any further. She moved on.

Olaria's challenge destroyed the delicate balance of curiosity and uncertainty. In one simple act, the Olarians took the upper hand. The Captain's ethical position dissolved. It was apparent he knew he had lost the ability to be in any real control. Though the Olarians had not threatened the Sunstreamer nor her crew, John had reached a decision and I thought he had just drawn a line in the sand, and if he had wondered what that would mean.

John evidently felt in no position to make demands and appeared to me uncertain as to our welcome. The Olarian demands were reasonable in the circumstances. However, being unable to have control of the situation was disquieting. John looked first at me and then Olaria and asked,

'What do either of us have to exchange apart from knowledge?'

I thought he had to be wondering,

Could they also hold Sunstreamer and the crew captive if they wished? If they could, power was truly unequally distributed.

I watched John's body tense as he dealt with these two powerful Alien intruders. He was carefully controlling his anger, but the darkening expression on his face did not bode well for the next interchange if these two individuals attempted to take more control. He seemed to me to no longer be taking cognisance of the fact that they knew what he was thinking and feeling. My discomfort, for the first time, went up. There was a sense of urgency in John's stance. He turned to the two intruders. That was how he felt about them at this moment.

'This is my ship.' His voice now forceful, they could not mistake his mood. 'You've gone too far. You cannot come on board my ship and issue commands, no matter how gently and silkily you make them. Leave my computing systems alone. Stop pretending to be caring and gentle when it is clear to me that you are not. This is a human built and operated highly sophisticated Spacecraft. You cannot come aboard by whatever magical means and issue orders or attempt to take control unless you are planning to destroy us. If that's your plan then do it now, or please leave whilst we decide what to do about you.'

He stopped, Olaria and Jald looked briefly at one another. I wondered if he had gone too far.

'Of course, Captain, Olaria's voice sounded cool but not unfriendly. Please invite us aboard should you wish to speak with us. In the meantime, we are holding your vessel where it is. It would be unwise to attempt to leave your orbit.'

With that, she and Jald vanished. John spoke immediately to the computers,

'Yuri, on my mark destroy, immediately, all data about this vessel and about the human race in all data storage locations.'

Nooo, please stop, we will not harm you I give you my word. Olaria's voice was distressed. Even telepathically, the tone was definitely pleading. The entire crew knew it would take only one word now to destroy the entire ship and human species data stored in the computer system. Of course, it seemed certain the Olarians knew this as well. However, the Captain was being careful not to identify his mark, and I was certain he would deliberately be not thinking about it. So, for now it seemed it was safe, and he held off.

'Number one.' He was speaking to Peta, his first Officer. Peta Lei, Sunstreamer's First Officer, was also the Science Officer, 32 and arguably the most sophisticated Astrophysicist and Quantum Mechanic in the fleet; attractive medium length brown hair, slender, fit, with distinctly Asian features. However, he was also looking at Tanzin. 'If I should suddenly appear ill, fall, die or begin to act inappropriately, immediately destroy all our tracking data from here to home. Is that clear?'

Both looked at him. 'Set both your systems up for my mark. Should any of the prerequisite indicators be evident, act immediately, without hesitation, without any other communication from me.'

The two looked at him, knowing he was preparing to totally isolate them in deep space. When they carried out these instructions, there would be no route back to Earth. The Olarians got that, and there was one final word from Olaria.

Please John, do not instigate this action, we absolutely give you our word we will not kill nor destroy nor harm you. Absolutely, every member of this Council will separately confirm what I am saying.

For an instant all eight appeared, ethereally on the Bridge and confirmed Olaria's promise. They vanished again, and John did not give his mark. Slow sigh of relief from the crew and a heartfelt thank you from Olaria. An unprecedented and terrifying stand-off. No memory by any of the crew, no known record of this situation having been used by a Starfleet Captain was known to exist before this moment. But then, as I thought about it, there would be no record, would there?

CHAPTER 2
Consequences

I looked around, conscious I was being explored, it felt creepy, then it went away. Just for a second, I had had a sense of a person in my head, and I muttered under my breath,

'What the hell?' Then I heard Olaria speak quietly and telepathically to me.

My apologies Zed, we are with you all the time, it's just that you are far more... sensitive than your companions.

I shook my head, and her presence and my sense of being possessed disappeared. I turned my attention back to the crew. There was chatter everywhere, some raised voices, minor arguments had broken out between friends. I watched, feeling undisturbed by the Olarian challenge, and wondered what that was about? I was actually more disturbed by John's last action than by the Olarians, but I was finding it difficult to understand why. Strategically it had been a good decision, in the circumstances. He was keeping the five-day time boundary clear in his mind. Within four days of our failure to return a fully armed Battlecruiser would appear in the skies above Olar and with the information they presently had, I could find nothing positive about that. I also knew the Olarians would now be aware of that.

Gerard raised his voice to be heard over the noise, 'Captain, I think we should just leave orbit with a full power burn and return home. This is not the mission we were given.'

Gerard was a strongly built man, but slender and immaculate. He had been a member of a Chechen Guard unit, and this was still reflected in his stance and bearing. When he spoke it was with style, but not a great deal of flexibility. As an engineer, he was brilliant. A graduate of Moscow and then Caltech, he had been deeply involved with the design of Sunstreamer's engines. Their design had involved technology that had not previously existed, their power output, unique fuel and fuel processing totally novel. Much of the novelty had come from Gerard's creativity.

Peta turned, looking directly at him.

'Gerard, please tell me your concern is primarily for Ghia and your unborn child.'

It was a strong thrust from the First Officer; it seemed the crew were collectively holding their breath. For a moment I thought that although she was probably correct, Gerard might not manage so direct and strong a challenge. That was wrong. In an instant Gerard's professional self seemed to regroup. Ghia was looking at him with concern and was gently shaking her head. 'No Gerry. We agreed, if my condition looks like highjacking operational decisions, I should not be here.'

That got his full attention. He shook his head,

'You're right, cancel that and accept my apology, that will not happen again.'

He was apologetic, fully professional, although I could see he was agitated. He briefly focused on Ghia, then looked around at the rest of the crew.

'Sorry all, bad call.'

John looked at him, then turned to the rest of the crew.

'Nevertheless, does anyone else think that might be the way to proceed?'

I focused on Ghia.

'What's your feeling about this?' She turned to Gerard.

'Gerry, so far as we know, these are the first aliens the human race has ever met. I don't want to walk away because they are smarter and apparently more powerful than us. I don't think SFC would want us to. And Oh, incidentally, does anyone actually believe we could just leave?'

It was clear to Ghia and I that no one except Gerard felt that way, and he was definitely no longer willing to acknowledge it. And John had, metaphorically, loaded the gun. One word and an extraordinary quantity of not insignificant data would perish instantaneously. Was I, I wondered, the only one cognisant of the five days we had been given for this mission?

Before anyone could answer, Olaria's voice came over the intercom.

'People of Earth, I regret that at this time we do not feel it is safe to allow you to simply leave. We absolutely intend you no harm, absolutely, for what it's worth, I guarantee it, but you frighten us and we do not know how to proceed. We are holding your ship in orbit. We believe we have a great deal to learn from you and I am certain this must be true in reverse, so having only recently met I think we need a more acceptable way to get to know one another before we can feel safe in freeing you to return to your homes. I am genuinely sorry. But I am certain you appreciate our concern for our world and its security. Please do not see this as a hostile act.'

I turned to the Captain.

'John, let's not get trapped in emotions we can't manage. I suggest we continue working the problem. We know that as we do this our hosts will be listening in, both to what we say and to what we are thinking and feeling. It would be useful if all of us kept this in mind. So, being anything except honest will be a bad strategy here.'

I looked around the crew,

'I'm hoping we all get that.' I did not wait for a reply. 'Okay, I would like to begin.' There was no dissent. 'To restate the obvious. We came here to survey the planet we now know to be Olar, to establish its ability to act as a human colony. We came to do this task because, apart from the reasons back home, the inhabitants of this planet intentionally misled us as to the actual state of animal life on their planet. Because we were misled by them, we brought an unweaponized Explorer vessel to engage with the task. Ironically, had the Olarians not blocked life data, SFC would probably have sent a fully armed Battlecruiser. Would anyone care to imagine the consequences of that engagement? ' I paused and looked at each member of the crew. 'If we were to return home, assuming we could, does anyone here believe the outcome would necessarily be constructive?'

I shook my head, and I knew they all got it. 'I mean, we are not here because, as a species, we have made high-quality decisions on our planet, about our lives!'

I stopped. This was a Captain's call, and I did not want to overstep the mark, however, John's nod made it clear he wanted me to continue. With the exception of Gerard all eyes were on me and urging me to continue. Gerard had slid away to some place brilliant Engineers go when they cannot tolerate what is going on between people. His face was red and when the others were looking at me, he was just slowly shaking his head. Ghia seemed to know how he was feeling. The rest of the crew were focused on me, they seemed not to notice. I continued.

'Here we are, weaponless, defenceless, and apparently at the whim of the telepathic and telekinetic inhabitants of the planet below, who, nevertheless, do not feel hostile and do not appear intent on doing us any harm. My first response is to be glad we were not a Battlecruiser. My second is to be seriously pissed off that apparently because they can, they have decided to hold us prisoners at their discretion. That annoys and distresses me, and is, for the moment, leading me to have doubts about their integrity, intentions and our options. If they were a friendly, wise and relationally sophisticated telepathic society they would know we were not aggressive nor hostile nor a threat to them. However, their ability to protect themselves from one of our Battlecruisers is an unknown, and for now, I would like it to stay that way.

My final point is this. We came to learn about their planet. They have, for the moment, stopped us learning from our scanners. The only other way to learn is if either we go visit them or they visit us and we share information. If SFC knew of our situation, I believe they would be encouraging us to try to avoid being killed and to learn as much as possible about our hosts, their way of life, their abilities, their situation. None of us know what they want, nor what they intend. I believe we need to get to a point where we know enough about one another for us to decide what is and is not safe. For this we will need to build a relationship with them. I believe they will need to set that up. We still don't know whether any kind of human settlement might be a possibility. That's how I see our situation.'

I watched John comb through my scenario, realise I had deliberately put a sting in its tail, and all things considered, seemed to accept that the argument was sound. John looked around the crew. Was anyone in violent disagreement? He paused at Gerard, knowing he had been one of the design team of the incredible engines that powered the Sunstreamer, that he was brilliant but also that people and interpersonal situations were rarely on his radar. Gerard was no longer showing open hostility but had withdrawn from the fray. There was little else to say. At this moment, the next step was up to the Olarians. Moments passed.

Peta was frowning at me. 'That was a pretty direct hit Zed. I know they are listening from afar. Given the nature of the information we have so far, all supplied by them, it seems possible they could eliminate us or imprison us. I don't yet know if they could actually stop us from leaving. However, in the absence of evidence of their good intentions, I feel ambivalent about what I want to do.'

The Captain watched the interchange.

'They know we are vulnerable. I don't know how vulnerable we actually are, however, not only are we short of information, but we have multiple issues to consider. We might be able to pull away from the planet and escape what I will for the moment refer to as the Olarian System and make it safely to the first wormhole. But, if we could, would we want to? There is, as yet no sign that these are a warlike people.'

The next move was made by the Olarians.

'Captain, this is Olaria. For reasons we will be pleased to share with you shortly, we are going to adjust your orbit to a geosynchronous one over our present location. Please assure us this will bring no harm to you or your vessel and identify the required altitude.'

John looked at Tanzin and Peta, both raised their eyebrows and shook their heads. Peta spoke as she looked at Tanzin,

'So long as they do nothing more than reposition us, we should be quite safe, but we will need to make some adjustments to our power and the Astronav Positioning System, I think that's it, Tanzin?'

Tanzin nodded her agreement and gave Olaria the desired altitude for a geosynchronous orbit and Peta the adjusted power settings.

A moment later, Sunstreamer's attitude was being adjusted and within seconds the telemetry and positioning data streaming down the Holo screens had stabilised and Sunstreamer was indeed being gently repositioned into its new orbit which it eventually became clear as the next orbit was completed, was over a very large clearing on the ground, one the crew now assumed to be the location of their captors.

What the act showed was that Sunstreamer was probably not leaving any time soon. Not really subtle, but unmistakable. They could almost certainly prevent Sunstreamer from leaving, although what the effect of a full power burst would be on their capabilities, from the astonishingly powerful and entirely new engines, was something no one would be wanting to test out.

The next instant Olaria's voice, still warm and friendly, 'Captain, be assured, we could easily hold your vessel regardless of the capacity of your power unit. However, we genuinely do not want to be in a power struggle with you, this is absolutely anathema to everything we hold to be important about life and our existence. We are as confused as you about what is the best way to proceed in our mutual interests.

We have never met an alien civilisation before, so no one here has any experience to lend towards a solution. We truly are not hostile. A bit cautious at the moment, as we can see that some of you are quite violent, which is not a quality allowed to continue for more than very occasional brief and temporary situations, in our society. We do acknowledge the inequity we have established, but it was you who came here, although I fully accept Zed's statement that you are here as a result of our deception.'

Olaria paused and there were glances around the Bridge, but no one spoke.

'As I said before, there are eight members of our Council and we would like to meet with you face to face. You have met my son Jald and myself. We would like to end this impasse without putting our world at risk. You are correct that we are curious about you and are aware you are curious about us. We too have hoped to find other sentient beings in the universe. It seems absurd that fear might prevent this from being a constructive and satisfying meeting. So, the Council has decided to assure you we will not make any attempt to prevent you from leaving here at any time you choose.'

There were more non-verbals among the crew, but still no one spoke.

'We are confident we can protect ourselves from any act of hostility that might result from your returning home to speak about us. We are not clear why you would want to continue scanning our planet when you know it can never be used as a human colony. However, we are interested in what you can learn about us from your scanning process. If you will agree to fully share the results from your scanning, we would like you to continue. We are genuinely curious.'

Olaria paused, and we knew she and the Council members and apparently others were watching and listening. I believed what they were seeing and hearing would disturb them, but I could not be sure. Did she realise that essentially there was no trust from the Sunstreamer's crew, no belief that the Olarians could be trusted, that their word was good? I put myself in the Olarians' shoes. Would they see the crew essentially examining the situation for ways in which this might be some kind of trick to lure them out of the safety of Sunstreamer? They would know this because it was one of the scenarios being discussed on the Flight Deck. The Olarians had given the crew the assurances which to an Olarian might seem like a commitment to safe passage. But we aren't Olarian, I thought.

Ours is a world of scepticism, more than that, cynicism. Why would we trust them? Open and freely given commitments are definitely not human style, were they Olarian style? I wondered. We live in a world of extraordinary self-interest and duplicity and expediency at every level, personal and institutional, of government and private enterprise. We could easily be falling into a trap. In our World, the idea of blindly accepting the Olarians' word would be considered naive and probably: stupid. Here? I wondered. In our Capitalist and economically rational world, profit, power and greed manage a majority of decisions. It is more than likely we are here, in large part because of them. Personal relationships were also really steeped in the management of power. How could we possibly trust the word of a people about whom we knew almost nothing. A people whose power was demonstrably greater than our own? This impasse lived firmly in our mistrust of the relationship between the two alien groups we represented. There were no precedents for what should happen next, no history on which to draw that related to the two groups and for the human crew, as yet no grounds for trust. However, the Olarians had taken a step to try and break the deadlock. They had offered what appeared to be genuine goodwill.

John returned to our usual tried-and-true procedure,

'How?' he asked, 'Can I trust that what we have been told is true?'

Peta thought out loud. 'If their offer is genuine, we are much better off assuming there are no hidden strings attached. But can we actually do anything except take them at their word? We plainly cannot sit here and not act. However, if we were to blast ourselves out of orbit to escape and we failed, would we not then be in a worse position than we are now?'

I looked at Peta, who gently raised an eyebrow.

So, I picked up her thread. 'Suppose we just follow that piece of string. We are here to do a task that now does not seem possible. We would never be the crew authorised to negotiate with the inhabitants of an occupied planet. This mission would not be happening and if a mission was to be launched, it would almost certainly not be with us. But we are here, and it is us who must do whatever can be done.'

No one disagreed.

'We could try and make a run for it but the evidence we have suggests that if the Olarians are not fair dinkum, we would fail and then how would that improve our position with our hosts/captors? It obviously wouldn't. We seem to have come in contact with the first ever alien life in the universe, certainly, so far as we can tell, the first humans have ever contacted. So, the question must surely be, what would SFC expect us to do? We have had many, not particularly serious discussions about this, mainly because most people secretly hoped but have not believed there were others in the universe. We now know there are. So, this is no longer an inconsequential discussion, it is deadly serious for us. My belief is, we would be expected to learn about them and for us to do that we will have to be willing to share our knowledge with them. And, if I understand the biggest elephant in the room, it must surely be the question, if we make clean contact with this race, might they not overwhelm us? Then, they might well be able to take over Sunstreamer, force us to take them back to Earth and pose a threat to our species and our world?? And is that not the bottom line leading us to shy away from a final decision? So, the end of that piece of string is, we either try and learn from and with them or if we think we are putting the human race at risk destroy ourselves and Sunstreamer now whilst we still believe we can.'

The Olarian Council listening in were horrified. Almost with one voice they spoke to the crew.

NO, please do not take that course, we would NEVER put you in so invidious a position, please speak with us.

And so, it seemed, I had tabled the ultimate challenge and we had received an unambiguous response. The question was, did that really change the options?

All of us were in our seats on the Flight Deck, I was now sitting quietly in my seat. This was, I thought, a strange and disturbing stand-off. Sceptical, even cynical humans, and aliens seeking goodwill in the face of a dramatic disturbance to their lives. But I had not quite finished.

'Captain, my recommendation is simple. Do a full power burn to exit from this planet, tracking directly back to and through the last wormhole.'

I paused, looking directly and unblinkingly at the Captain.

'Our hosts assumedly cannot follow us and on the other side, if we are allowed to undertake this journey, we can make a decision, in private, about our next steps. If we are not permitted to leave, we know we have been experiencing duplicity and so will in fact be no worse off.'

I continued looking very intensely at the Captain.

Every member of the crew was looking at me in disbelief, then one by one, as they watched me and John, they grasped the terrible logic of my suggestion. I had worked the problem to its logical conclusion. As they think it through, I can see them acknowledge the strength of the argument.

The last word they heard before John nodded his command to Tanzin and Peta was Olaria. *Oh, please don't go.*

Then the full power of the gigantic engines hurled the Sunstreamer out of orbit and toward the wormhole, still hours away, at an acceleration that was testing her limits. John looked at Gerard,

'Can I safely push us to their limit?' Gerard nodded and disappeared down to the Engineering deck.

Two hours three minutes later, not a word had been spoken on the Flight Deck and Sunstreamer exited the wormhole and reduced power to zero thrust whilst Tanzin and Peta turned her around and using the incredible power plants again brought her to a full stop in space. Gerard returned to the bridge, smiling. Every face looking at me and then John. I was obviously expected to say something.

CHAPTER 3
And Then

'Okay, now we know, either they could not stop us, or they honoured their word. We have our freedom. What we do not have is any really new knowledge about the only other sentient life ever known to exist, and,' I repeated, with edgy uncertainty, 'So far as we know, in the Universe. However, Captain, right now, I believe, we have the ability to return and can make our decision without external observers.'

Raille was looking at me, an eyebrow raised, the quirkiest smile on his lips and was shaking his head slowly from side to side. 'My god, Zed, what you just had us do, that was mad. The maddest thing I have ever heard you suggest in a long friendship of mad things. I just love you for it! And Captain, forgive me, but ... that took some guts.'

There was no disagreement amongst the crew, Peta an expression of incredulity cast in stone on her beautiful face did a mock bow of deference to me and John and the rest just laughed and laughed more with relief, I thought, than anything else.

And it was John who then looked around at his crew, at Tanzin who had just followed his unspoken instruction to the letter and without hesitation supported by Peta, also with no hesitation. He said, 'Okay, now we can have that conversation in private. Zed, I believe this is your play?'

I looked around at the crew.

'I think for the purpose of this exercise Captain each member of the crew should be given permission to speak for themselves as individuals and not as members of SFC. I know this is way outside protocol. But, meeting a new species who appear to be almost identically human who are able to speak with us in English and telepathically is not really covered in our operational manuals.

I believe we could justifiably return to Earth and allow the powers that be decide who should be on this mission. However, that said, I believe we have stumbled on an alien race who interest me enough to want to explore with them, even though it seems highly improbable any human colonisation will be possible here and so we may not be able to maintain our mission parameters.

We were sent here to do a task that we now seem no longer doable, at least for its intended purpose. However, the Olarians have told us that we can continue a key aspect of the task. We would almost certainly not be the crew authorised to negotiate with the inhabitants of an occupied planet. This mission would not be happening or, if it was, as we have said before, it would probably not be with us. But we are here, and it is us who must do whatever is to be done.'

John looked around the group. 'Alright, I take your point Zed. We still do not know for certain that the planet is ideal. We also do not know for certain we could not set up a colony here. Given these truths, we will be well within our mission parameters if we return and finish the job for which we were sent here. However, the circumstances are changed, and I agree that in these unusual circumstances each member of the crew should have their say. So?'

Each crew member spoke, no one said they did not wish to return and complete the mission task. Even Ghia who, bearing a child, probably felt most vulnerable, and Gerard, who was seriously concerned for their child, agreed together they should not miss this opportunity. I was watching Gerard very carefully and could see he was, in fact, lying. However, he would not upset Ghia. I watched for a moment longer. Yes, I thought, she knows. People who travel in space seeking new worlds are unlikely to pass up the opportunity on offer here. So, the question from the Captain to me was, 'How do you propose we go about this?'

I sat silent for several moments. I had known this would again come back to me.

'I am feeling more than a little responsible for our present position. However, before I put any suggestion forward, I need to place a caveat on the table. I don't feel I have the right to withhold a concern. We may have just been skilfully duped. And, I could be wrong about this, I seriously hope I am. But suppose they are inherently as duplicitous as our politicians and Dynastic and Corporate leaders. Suppose they are banking on our curiosity. Our desire to learn new things. But are in fact of evil intent, what then? We will be putting ourselves and our world, at unknown risk. Should it be us that makes this decision?'

I paused. 'My intuition tells me they are playing from a straight deck. If this was not so I believe I would have had at least some feeling, some intuition, leading me to feel uncertain. And I do not. So, I'm placing my vote for a return, but in the words of another era, I am also planning to keep my powder dry. This may be of no value, but it's all I've got.

I think we should return as soon as possible. That we should speak openly with the Olarians about our concerns and our interest in them. They should know we want to learn about them, and we would like to help them understand whatever they want to know about us... Keep it seriously simple and direct and see where it leads us. So far as we can tell, they have shown themselves to be creatures of their word. If down the track this proves to be incorrect, for me I feel—so be it.'

John stood quietly looking long and hard first at me, then at each member of the crew. Paused for nearly a full minute after looking at Gerard, sat in his seat and closed his eyes. The only sound on the Deck was still the hum of the power plants and the very gentle hiss of the life support system. Then he reached his decision, turned to Tanzin and said; 'Before I issue any orders, does anyone want to change their mind?'

However, the flight deck remained silent. One more glance around and then he said: 'I am going to cancel my instruction to the computers,' and he cancelled the 'mark' he had made with Yuri. 'Number One, Tanzin, position us for re-entry into the wormhole and orbit over Olar, manoeuvre us to the geosynchronous orbit where they placed us before we departed, Tanzin, but program us to be able to take up our scanning pattern from where we left off. Number One, take the helm. I will be in my cabin if you need me, I need to record this event now before any details are lost to me.'

With that, he left the Flight Deck.

Extract from my Holo diary. (September 28, 2096)

"My name is Zed Eko, I am the crew PsycHologist, and I'm starting this Holo record as Sunstreamer sits stationary in space just beyond the wormhole that will take us into the Olarian Solar System. I just agreed, together with the other seven members of the crew, to return to Omega5Z3 called Olar by the Alien race that inhabits it! I agreed because... we just stumbled across the first Aliens the human race has ever found and we are an Explorer spacecraft and these aliens can communicate with us, in English! So, if

you are reading this, it's possible we did not survive, and probably should have made a run for home when we could."

A little more than five hours after leaving orbit over Olar, Sunstreamer slid quietly back to its original station. John had returned to the Flight Deck and now with a nod to each of us spoke out loud.

'Olaria, we have decided we need to trust you if we are to meet and share knowledge from our worlds. We would like to meet with your council and your people and learn what we can about you over the five days we are permitted to be here on this mission. I feel it would be most appropriate if you were to let us know if you would like to proceed and how you would like to do that. This unique situation seems to have no rules, no protocols, so this being your home, us being, as it were, your guests, I believe these matters ought to be in your hands.'

Several moments passed. Then Olaria's voice came telepathically to all of the crew.

Sunstreamer, we are absolutely delighted to welcome each of you to Olar. Thank you for returning to us. What you did was clever, courageous, and your return is most welcome. She paused for a moment. We are not duplicitous as we understand some of you are wondering, but you will find that out for yourselves as you learn about our world. We assume you have a way to reach the surface that does not involve bringing the Sunstreamer down through the atmosphere?

'We have two Landers you will see in a hangar above the crew cabins. They are small stubby winged craft, capable of flight both in and outside planetary atmosphere, each can transport around twenty people. Peta, Tanzin or I will pilot one of these to a position you designate. For the moment, one crew member will be required to remain on Sunstreamer at all times as Officer of The Watch but will be able to communicate with us with full visual and audio capability using our mobile Holo units.'

There was silence, however, we knew immediately Olaria was engaged with Tanzin in setting up the landing area co-ordinates. A few moments later Tanzin was able to tell us she had programmed the landing co-ordinates into the onboard computers and copied these into the Lander's navigational systems.

Another silence and again Olaria was speaking, this time with Ghia and the flight Medic/ Biochemist, both of whom were responding in speech. And shortly both agreed the environment of the planet and the atmosphere were entirely safe for the crew.

I sat back in my seat. I felt the Olarians in my mind. I had felt them leave when Sunstreamer exited the Olarian System and felt them return when Sunstreamer returned to it. I was feeling... unsettled. I had been calm and comfortable since arriving in orbit over this strange and beautiful planet. The people felt more settled, more connected, and I felt disturbingly at home with them. But still, I was definitely feeling unsettled and wondered why. I'm 38 years old, why on Earth did I argue to return here rather than to return home?

I settled deeper into my seat on the bridge and allowed my mind to drift. At the start of this mission, as Sunstreamer had slid gracefully out of Moon orbit I had felt the slight pressure increase on my back as we accelerated toward our travel speed and wondered even then whether I would feel the slight pressure decrease that would herald our return home. That had been my usual pessimism about these voyages, not the uncertainty I was feeling as a result of our contact with the Olarians.

And the woman Olaria, *Zed, why did you not speak to us?*

What had she meant? I continued to let my mind drift.

Although she had died more than a year ago, I could see my mother now, standing on our front porch in New Canberra. I was about to go to work with my dad and she was in my face.

'Remember Zed, never ever speak to people about what you think about them, keep it to yourself. That is the only way to stay safe!'

It was a mantra she had given me since I could speak.

I saw myself sitting squarely on the pillion seat of my father's giant motorcycle, giant to me then. Old and fully refurbished and ridiculously powerful. Today a rare sight. Over 90% of all personal transport was airborne, fully automatic and satellite controlled. Diga, my father, loved the powerful old bike, the very last of its breed. A 'New Era Indian'.

I was five years old. Rebecca, my mother, had come out to the front porch of our country style farmhouse, built on the edge of a recently created estate on the outskirts of New Canberra, a satellite of the original Australian Capital Territory. For Diga a 20-minute ride to the Australian National University. My whole being hummed with pleasure. My arms clinging tightly to my dad, the wind streaming through my helmet. I felt safe. My father and I had a bond on the bike that existed nowhere else. I breathed in the cold air and the familiar scent of my father's heavily stained and well used thick leather motorcycle jacket. The world flashed past, and the powerful roar of the engine vibrated through my entire body. My father had been absolutely clear to me about the life I must create.

Rebecca had fallen hopelessly in love with Diga on sight, the first day on the ANU campus when they had met, two strangers, new members of staff. Diga totally dominating and certain of himself. I was remembering my mother's stories. I could almost hear her speaking. I was uncomfortably aware I had absorbed my father's expectations, his strange unspoken fears and some of his definite core values. And that my mother somehow had been Diga's mouthpiece even after he died in a terrible accident on his bike, and when she later remarried. I realised I had absorbed more about my father and mother, especially their unspoken fears than I had ever been aware of before this lightbulb moment. Realisations, I knew, had consequences, I just didn't know what they would be.

It was my final memory of my dad. I had never seen him again.... My mother, too full of sadness, and pain, did not immediately have the resources to focus on her son. She rationalised I would get a better education in a prestigious school in Sydney. And so, full of fear and distress I found myself alone in a world of strangers, my only real anchor, an ancient woman, Mrs. Frazier, the linen lady responsible for sheets, pillow slips and towels for two hundred boys, and me, the youngest boarder in the school. Knowing unconsciously, I was not really like the others.

Each morning sent to the kindergarten, a small alien; at first, she took me by hand, but soon they knew I could find my way after breakfast, and I was left alone once she made sure I was properly dressed, my bed made, and I knew the rules and where to sit at the table.

I thought about who I was now, sitting quietly on the Flight Deck of this massive spaceship. I definitely was not the five-year-old sitting in the kindergarten. I was no longer alone, my friend and companion of nearly two decades, Raille Korzyst, who was also my martial arts sparring partner, almost in reach. But I knew it was true, I was a serious loner, a certified maverick. And I remembered, as if it was yesterday, my mother picking me up from the Boarding School on my tenth birthday, and finally taking me home. It was at that moment that I felt my life picked up again.

She had loved me, but then I had a new father with whom I would never really bond. And she was stricter than Miss Frasier: every day there was music on a small but exquisitely created Harp, martial arts and study. Relentlessly. She needed me to be the best. She had been a loving but unrelenting task master! Master! I still thought of her that way. But her unwavering expectations and love, in her way, were with me still. She had succeeded with me; I knew.

I was unique, my own man, and not unsuccessful. But and it was a big but, I never quite trusted myself with others. I always heard the whisper of my mother's warnings and in spite of my successes, I always managed to feel a fraud, the feeling never quite left me. I was truly that man for whom an old song spoke. I did it my way! And I had so often. But at a price.

I stopped; suddenly aware I was being led to these reflections.

'Olaria?' I could feel her in my mind. She acknowledged my silent demand for confirmation, and I asked her not to do that again without my conscious involvement and she agreed. I shook my head with irritation.

CHAPTER 4

Landfall

Tanzin eased the Lander into the Western edge of the field precisely at the co-ordinates she had calculated from the instructions Olaria had given her. Eight Olarians were gathered together approximately fifty metres away. The crew left the Lander and Tanzin remained to power the small craft down and activate its Automated Management System. She then picked up her kit and walked down to the planet's surface. I was waiting for her as she left the little craft; she did not look her usual self as she moved toward me. Her luxurious red hair blew gently in the surface breeze, which had been at five knots as we touched down.

I thought she looked a little uncertain, disoriented and tense now her tasks were completed. But I noticed she seemed to pick up when she saw the amazing clothes of the eight members of the council now approaching the small cluster of crews awaiting them, and, in a moment, she was chatting to the other women about the clothes whilst the men listened in, most of them smiling at the sudden burst of energy and enthusiasm, to which they were in the main, observers.

I imagined how she might be feeling, Tanzin would normally have avoided feeling vulnerable or powerless. Yet this wasn't the type of situation any of us could avoid. My heart went out to her. She was standing still now, a few metres from the group of crew members. All of us were standing under a cloudless sky and the place was quiet and peaceful, but I did not imagine any of the crew were feeling peaceful. I knew that none of us really knew what would happen next. More than the others, Tanzin would have been feeling vulnerable and powerless and would be hating it. I knew this was the kind of situation she would usually make certain to avoid.

She had described for me, in one of our early sessions together, how she had felt the day she became a cadet at the Astronav Training Centre. Here today she stood as one of the top two Astronavigators in the world. Then, she had been alone, standing outside the enormous white building which housed Astronav, a bubble of excitement filling her chest, but unsure what would happen to her next, what was coming. Then she had felt alone, now she would know she was not alone, but none of us would be easily able to shake off the discomfort that was associated with our loss of privacy. We would, I thought, all be a little unsettled by the completely unknown nature of our situation on this strange, yet beautiful, planet.

I looked up. The clear blue sky was not unlike home. But the trees and vegetation were undeniably from another world. Tanzin turned suddenly and looked closely at the group of Olarians, and I guessed one of them had spoken to her. As I watched, I saw the man who had boarded Sunstreamer break away from the others and move toward her.

Then I heard him speak to her telepathically, are you willing to be my guest for the next five days? and I wondered if the others had heard the telepathic message.

No, it was Olaria speaking to me telepathically. *You are more tuned to us than the others of your crew, have you not realised this yet?*

I felt strange but simply shook my head. What I did know, as did Tanzin, was that the feeling had travelled with the message. It had contained warmth and friendliness in the way a human could never reproduce. Here on this strange world with these even stranger people it was unnecessary to hear the tone and be familiar with the context in which it was being said to understand the emotional content, Jald had simply included it with his request to her.

Tanzin had responded but was still fascinated with the clothes. They were a seriously inescapable distraction and even I could not take my eyes off the beautifully arranged energy fields through which the colours and patterns and shapes flowed ever so slowly. I heard her ask Jald whether humans would be able to wear them, and Jald's chuckle as he replied.

You could wear them once the energy form has been established; they exist like the material of your clothes. They cease being simply energy streams when they are formed, I'm just not sure how you would get them on and off.

Her smile of delight pleased him, and the lightening of her mood left me feeling a little better. I kept watching the couple and wondered how five days would shape up as a time frame in which they needed to learn about each other. It seemed a very short time, yet I could not help wondering, hoping it would be enough. Then I caught the end of the thought. Enough for what? For us to return home.

I became aware of Olaria offering to make the introduction of the other Olarians. They made contact, hosts and guests, and names were exchanged.

But Tanzin, still curious, asked her final question regarding their clothes.

'Are they related to the status of the group?'

Olaria smiled and shook her head. *No Tanzin, as you will see, they do not differ in any particular way from the clothes worn by any of the several hundred millions of us.*

As I watched, I noticed John had responded to the several hundred million with an expression I identified as a spark of hope. Several hundred million on a planet this size was nothing. Olaria, I noticed, had picked up John's unspoken thought and frowned.

I wondered how John had felt about the discussion of clothes, suspecting he would have thought it almost insignificant. But not so the population data. I wondered what John thought they ought to be talking about at this point. I kept being drawn back to the clothes. They were, remarkable. I could see that they were slightly illuminated, and the patterns and hues underwent continuous but very minimal change, but they were not what I knew was the undercurrent amongst the entire crew. Were we really free? Or were we actually prisoners? I wondered if the tension amongst the crew about our status was understood by the Olarians.

Whilst the Olarians for their part appeared relaxed, the crew did not. On board, Peta watched through the crews' Holo-communicators, now clipped to our uniforms. They had the range needed for very long distances and were not subject to interference by physical objects. Although the Olarians had decided they were interested in the data, Sunstreamer had not recommenced its planetary scans but remained in a geosynchronous orbit over the small landing field.

At this point almost nothing was known about the Olarians and I was pretty sure, knowing most of the crew were Sci Fi readers, they were probably having their various fantasies about our hosts, depending on I imagined, what they had read last.

The group was about to break up and move away with their hosts. John, feeling uncomfortable at seeing his crew about to be separated and yet feeling little confidence in our hosts' integrity, looked at Olaria and voiced an issue that was disturbing him.

Olaria was certainly already aware of his tension and anxiety.

'Olaria, before we leave here and separate, I am pretty confident you are aware how uncertain I am feeling about our future.'

I was watching him, clear about the central nature of his concern: vulnerability. And to a lesser extent, control. Separated from his crew and his spaceship he had to be feeling vulnerable, out of control, alone and so, very uneasy. His feelings were understandable. He was responsible for this mission, this vessel, and his crew. When he spoke, his solution was more novel than I would have guessed.

'I wonder if you might agree to all of us sitting down here with our hosts at our side and having our first introductions and serious engagement, together?'

It was phrased as a question, but no one hearing it would be confused. It was a statement of requirement. He was around six feet three inches tall with an appropriate build to match. When he spoke forcefully, the impact was impressive.

Everyone paused. Some had been speaking, others simply preparing to move off, none of the crew quite sure where. John was standing still, his host beside him, both looking directly at Olaria. There was a momentary rise in the tension amongst the crew, and it became immediately clear the Olarians were engaged in a telepathic communication amongst themselves. John did not hesitate. 'Olaria, it is evident that you are discussing this amongst yourselves and in this process, I believe we are being isolated from you and disadvantaged in this beginning relationship. I do not want to appear un-cooperative, but that's how it feels, to me. Excluded.'

He paused and looked directly at me. I made just the slightest suggestion of a smile, raised my eyebrows slightly made a small movement pushing my lips out just a little and nodded. John continued. 'As though you are having a secret meeting about us, whilst we are actually here but unable to participate. As though you are using your telepathic abilities to our disadvantage.'

The Olarians and then the rest of us could feel the undertow of his hostility.

'I would appreciate you granting my request to see if we can't manage some equity in what I feel sure I am not alone in experiencing as disturbingly one-sided. It feels as though it makes the gap between us wider, harder to cross.' I could see that she knew. Although he did not add, it increased his discomfort and feelings of vulnerability.

Amongst the fourteen of us on the ground, there fell a hush. Most of the crew, at first surprised, felt a sense of relief. Between John and I stretched a connection, a strength. Made clear when he turned and looked directly at me. I smiled quietly at him, nodded, and turned to also observe Olaria. I added my weight to the captain's words.

'Olaria and to the rest of the members of this Council, surely, in an equitable society, this will be the better way for us to begin a collective relationship with you, together, where all of us, as well as all of you, will know what common cultural things need to be known and perhaps what might be the best way we can share knowledge?' Whilst I was speaking, Olaria focused on me with an expression I could not interpret. With barely a hesitation, Olaria nodded to John and turned briefly toward me.

You agree, this is a good idea?

It sounded like a question, I simply nodded.

Within seconds a circle of lightly glowing low-level seating appeared, and the Olarians led us to them. They looked a little like foam blocks with a seat carved into them but appeared to have no substance, and none of the crew seemed comfortable to actually place their weight down on them. Olaria just sat. It was immediately clear the object was capable of supporting her weight and each of us tentatively lowered our weight onto the seats or perhaps into the seats would be more accurate. The energy seats adjusted to our shape and provided comfortable support. I turned to Olaria.

'How exactly did you do that?'

She stared at me for a long moment. It appeared though she was about to say something, but she paused and turned to the group.

We are creatures of energy. We see it everywhere; our brains are attuned to it and we are able to manipulate it in almost any way we desire. Also, we noticed when you left your small Lander, each of you was carrying an object containing clothes and some other unusual objects. You hefted them on to your back.

'Backpacks,' Tanzin said.

'Backpacks,'

Olaria mimicked the word, speaking the word out loud and getting its meaning. Well, it was clear they weighed a little and only small effort was required. When we use energy to move something, no effort on our part is required. Regardless of the actual weight of the object. Perhaps if you would let me demonstrate? Most of the crew were nodding. So, Olaria continued, I will, if you will permit me, lift all of us up off the ground just a little and then put us down. Is that acceptable?

She looked at John who nodded.

The next moment the fourteen were half a metre off the ground with no sense of instability, and then after a few seconds when the amazement and delight of the crew were clear, Olaria returned all of us to the ground. A silence ensued. Some nodding and head shaking around the group. Olaria continued, you see, weight is of no significance when our minds are manipulating energy. It is as if whatever we are wishing to move has no weight. However, if I tried to lift you with my hands and using my physical abilities, I would be hard pressed to even lift one of you off the ground. Perhaps I could manage Tanzin who is arguably the lightest of you.

Tanzin smiled.

Peta, who had been observing from Sunstreamer using the activated Holos of each of the group which images were visible on one of the large Holo screens on the Bridge asked, 'So, Olaria, is that how you moved Sunstreamer into this present geosynchronous orbit?'

Olaria confirmed it was.

'So how many of you were needed to do that?' Peta asked.

'Oh, I did that on my own. As I said Peta, the part of our brain that manages energy allows us to see and connect with energies of many kinds, and act by using them. However, the actions are managed by the energies and not by any muscle activity on our part.' Olaria replied.

A deep silence settled on the group and Peta could be seen clearly on each of the crew Holos and on the large Holo screen we had taken from the Lander, eyebrows raised, jaw dropped and shaking her head gently from side to side. I picked up the thread.

'We have objects we call Drones. They have their own power, and a single operator can control them over many miles using electronics and radio connection. It seems your telekinesis is something like this?'

Olaria looked at John. He was picturing a robotic drone working on a space platform. The Olarians saw the image and understood his analogy. Olaria smiled, expressed her confusion at what she was seeing, but she and the other Olarians quickly grasped the parallel he was drawing.

'You said you did not have telekinetic powers. How is that being achieved?'

'Machines are generating the power and signals are passing between the operator and the unit. It's like a mechanical-electrical equivalent of your telekinesis.'

The Olarians were impressed, and a little confused. However, John was satisfied we had made our point. From his perspective, honour was satisfied, he no longer felt as unequal. He could see Olaria understood.

'How would you like to proceed?' She asked.

But John had reached the end of the pathway he had created. He turned toward me, so I picked up the thread.

'Olaria, I believe it would be a really helpful start, if you and your Council are willing, for you each to tell us who you are in the Olarian world and perhaps how you became members of this Council which appears to manage this planet.'

Olaria immediately looked around the group and it was obvious she was in discussion with the others. 'Might I interrupt, please?'

I felt a strong need to be very clear here, and it was about one of the central aspects of John's distress.

'I am anxious not to cause any unnecessary ripples in the tenor of our relationship, especially at this early stage, but, when you speak with your Council members and we cannot hear we feel a little offended and uncomfortable, perhaps even vulnerable and a little insulted.

In our world this would be like turning and whispering to the person beside you but not letting anyone else hear, even though they would know you were speaking about them. We would think of that as insulting and bad mannered. Now I know you cannot possibly have this experience because you always hear one another, but this is quite new to us and it seems important you understand.

'Do you feel willing either to speak your telepathic communications a loud so we can hear, or perhaps in some way help us to hear your telepathic communications?' I paused for a moment. 'There is another alternative I think might work. Are you able to communicate with one another and with us through spoken language, in English, without using your telepathic abilities?'

I could feel the crew almost cringe as I spoke. However, Olaria's response took the potential offensiveness out of the words. She sat for a moment, and it was evident

41

that several of the Council members had begun to speak telepathically to her, but she held up her hand and they visibly ceased.

I am speaking to the other seven of us telepathically, she said, *telepathically, and aloud so the crew were able to hear.*

I think I understand what Zed is saying and what John has been concerned about. I think they are right, and I apologise. We have never been in this particular situation before—it is not like the situation we experience every 50 years with the Cretians, a race who also live on this planet and about whom I will tell you all later—. It is almost incomprehensible for us to not speak telepathically, however, we could certainly try it if you think this would—how are you saying it—level the playing field?

I nodded. Smiled. Then continued. 'Olaria and members of the Council, if you speak to us out loud, and you agree not to use your telepathic abilities at all, whilst we are together here speaking with one another through your initial introductions, you will quickly come to understand pretty much how this is experienced by us. I suspect, should you agree to this arrangement, you will be excruciatingly uncomfortable because you will be deprived of information which, it seems clear, you use constantly to smooth your relationships, but you will gain an insight into our limitations in communicating with each other.

I'm wondering if you would agree to do this, for say the time you take to introduce yourselves to us. Then, perhaps you could find a way that would allow us to know what is going on in your minds and in the minds of each of us. I feel certain this will leave us excruciatingly ill-at-ease. Nevertheless, we will have gained some cultural understandings that may be possible no other way!

Fourteen individuals plus Peta and her host from Sunstreamer, individuals from two very different worlds, looked at one another. Whilst not everyone was enamoured of this idea, pretty well everyone was, to some degree, taken aback. I smiled to myself. What I was thinking was, I thought, an extraordinarily creative, if disturbing and uncomfortable suggestion. But could the Olarians arrange it? And if they could, would they? Certainly, we could not.

A silence settled on the group. Breathing was shallow and quiet, everyone poised, awaiting Olaria's response. She sat very still, looking at me with a slowly spreading smile and then around the group at each of the crew and asked, out loud,

'To the members of my Council, please nod if you agree with trying this extraordinary experiment.'

One after another, they did, including Peta's host on Sunstreamer. This was facilitated by the presence of a large Holomonitor we had brought from the Lander. It was sitting between Olaria and the crew Bio-med.

Olaria looked then at each of the crew, who, one by one, added their agreement. And so, turning to me, she spoke aloud in an amused but friendly tone,

'Mr. PsycHologist, you have your wish. Then, I assume Zed, you would like us to begin?'

I smiled and nodded. Something novel and extraordinary was about to be enacted on this small and beautiful piece of land on this strange unknown new world.

CHAPTER 5

Meeting

Olaria glanced uncomfortably around the collection of people from two worlds, all now looking at her. This was a seriously novel experience, and her first glimmerings of uncertainty were visible to all.

Nevertheless, she began, 'I am effectively 38 years old, but I have been alive for 1825 years.'

'Excuse me, Olaria?'

John made his comment almost immediately after Olaria had spoken her first sentence. He shook his head. I realised he had spoken to the incongruity. Looking around there was little doubt the entire crew either thought they had misheard or that Olaria was joking, or perhaps that there was a large discrepancy between a year on Earth and a year on Olar yet that hardly fit with I am 38 years old but been alive 1825 years.

'This year, how is it measured?' John realised they may not be speaking about the same length of time, perhaps the time scales were different.

'Well, using your timescales, which we derived in part from your tiny spacecraft and confirmed from your computer language dictionaries, your day from sunup to sunup is very close to ours. Your seasons with the names of Summer, Autumn, Winter and Spring cover 365 of your days. Our words are quite different but for seasons and durations there are but a few of your days difference.'

I could see that Olaria was feeling uncomfortable; her normal interpersonal resources no longer available to her. She looked around at the other members of the

Council, but apparently remembering her agreement, she did not appear to communicate with them telepathically. However, the crew noticed one of the Olarians appear to begin a telepathic communication to which Olaria shook her head and again spoke aloud.

'No!' She said, 'We have agreed to only speak aloud and think our own thoughts and not share these with one another. Already I can tell you I am on edge. The act of not entering your minds to check on how you are feeling and thinking about what I am saying, is stressing me more than I would have believed possible and so far, I have said almost nothing.'

The crew were bewildered by this interchange, yet it was Kyuto, Ghia's host, another of the Olarians, who spoke.

'I'm sorry, but I have to say how uncomfortable I am feeling. To you our human visitors, you should know that what Olaria said is precisely how I am feeling at this moment. I have never sat and talked with someone when I did not know how they were feeling and what they were thinking about. This is extraordinary. I am feeling trapped in my seat, confused about what to do or what to think about.'

There was evidence of agreement from all the members of the Council. Nevertheless, Olaria continued.

'Well, we will all have to wait and constrain ourselves; everyone will have their chance to speak in turn. Already I am getting some insights I have never imagined; maybe for the first time in a very long time. And. And this is quite difficult, but I am saying this for the sake of our visitors.' She frowned, touched her forefinger and thumb to her forehead and shook her head. It was quite evident how strongly this process was disturbing her.

'There are many hundreds of thousands of us Olarians listening in to this conversation, and to them I need to say as I speak these words out loud to our visitors. We need you to NOT communicate with us whilst we are doing this. I'm sorry, but this is more difficult than I could ever have imagined, and I need not to be hearing you whilst we try to learn how this works.'

She looked at the crew, seeming to search each face, looking for something, but what she needed—access to their thoughts—was presently beyond her reach.

I'm sorry if this sounds strange but whenever Olarians speak there are almost always several, but in our case hundreds or even thousands, sometimes millions of others listening in, which they can do without disturbing us. However, because I have agreed not to be telepathically in contact with them or share anything with them that way, hard as this is to say, I need to tell them not to communicate with us whilst we engage with you in this experiment.'

It is difficult to say if any of the crew really understood what she was trying to tell us, but everyone nodded politely. Olaria continued,

'So, to continue, John. My father was a man named Jard, he married Leiti, my mother when they met 3000 years ago. I was born when my mother had been with us 1175 years. And just to clear up the way we speak of this, we think of our age as 38 years old, but we speak of the time we have been alive, and we do not call this time our age. My body is and will remain 38 years old except for some aspects of my brain. Now you all look young to us; however, we have been assuming you are much older than you look because we cannot imagine people so young but also attractive being in charge of so powerful and complex a vessel as your Sunstreamer and being able to travel across Galaxies to find us. Can I just pause for a moment to ask how long you have been alive?' Olaria paused.

The crew looked at one another, and I spoke. 'I am the oldest member of the crew and I am 38 years old and have been alive for only 38 years.'

The Olarians all looked at me and as they realised, they could no longer check my statement telepathically, they looked at one another until finally Olaria said, 'How can we know that you are telling us the truth about your age and how long you have been alive?'

'Well, that's the thing about us and not being telepathic. You can't. But if you could see my file. On it exists a copy of my birth certificate, you would see what the written record shows. However, in this conversation you have to take my word, observe me to see if anything about my behaviour or the way I speak would suggest to you that I have lied. I can tell you that the crew's ages range downward from me to Ghia—' I looked at Ghia who simply nodded her agreement to me '—who is the youngest of us at 28 years old.'

The Olarians were puzzled and more than a little disturbed. Each looking carefully at their visitors. Finally, Olaria smiled and shook her head, looking directly at me.

'That was clever. I think I need to continue. I will tell you in the broadest terms about the history of my family and the simple reality of Olarians today. I also want you to believe me, to recognise that I have no reason to deceive you, that as an Olarian, because we are telepathic, normally, we simply could not deceive one another. But I am feeling the need to say this to you. When we are being ourselves, we all know or can know what another is thinking and feeling, it creates the way we relate, makes it entirely different from what we are just beginning to understand about you and your people.'

She shook her head, an indication I thought of her growing frustration and realisation of just how different and perhaps difficult this might be.

'3000 years ago, my father, and three others including my mother who lived in a distant village and whom he had never met, left their homes seeking other telepaths. They first found each other, then another four during a year of searching. They were the original eight telekinetic telepaths on our planet from whom we descended, all 600 or so millions of us.' The Olarians were looking at us with expressions of strained intensity, trying to establish the reaction Olaria was having and seeing, what, so far as they could tell was simply incredulity, but also so far as they could tell, not disbelief. Olaria went on. 'My father and his originals did some frightening things to ensure our survival. Things you may find difficult to understand. There is on our planet another race. They are called Cretians and we almost never speak or think of them, have not for 3000 years, we know virtually nothing about them. The Originals, my parents and six others, put them out of reach of us. They built a wall of almost complete silence around them, which we treat very seriously. I probably would not speak of them further except that you need the information. They were warlike.

They threatened the survival of the Original Eight who protected themselves and future generations by an act of astonishing magnitude: first they needed to get the Cretians to stop attacking their settlement on the Olarian mainland. When the Original Eight visited Cretia, the Cretians sent what you would I think call a Cavalry unit to wipe them out. The Cavalry unit was destroyed by the simple expedient of rolling huge logs down the hill up which they were advancing. They killed all hundred men and their beasts.

The Cretians were still not willing to capitulate, so the Eight destroyed their entire fleet of ships and promised to do it again every time they rebuilt unless they signed a peace treaty. The Cretians were frustrated and confused. Still treating our telepathic parents as a joke, they signed the treaty agreeing to meet every fifty years, and, to the creation of a wall that would seal the Cretian continent from the rest of the planetary continents. They did not for a moment believe these strangers could do any such thing. The Council of Eight, the Originals, having established that Cretia was huge and more than capable of supporting their population, created, in the Ocean one mile from the coast, an energy wall that surrounds the entire land mass of these people and prevented them leaving their continent to attack Jard and his little community ever again. It was a monumental undertaking which took more than a year to complete. Unfortunately, while they were doing this, some Cretians were waging a war on the original Olarian villages. Including the villages which were the homes of the Eight. When these warriors could not return to Cretia because of the wall, they returned to the Olarian continent and fought and overran many of the original non-telepathic Olarian villages and took control of them, raping women, taking whom they wanted for wives, and enslaving them and the entire community. Subsequently, they became a new and constant threat to the telepathic community.'

The story was having its impact on the crew: the distress and disgust of the crew was evident from their agitation.

'Finally, during their ninetieth year, in utter desperation, the Originals used their abilities, to sterilise the entire non-telepathic population on the Olarian continent, so that by the time the telepathic elders had reached their one hundred and thirties the original Olarian village communities had died out. This act, a decision to which all had agreed, in order to ensure their survival, nevertheless horrified the small telepathic world who very nearly did not survive the enormity of what they had done.

One more thing I need to tell you, then I will have said more than any Olarian has spoken for thousands of years except every child is told the true story by the Knowledge Holder Group once in their early life, so they understand. You need to understand and realise, this is a painful and horrific memory we all possess. My father had done one more thing that changed the nature of our world. He and my mother, Leiti, whilst exploring the structure of their brains in order to look after their health, discovered, by accident, the secret of ageing and how to prevent it. As a result, the vast majority of Olarians freeze their age at around 38 years and stay at that age. During the time since, once death was no longer a part of living for us, we have devoted very substantial numbers of people and amounts of our time and resources to understanding how to manage our health and well-being. At this time in our history, we believe we know how to maintain near perfect mental and physical health for as long as we wish to live.'

She finished speaking, and the crew looked at one another. The frustration of the Olarians was palpable. They wanted to know what the impact of Olaria's story had been on us but given they could no longer look inside and find the information. They were watching the different expressions on faces but were not yet able to accurately identify or sort what they were seeing. Their experience at reading faces and bodies had not been developed to the same extent as the crew, they had had no need. They glanced from face to face around the crew evidently waiting impatiently for comment.

So I began; 'I think I am probably speaking for all the crew when I say that I find your story very disturbing.' There was acknowledgement from everyone, including Peta on Sunstreamer. The agitation from the Olarians was equally clear. Without access to their usual sources of information, they were seemingly at a loss as to how they ought to proceed to get the information they wanted. It was Peta's host on Sunstreamer who broke the silence. Perhaps he felt slightly less embarrassed or disabled because he was not physically sitting in the circle.

'I don't really know how to do this, but it feels right that I should ask the crew whether Zed was speaking for all of you, and if you are actually feeling disturbed, what does that mean for us here?'

Tanzin was shaking her head and to the crew it was clear it was not with the intention of expressing disagreement with what I had said. She was agreeing with me and adding disturbed emphasis to my comments.

'Olaria, perhaps I can just say how I am feeling about your story. It seems that at heart you are just like us. You are willing to kill to save yourselves. You are as a race ruthless in pursuit of your safety and survival. I find your story frightening and I am feeling vulnerable here.'

Suddenly it was as if everyone on the Council was trying to speak at the same moment. The babble of almost incomprehensible sound stopped when Olaria burst out laughing.

'Right now, I am filled with curiosity. We have no idea how to proceed, without our telepathic ability we are floundering, we seem to be without the resources to disentangle meaning and feelings here. We need your help to know how to understand what my story means to you and how to correct the impression we appear to have given. Our early history is not an accurate reflection of us today.

To deal with your point Tanzin, there have been consequences resulting from the actions of the Original Eight and the early telepathic community's response to the threats to their survival. We have not been involved in any violence for over twenty-eight hundred years. We are a deeply peaceful, non-violent people. Our society works relentlessly to instil peaceful and interpersonally sensitive processes for all our children and our way of life is without violence. I think this is a consequence of our own distress at the actions of our parents, although we see the reasons they acted as they did.'

Raille, my closest friend, my martial arts sparring partner, the crew Vegetation Analyst and one of the top Linguists in the world (his real hobby and interest) had been nodding quietly. He cleared his throat to get everyone's attention.

'Olaria, members of the Olarian Council of Eight; please forgive me for pointing this out, but it seems to me the only reason you appear to be peaceful is that you have sealed off, destroyed, and simply removed, anyone who could threaten you. You have no enemies. You appear to be an extraordinarily homogeneous society. Absolutely no one threatens your way of life. You have made certain of this. So, when you speak to us of being a peaceful society, we are not likely to feel re-assured. If you come to see us as a threat to your way of life, you may well decide to respond with extraordinary violence as your parents did in the past. Is this not so?' Having made his point, Raille fell silent.

The Olarians looked at one another. With their usual means of sorting out such a situation no longer available to them, they were temporarily and uncharacteristically silent and distressed. It seemed evident many of them wanted to speak, but no one wanted to begin. With no access to instant and accurate information about what the others were thinking and feeling, they seemed temporarily disabled. I looked directly at Olaria,

'Are you beginning to understand what it means to be not telepathic, to have no immediate access to the feelings and thoughts of others? Can you see how hard it is to take a single step to find out how someone else is feeling in a way you can believe, especially when you cannot reach into their mind?

You have, instead, to look at them and read their face and body language. This is more difficult when you cannot get them to speak at all, or, if they do, to know whether what they say is accurately what they mean. You do not know whether you are getting what they are feeling or just something they want you to believe?'

She looked at me.

'Unless I am mistaken, you do not have this problem, at least not to the extent of the others of your crew, and not to the extent we are having. Do you know what we are feeling?' I raised my eyebrows in surprise.

'I believe that to some extent I do, or at least can guess and can test my guesses.'

Olaria was drawn in.

'Please tell me.' I looked at her more intently and more carefully.

'If you will speak to me with no deceit. Will you do that?'

Every person around the group, as well as the couple on Sunstreamer, were intensely focused on the engagement between us. It was the strangest conversation in these circumstances, and it was impossible not to feel more was at stake here than anyone could see.

Olaria nodded.

'Of course,'

I began,

'I can see some of you are getting it. Your facial expressions are less full of frowns. You are no longer screwing up your faces. Your raised eyebrows and nods suggest your concern at what you are learning. You see how different we are, in some ways. I can also see, as you assimilate what is happening here, your faces again darken and become less mobile and tighter than before. Your body tensions are increasing and... most are breathing more shallowly than before, and I am guessing most of your Council are feeling a new level of uncertainty and concern you would not normally experience. Two or three of you—forgive me, but I do not remember everyone's names—are feeling the edges of annoyance, perhaps anger at the constraints you have imposed on them, even though they initially agreed to participate on the terms you described. I am guessing from those expressions they wish you would stop, what they are probably thinking of as a charade. I believe they are not pleased with this experience, this is not the way they would explore our differences, are not, if I am reading correctly, convinced this is a good experiment. And now, if you wish to see how far this accurately reflects their reality, they should speak and confirm or deny my reading of what is going on here with them, without returning to their telepathic reality.'

Several members of the Council began to speak at the same time, then spontaneously stopped.

They looked at one another, obviously a little bewildered. Olaria did not interfere. One of the council members looked around the group, then focused on Olaria.

'Unfortunately, I believe he is substantially correct, certainly for me, and I think for several of us. I want to say, this is the most appalling way to carry on a conversation I can imagine. When I don't know what the rest of you are feeling or thinking, when I can't get access, I feel constrained not to speak and to make demands that you tell me truthfully what is going on for you. This applies to you, my colleagues and to our visitors. It is an awful feeling, really disturbing. I am thinking that if I had to proceed this way, I might begin to cease speaking to you at all. I would just stop and withdraw into my anxiety. I don't know how you ever get anything done, anything discussed. What is worse, I realise that if you spoke, I would not know how to establish that you were speaking from the heart, that you were speaking the truth, although if any of us spoke I believe I would trust what they said, even though I could not check it. However, even as I say this, I am not certain that would long remain true for me. How, by the light of the moon, did you ever get to build your spacecraft and fly it here?'

She stopped. John remained silent for a moment; his brow deeply furrowed. He turned to me, whose instincts and professional competence he trusted. My arms were crossed casually across my chest, my head tilted, taking in everything that was being said but showing no great concern. John took a deep breath, his familiar relaxed expression returning as I continued...

'I think this experiment is working just fine. You are beginning to understand the kind of difficulties we have in communicating with one another. However, we have developed considerable facility in getting our messages across to one another. Because we can't read each other's minds, because we have never been able to, we have developed rules that are mutually understood for sharing information.'

I looked around the group. Heads were shaking, facial expressions were sometimes almost comical and whilst this was a very limited conversation, I was quite astonished at how much low-level tension was visible in the group. I shrugged and just kept going. 'Some people are better at using them than others. Sometimes, when a person does not fully understand the rules or does not have the skill or intelligence to engage satisfactorily with another and is unpractised at managing their feelings of discomfort, they will resort to violence or abuse or will simply lie or try and mislead by saying things that will be intended to mislead the other. We are very skilled in being dishonest, disingenuous, and misleading. Sometimes when this is happening one or both people know it, sometimes not. As a consequence, we have a great deal of more or less continuous misunderstanding of one another, and again violence often results. Further, we exist in many sub-groups: religions, geographies, genetic collections, localities where we were born, but also many others.' I stopped.

'I would like to suggest we simply continue as I believe you, our hosts, will gain considerable insight into us from this experience. I am definitely looking forward to experiencing the other side of this coin.'

At which point I was required to spend several minutes explaining about coins. Finally getting agreement to discuss money and an Economy later. The Olarians, however, indicated that they had no idea what I was talking about. It took several moments to find out that the Olarians did not use any form of barter and had no monetary system! The curiosity and puzzlement of the crew would have to wait.

One after another, the Olarians introduced themselves.

'I am Kyuto, Ghia is my guest, this year I have been alive for 1220 years.' Kyuto explained with a little difficulty that he was responsible for Special Projects and that these were essentially activities that slipped between the cracks of the activity areas of the others.

Peta's host spoke next.

He began, 'I want to begin by saying how strange and disoriented I am feeling. I think you must have developed some very robust ways to manage your lack of information. That you were able to do all that would have been necessary to get you here strikes me as pretty impressive, given my experience of your communication processes at the moment. I am responsible for planetary weather and like Kyuto there are around thirty-five million people who operate in my groups. Like all the other groups, we study the weather and only manipulate it when we can see the patterns changing in ways that could be harmful, usually to our agriculture. The other exception relates to weather exiting (departing from) the Cretian continent.

This requires continuous cleaning, something to do with some of the material they put into the atmosphere but also into their waterways.'

The next host picked up the thread. 'I have been here for 1312 years and my responsibilities relate to the Knowledge Holders. I have considerably more than thirty million members of my groups and they divide roughly into three groups, each in different time zones. We do this to ensure that one group is available to everyone at any time whilst the others are either rebuilding or sleeping.'

It was clear to her from the frowns and obvious confusion amongst the crew that she needed to say some more about her groups. 'We do not have computers such as you use to store knowledge, we use people.'

The surprise and exclamations of confusion from the crew led her on.

'Back in the beginning, soon after it was clear we were not going to die anytime soon, we had to figure out ways to store the important knowledge we were accumulating. We have writing and we use it for recording some things, for recording stories we tell, but only short ones. We sometimes write, using a treated bark on which we also paint, using colours from various organic substances and from energy sources drawn from various specific locations. In addition, we create what we imagine you would call energy art. But writing has never been very important. We tend to use ourselves, our bodies and our minds whenever possible for the things we need. Except, that is, for the communities of artists who have found ways to use almost everything in our living world to express themselves.

'So, we created a group of people who would store our knowledge. Initially, a small group who would take responsibility for remembering everything they were told. However, it quickly became evident this was not going to work. Leiti and Karen, two of the Originals, whilst working with Jard, came up with the idea of using unconscious processes. Leiti and Jard had been exploring each of the areas of our brains when they discovered how to control our ageing, they used a similar process to explore how we stored information in memory and then begun an exploration of ways to use this to expand the accessibility of unconscious processes. It took more than a century to perfect this. During that time, we lost a lot of knowledge and a considerable number of knowledge holders went mad or died. Finally, we learned how to take care of them and for the last two and a half thousand years we have lost nothing and have developed these unconscious control processes to a very high level of effectiveness and safety for the members of the Knowledge Holder group.' She stopped.

The crew looked bewildered, but it was Peta from Sunstreamer who asked the question. 'Are you telling us that your entire library of knowledge is stored in the unconscious minds of your people, living knowledge holders, a Living Library?'

'Essentially, yes, and I do love your words for us... A Living Library!' she replied. The incredulity of the crew was palpable. Raille, however, who was her guest, was burning with curiosity and now very keen to get her alone to explore further. She, however, who was looking at Raille could not decipher his expression. Having agreed not to use her telepathic abilities to get inside his head, she was concerned that he might be showing displeasure. She need not have worried.

Raille noticed her distress and accurately assessing what was happening for her, looked directly at her, smiled and said, 'I am delighted to be your guest and seriously interested in us to talk.' At which point, she smiled, and the next host picked up the thread.

She introduced herself and said, 'I have been alive for 1350 years and am responsible for the Sub-surface geology of the planet. Everything from the Olarian Core to the surface, excluding water, and I have a similarly large collection of groups to the others, I never actually remember how many groups of how many millions are involved, but the majority of our groups are of similar size.'

At which comment, the other Council members smiled. She wore her hair wound into a turban shape which was managed by cleverly woven energy strands. It was a rich brown colour and cast her soft even features into a backdrop for her greenish eyes, which twinkled as she smiled.

She is, John thought, very elegant looking for a geologist. And, since I can, at least for the moment, think my own thoughts without being listened in on, I am also finding myself thinking of her as an interesting-looking woman. Like the others, she feels friendly. The thought was his alone, and he felt a sense of relief that she could not know what he was thinking. Then he realised they were allowing him this privacy to learn about humans, not because he was being given any privacy. The thought that stayed was he was going to have to learn quick here. This planet was very distant from, yet disturbingly like, his home. She had one other comment to make, one which got the total attention of the entire crew.

'Some five or six hundred years ago, one of our exploring parties were working at a considerable depth. They came across skeletal remains of what looked suspiciously like an Olarian or a Cretian skeleton. We believe about 25 million years old. We have been seeking more since then, but so far without success. However, we feel certain we will find more evidence of an earlier civilisation and that is one of our truly exciting projects, it always attracts new members.'

Next was Gerard's host. She had been alive for 1400 years and was responsible for Education on Olar and like the others was involved with many millions of Olarian Educators. Jald was Tanzin's host, and it turned out he was Olaria's last child, born 788 years ago. He was the Cosmologist responsible for the space between the surface of Olar and infinity. An area, he explained, filled with an astonishing quantity and variety of energies that his group studied. The many millions of members of his team worked in thousands of groups, each with their particular energy strands. Tanzin realised there was so much information she was not getting she was going to have to think very carefully about how to probe deeper into this alien yet seemingly familiar world.

The final introduction was from the Bio-medic's host and he said,'I have been around for 1423 years. For as long as I can remember I have studied our minds and our bodies, in ways that have often been quite bizarre. It will not surprise you to learn that once we realised, we were living long lives our health became a top priority. Illnesses and disabilities occur in our population much as they always have, so understanding their causes and how to deal with them remains a priority for us.

A very high proportion of physical dysfunctions are initiated and are consequently managed by engaging with changes in the brain. However, there are literally hundreds of intelligent behaviour centres in every organ and in every part of the body, even blood vessels have a manageable form or intelligence and perhaps even more so the billions of tiny organisms that inhabit our gut and every tube and cavity in our bodies. We have often thought of our bodies as an assembly of tubes!

Whoever designed us or if it was not a who, then however we were designed, the complexity of the plan layer by layer down to what you appear to call the 'sub-atomic' level has an astonishing level of understanding which we believe we will probably never be able to achieve. But we move constantly toward it.'

This was calculated to catch a Bio-medics attention as well as the rest of the crew who were totally fascinated with the idea and wanted to know more.

'I honestly don't know how many people are in my group, it was over thirty-five million when we tallied it last, but many young people join us to see if they can get a fuller understanding of themselves. At first, they get overwhelmed when they find the extraordinary breadth of things we are studying, still we think of our knowledge as primitive. Most of us want to understand more about sentience and what exactly happens to our life energy when someone dies. No one has yet reached satisfactorily into that well of understanding.'

He stopped. The entire human crew were looking at him. He had continued to engage everyone's interest. But that was it for the moment, and attention shifted back to Olaria. However, before anyone else spoke, I had a question.

'Olaria this is addressed to you but also to the entire Council. You have just had the experience of sharing information without your usual ability to identify what the recipients were thinking and feeling about what was said. Now it's true that the information you all gave us was not really emotionally charged, but I am curious, before we move on, to know what each of you has thought and felt about what has just happened here, especially if you could do this before you return to your normal telepathic reality.'

Olaria did not immediately pick up the thread but turned to look at her companions, eyebrows raised.

Raille's host spoke first. 'My feeling is of walking in the dark, no light ahead, no light around, yet I can see, but only dimly. It's as if my world has been closed in and I can only see some of what is around, much is out of sight, and I am able to make sense only of some of that world.

This is definitely not a comfortable feeling. Frankly, I am having enormous difficulty believing you are aged between 28 and 38 years of age. I have an almost uncontrollable desire to return to my telepathic reality and check that out. It seems incredible if it is true. It raises issues about our assumptions and our education I am hardly able to articulate. How come we take so long to learn?

Zed, I see you looking at me with a puzzled expression, but I don't know what is concerning you. I would really like to know.

I nodded. 'Like you, I am wondering about the learning. I think the length of our lives might be the biggest factor. We have to get on with our education and get down to work because shortly we will be ageing and less able to achieve some of the things we wish to achieve. I'm not sure it's really much more complicated than that?' She nodded, doubtless thinking about what I said, and finally she appeared satisfied.

Olaria was watching me, then looked around at the crew, one by one, and finally the Council members. 'I feel as though I am walking in thick oozing mud.' She spoke. 'Without information I am feeling not only uncomfortable, but uncertain about how to proceed. I desperately want to look and listen without these appalling restrictions.'

'Exactly,' I responded. 'Right at this moment you are living in our world.'

'But it is so barren. Please accept in advance my apology for the insult this must seem to be, but if I had to live in this silent world, I think I would soon go crazy. I can already feel myself getting desperate to return to a saner and more informative place. I am barely tolerating holding myself back. I don't know what's really going on, what people are really thinking and feeling. I hardly know how to proceed.'

It was clear looking at the Olarian Council members they were in complete agreement with what Olaria was saying. I continued; 'Please don't return to your telepathic world for a few more moments. I am feeling uncomfortable asking you to remain in this disturbing state, but I really want us to understand each other, and I do not know a way to do this without the discomfort. I am sure you understand what we are trying to achieve, and I believe it will turn out to be really helpful if you can actually understand our dilemma here and what you experience as our limitations, if we are to genuinely share our two worlds. This is our normal. This is how we experience life. We don't feel the distress you seem to be experiencing because we have no real understanding of how you experience the world. This is how we engage with one another all the time. Our political processes reflect this inability to verify information and identify true feelings.

'In all of our ordinary working and personal lives, this is the amount of information we have to work with. I don't think any of us can yet even imagine what relationships could be like from your perspective. However, I believe you are getting a very clear impression of what it might be like living as we do. I am hoping it will help you understand why we have so many of the problems we have, how easily many of us slip into duplicity and lying and how fraught are most of our interpersonal relationships; relationships of all kinds, even intimate ones.'

Kyuto, Ghia's host, looked across the space directly at me.

'It must take time you seem not to have to construct your relationships, it surprises me you can work together, as you must have, to bring your spaceship here, to even have been able to construct it.'

I heard in the tone and fashion of his comment what seemed to be a hidden challenge. The mere whisper of disbelief and I felt a powerful almost desperate urge for them to get it, to understand what happened in human lives. But having nothing to give but information, I decided to continue.

'We are able to lie and misinform one another about how we are and what matters to us, usually to protect ourselves from our own feelings of inadequacy and our fear of failing.' This time I paused and wished I could show them one of the experiences of human relationships coming apart, so they could see and experience the problem as I knew it. But I had taken that resource away with my clever process and now wished to get it back, so I could convince them. But reluctantly gave up, for the moment, and continued. 'We are generally uncomfortable with our own and other people's feelings and tend to avoid engaging with them because we don't know what other people's truths are, frequently we are not certain about our own. We grow up learning to manage with this amount of information. We watch people and we listen to how things are said. And this is magnified by our uncertainty about the appropriateness of our feelings toward others and our feelings about our own adequacy.

So, I would like to welcome you to our reality, our world and its limitations. We compensate a little for this lack of accurate, real time information, by using ourselves as a reference point for how others probably are. We hear quite subtle changes in tone and pitch and loudness in other people's speech and we notice changes in body language and skin colour and some other non-verbal cues, however, this information is not always as accurate as we would like, and nowhere near as accurate as your information about one another. Sometimes we get clear strong bursts of emotion from others when we express ourselves strongly to one another, but we feel usually uncomfortable when we do this. I suspect you do not have this problem.'

Facial expressions and nods suggested that most of the Olarians seemed to be indicating their agreement.

'I believe you needed to experience our limitations. As individuals we simply do not easily understand one another, you now know this. So, for us to really get acquainted with you, we are going to need your help. But and this is a big but, we have been able to overcome much of our inability to understand one another by turning our attention to things, so we study the world with a kind of objectivity, using what we call Science, a seemingly objective model for the collection of information and its processing. This process, with all our limitations, has allowed us to find and visit you here in a piece of the cosmos we have never previously known.'

I was now sure Kyuto, Ghia's host, did not get it. The frowns, the slight shaking of his head, it looked like this was just not quite believable to him. 'In a moment, I know you will need to return to your reality in which we cannot fully participate. It might prove helpful if you recall this experience. I wonder if you are able to think of ways you might help us understand your reality. And, before you return there Olaria, would you please consider whether there is some way you might include us in your awareness of everyone's thoughts and feelings? It is quite impossible for us to imagine what that would be like. Could we, in some way, get a sense of what it is like to be telepathic, like you. Is there some way for you to include us in exactly what happens when you return to your normal state?'

Looking around the crew, I realised there was a great deal of consternation, uncertainty, anxiety, and through it all, a burning natural curiosity. Excepting, possibly, Gerrard, whose natural instincts were heavily modified by his concern for Ghia and their as yet unborn child.

Before the session ended, Peta let out an exclamation, then apologised, 'It's just, when Olaria was discussing the wall and the Cretians I had a niggle, then I realised why the scans from the probe showed a whole section of the planet as empty, it was the energy wall around Cretia created by the original Olarians. Sorry,'

She said, 'Just got it.' And she smiled with pleasure, cat with the canary. expression on her face.

Everyone was looking at Peta, so no one actually saw the expression on Olaria's face, which was captured by several of the crew Holo recorders. It happened just seconds after the Olarians returned to their normal. Olaria turned slightly to look at me. I caught her and realised she too had just got some insight, something she wanted to tell me? Show me? I could feel the strong desire, but no more. However, it seemed, given our present situation whatever it was, was going to have to wait and I wondered what could be so important.

CHAPTER 6

The Roles Are Reversed

After Peta's outburst, the entire crew looked at me in apparent disbelief at my request to be included in the Olarians' telepathic process. Had they heard correctly? Then like a silent movie all eyes returned to Olaria, moving slowly to take in the other members of the Council. Olaria looked at first a little more than surprised, I imagined I was seeing something like delight and amusement. Then the entire crew heard, in their minds, the sound of her amusement, a delightful bubbly chuckle.

Oh, Zed!

All the crew and the Council heard it without external sound as she reconnected to everyone telepathically and without a break in the flow. It had been said with warmth and with what felt like a familiarity and affection! *Absolutely,* she spoke. Next moment, she was speaking to the Council, but the crew heard her words. They felt the surge of relief as she engaged both the crew and the Council simultaneously and telepathically.

If we all feed our thoughts and feelings to them, they will experience us, but we need to remember they will almost certainly be unable to sort our communications in the same way we do, nor will they be able to manage with anything approximating our usual speed, so please speak slowly and remember to deliberately feed your feelings out with your thoughts.

She paused for a moment, looking at them all. She felt... something. What was it? As she sat looking at all of us and then a glance at the Holomonitor, these humans... she knew Olarian lives were already changing, right here, and a shiver of fear passed almost unnoticed over her. She had felt it when the strange Probe had turned up in their system;

she felt it now as she returned to what she had been saying. In 3000 years no Olarian had ever had to deal with any outsider, ever. This was already an extraordinary challenge to such a homogeneous society.

I am pretty certain this will not be enough to properly engage them with us and there is no way you will be able to sort your reading of their emotions back to them with any clarity because it will be way too rapid for them to get the information or process it. So, I think to begin with, at least, we ought to keep everything short and terribly slow and if necessary, summarise what we are experiencing. Imagine them as our young children or as yourselves when you were very young.

For an instant there was a burst of what to the crew sounded like babble, which Olaria immediately suggested they stop. However, as they explored, it became clear that even the Olarians' slowest communication rate was too rapid for the crew. The Olarians did not need any conscious process to read, accurately, emotional states in others, their awareness of emotions was inaccessible to the crew unless the Olarians first made them conscious, then shared them. Because the telepathic process the Olarians used drew on pre-conscious thoughts; the thoughts and the emotions accompanying them were known to the Olarians a fraction of a second before they became conscious thoughts or experiences the crew could use. If a crew member decided, as they became aware of the thought, that it needed censoring before they spoke, it was already too late.

The Olarians had heard it. The altered spoken thought was immediately recognised as an alteration on the original. It might be heard as a lie, or at least as confused or somewhat misleading. When the Olarians were being telepathic, the problem was speed. If they engaged with the crew at their normal rate telepathically—in order for the crew to experience their telepathic communications—they seemed to be communicating so fast the information was overwhelming and hopelessly confusing to the crew. So, Olaria stepped in again.

I think we need to approach this experience for our human guests in a different way. Perhaps each of us should speak only to our own guest, allowing him or her full access to our thoughts and emotions and our awareness of theirs. We need to keep this process uncomplicated if it is to work. I fear they will be as overwhelmed with information as we were starved for it. So, I suggest that as one crew member introduces his or herself, their host shares telepathically whatever they are hearing and feeling from the sixteen of us. This way our guests will get some sense of what we normally hear and feel during a discussion.

I was thinking about it. Communication experiences with nowhere to hide!

Olaria had paused and fed my thoughts and feelings to the rest of the crew who now looked at me, and I felt their tension, confusion and uncertainty—connected to a deep stream of almost fearful excitement, anticipation and desire. The complexity of human emotions and thoughts being laid bare in the fashion of the Olarian normality was bewildering, yet I knew no one actually wanted the disturbing experience to stop! I shook my head, looking intently at Olaria. Her entire body posture was now relaxed and her face softer and more peaceful.

However, it was Tanzin who spoke to Jald. He was looking directly at her and as she told him her age, where she was born and what her job on Sunstreamer entailed. She became aware that he was intrigued by her red hair and the strength and warmth of her voice, and the intensity of her feelings which he was noticing she kept slightly hidden in the background of her thoughts and words.

Tanzin was intrigued, disturbed and overloaded with the information pouring into her awareness. Especially the emotional aspects of it were proving too much for her to manage, an entirely novel experience for someone who processed as much cognitive information and possessed such an extraordinary cognitive capacity as did she. She was finding it increasingly difficult to continue speaking, and when she picked up the concern and other emotions, especially from Ghia, Peta and Elise our Biomed., her ability to speak dried up entirely. Then Jald was filling her mind with the concerns and confusion both of the Olarians about where she had been born and the crew about how overloaded she was feeling. The result was, she simply froze.

Jald immediately stopped giving her telepathic information and she slowly relaxed and felt able to look around the group. In as much as the Olarians had been jammed up and frozen by the lack of information, the humans were hopelessly overwhelmed by the quantity, variety and rate of the communication of the Olarians.

Her next comment was, 'Bloody hell.' Then, 'I'm used to handling lots of information, but when you shared the emotions and the unspoken thoughts of all the others it just got too much. I mean it was a simple enough task, just name, rank and serial number really. But not with all that background information at the same time!'

It was Raille who summed it up, using the Olarians temporary telepathic gift to the crew. He thought, our computers let us understand how much sub-vocal information processing is going on when we speak, however, the actual experience of participating I found quite overwhelming. As Tanzin so eloquently expressed it. Bloody hell! I don't understand how you are able to do it.

Olaria frowned as she looked at him.

I'm struggling a bit with how to describe this. When you look, you are simply using your eyes. When we look the part of our brain that sees energy and the part that manages our telepathy both "look" and I am not too clear how to describe the differences for you. We see energy, it is a visual experience, each energy has a colour, but the information is routed to this other area in our brain.

Our telepathy works in a similar way, we hear the activity of your thinking and pick up, feel, experience, the energy vibrations which are your emotional responses. We have over the centuries given birth to three or four children who did not have the telepathic and telekinetic areas in their brain. We learned to help them grow up and live in our society, but none of them chose to have their lives extended, which we now know would have been fatal for them. None lived beyond their sixties, by their own choice. None who were alive when I was born are alive today. I don't really understand why we don't understand you. We had no trouble understanding them, solving this problem with them, but then they were ours and they lived in our world.

She could see our disappointment.

However, she continued, *our Knowledge Holders have a detailed record of their lives, so, if it is important to help you understand some aspect of us, they can help. All of us will be revisiting the lives of these Olarians held by our Knowledge Holder group.*

When Olaria had finished speaking, Ghia who had been watching her intently became aware of the tension amongst the crew. She was sure Kyuto, sitting next to her, was doing what Olaria had asked, feeding his awareness to her. Ghia was not a shrinking violet. She turned and looked at him, immediately knew he was expressing his curiosity and so, in her direct and confident way, began to speak to him. She followed Tanzin's lead, telling him her age, where she was born and her role on Sunstreamer. Throughout these few moments she was looking directly at him and thought, as she did so, I wonder what you are thinking of me? This thought popped into her head before she had considered the consequences, and so, when in a flash she knew he was thinking courageous and interesting and unbelievably young and that he wanted to know that she really was 28 years old and got that information from her thinking about it, she knew he was incredulous that she was in so important and complex a position and pregnant at so young an age!

Thing is, in that instant she knew the others had heard the interchange and no words had been spoken. She felt weird, spooked and as she looked around, she found herself in each of the minds of her colleagues on the crew and when she experienced Gerard she burst into tears.

She knew he was feeling love and concern for her, knew he was desperate to hold her. Immediately these insights hit her she felt embarrassed and a whole panoply of emotions tumbled after it: outrage, anger and confusion at feeling so exposed. She dried her eyes, quickly pulling herself together. As she looked around, she realised everyone was looking at her and became aware of a huge wave of warmth, caring, concern and support. It was astonishing and very comforting. She felt responses from the crew way beyond anything they would normally have said or shared, and in that moment, she was grateful to the Olarians for their telepathic abilities.

With the help of the Olarians, each member of our crew got to introduce themselves, and experience, if in a somewhat reduced form, the telepathic reality. The experience was unlike any other in our lives. Even in this carefully reduced form, the telepathic sharing was exhausting, although extraordinarily caring and supportive in a way no one in the crew had really experienced before, except, and several of them found this surprising, as infants in contact with their mothers. It left all of us feeling comfortable yet very exposed and in need of some of the inner peace we normally got from privacy. We had, in the short time involved, experienced more about the Olarians and each other than we would have believed possible. It was certainly an experience we would remember.

I participated fully in the experience. However, I was looking ahead to what might be the consequences of what the eight of us were learning. In the ordinary course of events, the issues of the future would not have been my responsibility. But these were not ordinary events. So, I began a reflection intended to re-arrange our focus.

I'm just wanting everyone's help to work a rather novel problem in which we are, I believe, now, all deeply involved. I would like this invitation extended to our Olarian hosts if they are willing to join with us.

I could feel the Olarians exploring my thinking, but I was managing to keep it, for the moment, only in fragments and mostly outside my focused consciousness. Olaria was smiling. She and then the other Olarians seemed to know I was utilising an ability of which I was substantially unaware. There was no hesitation from them or the crew. Because of its complexity, I felt the need to say it out loud.

'Okay, here's the issue. We are all learning some important things about the differences between us. Your ability to operate intimately and with clarity in areas of emotional awareness far exceeds ours. Yet, we were the ones who found you.'

The crew were exhibiting signs of agitation, a bit of foot shuffling and occasional frowns and looking down at the ground.

Nevertheless, I continued. 'So, it appears we represent two divers yet functional ways for people to operate.' Everyone was focussing the frowns and movement had ceased.

'I am thinking we need to understand one another in order to speak and think freely and openly with each other. However, your ability to manipulate us disturbs me. You have posed a problem we need solved. For us to accept the credibility of your offer to allow us to return home, which I realise you have already demonstrated, I believe we need to know how you can believe it can be safe for you to permit us to leave here, in spite of the fact that we know you have already done that.' I looked around at the group.

'This experience has opened a new line of thought for me, which I don't believe is irrelevant, even at this early stage in our relationship with you.'

I could feel the crew watching me closely.

'I am saying this to the crew because it is something they will understand, but I want our Olarian hosts to hear it, and, in so far as they can, understand what it is that is concerning me.' I looked around at the crew and our hosts, then just continued. 'Our society is not usually generous nor supportive, it is more competitive than co-operative. Big organisations, like Space Fleet Command, are both bureaucratic and highly controlling. By their very nature, not enormously flexible. They almost universally protect their interests against other coming interests, especially for money, usually babying secretive about assets that might give them an advantage in the constant battle for funds, power and prestige.' I could see that I had everyone's attention, however, I was certain it was for two quite different reasons.

The Crew were anxious about what I might be going to say, whilst the Olarians were being barraged by concepts which might be quite unfamiliar to them.

'When we return, we will be debriefed in secret, away from any public scrutiny. When it appears, as I believe it inevitably will, that we have returned with a potential "gold mine" of information and possible resources, it is more than likely that the reality of or meeting with the Olarians might be hidden from the Public whilst the powers-that-be, those responsible for the running of and in control of SFC, are likely to decide that what we have learned is simply too potentially valuable to SFC to be released to the world, yet. 'I was aware of the growing looks of horror and distress on the faces of the crew. I was, I knew, speaking the unspeakable.

However, I was on a roll and I did not plan on stopping now. 'The free sharing of information will not be an item high on their agenda. I am trying to imagine where relatively insignificant carriers of potentially valuable information, "us" might find ourselves. Is my paranoid fantasy shared by any others of you? And I hasten to add, I know all this is on record, so this is also a very risky revelation.'

Nearly every member of the crew was staring at me, aghast. Everyone wanted to speak, however, simultaneously they were all aware of what I had just done. Recordings of most conversations were routine, I had not been speaking on any of the private side channels, and suddenly no one was too keen to be the next one to say what was now out in the open and potentially could carry disastrous consequences.

It was Olaria who first grasped the nature of what I had just done. Speaking telepathically to the entire crew, she said, *I think I understand the potentially hazardous action Zed has just taken. I am speaking to you telepathically in order that your devices cannot record what I am saying. I would like to invite you, Zed, and the rest of you to whom it is also important—and immediately everyone knew it was important to all of them—to perhaps hold this discussion until a later time when we have come to understand one another somewhat better.*

From every member of the crew there was affirmation, and this included me.

There is one other pattern we have noticed when we listen in to your discussions, and which we would like to understand. It is a pattern that we did not see when you were working together, flying your spacecraft when you seem to say what you mean. This other pattern, which we have decided is the one your language library calls 'being polite', makes it difficult for us to understand what you are actually saying, because you seem to be deliberately not saying what you mean! You lie to one another. You say "thank you" when you are thinking, "I wish he would shut up!",

It seems you want the listener to believe you feel more positive toward them than you, in fact, do. And we are guessing that because you don't actually know what others are thinking, both of you can carry on as though the relationship between you is okay, when it isn't. Is this right? Oh!

She had just picked up my understanding of it and shook her head.

You mean, at some undisclosed level, you know the person is not being honest. But their saying it this way makes it alright to say it. But it would be rude to actually say what you were thinking or what you meant, even though the other person actually knows you mean the opposite of what you say? Ghia was looking at Olaria with a puzzled expression.

'You are suggesting that when we are being polite, we are lying to one another?' I chuckled.

'Sure, from childhood our mothers taught us to say, "thank you" to someone for something they may have offered us, even if we thought the offering was unpleasant, like a sweet or food we did not like. It's one of the socially acceptable lies we all use. And, of course, we all know it is a lie, just an acceptably phrased one.'

Ghia paused, frowning. Then as she processed my comment, she finally nodded her agreement.

'That's true, I'd never thought of it like that.' Smiling, she said, 'I like the idea that my mother taught me to lie!'

Olaria was watching the two of us with a curious frown, shook her head, then with a twinkle in her eye continued, *I can see we have a lot to learn about one another.* I was staring intently at Olaria. *Ask,* she said, seeing my unspoken question and knowing the others would soon also be wanting to know.

'Okay,' I continued, 'How do you eight get to become the Council of Eight with the responsibilities to run the society?'

Olaria laughed and I could see that we again felt the contagion, it was infectious and left the hearer feeling lighter and wanting to grin from ear to ear, qualitatively unlike the majority of the laughter experiences of the human crew.

You are only meeting us as the Eight because of the timing of your journey. Had you come ten or twenty years ago, you would have met others. If you had come in ten— or twenty—year's time you would probably have met still others.

Most of us were either shaking our heads or frowning. However, the Olarian organisational pattern was becoming a bit clearer. People come and go from the Council, similarly, individuals who are taking overall responsibility for each of the special interest groups will change from time to time.

Most of us were affirming that we understood as she spoke. *There are no fixed arrangements, there is no special significance as to who is doing the organising role in any particular group at any moment in time. When someone is ready and the present person is ready to move to another role, it happens. There is no hierarchical status as there is with your Captain and crew. We saw that very shortly after you entered our Solar System. We make distinctions, but they are not hierarchic.*

On that note, the group seemed to have had had enough for the present, and without anything actually being said, paired off and by a kind of unconscious osmosis the couples seemed to know they were ready to move away from the circle. For the crew and the Olarians this had been a big awakening, for all of them Human and Olarian alike there were more questions.

I noticed as they rose from the energy seats that these disappeared and knew Olaria was doing it. She turned toward me; her face a study in uncertainty. I could feel she wanted something of me but not what, however, it did feel as though it was... intense? I could not put my finger on it and was definitely feeling confused. Her face was a study in tiny transformations, a bit like watching someone who wanted to say something but didn't quite know how to say it, maybe even what exactly it was they wanted to say. Was it related to me or something to which I had no connection?

Olaria turned, and I felt her hand gently in the middle of my back, guiding me, it seemed, toward the edge of the field, no sound spoken nor in my mind. This had been some introduction! It was so quiet as everyone left with their hosts; almost funereal, I thought, except the very air around us seemed to be vibrating with energy. My strongest feeling was "Everyone is changed" our recent experiences more or less ensured that.

'Well,' I mused, 'the last couple hours have definitely been a game changer.'

I felt certain I was not the only one, way out of their comfort zone, and wondered where this was going to lead. My confidence had been boosted and then depleted by the events of the last engagement and was quite badly shaken by everything that had happened. Nothing was really resolved, and in fact, very little had been learned that had not opened up more questions than had been answered. Were we really confident we could return home if and when we wished? And, if we could return, would we be believed? Was our credibility going to be challenged? Would my debriefers believe my account of events if I returned home today? I felt as certain as I could be, back home, I probably would not be believed! I repeated Tanzin's comment, 'Bloody hell' and for the moment I was, for all intents and purposes, no more than a leaf in the wind on an alien world.

CHAPTER 7
Moving Out from Safety, Tanzin & Jald

Tanzin

As the group broke up, I felt emotions far outpaced reason. The first two sessions of contact had stressed both the Olarians and us to the max. It was obvious the Olarians had never been without their telepathic awareness of one another; we humans had never had certain knowledge of what others were thinking and feeling. I was aware that disturbance had been the over-riding factor in this novel situation. Jald was walking us toward the boundary of the field, and I was keeping up with him, with some difficulty. There came a moment when he suddenly seemed to get a twinge of distress at his failure to realise, I had been almost jogging to keep up. He stopped. Apologised, slowed and his fingers came to rest lightly on my elbow. He now walked at a slower, reasonable pace, and I settled slightly closer to him. Within seconds, I began to feel uneasy from the warmth and apparent intimacy of the engagement. Jald immediately picked up on my distress and paused.

Have I behaved in some way inappropriate for you?

'Would you touch one of the men like this?' I asked. Jald smiled at me, not in the least disturbed by the question.

He paused for a moment. *I don't know. I think so. What exactly is uncomfortable about it?*

'When you touch me, it is too intimate, I hardly know you, you could be my gaoler. I don't know what you want. I don't know what I want except to be able to return home. I just feel a bit crazy in this situation.'

Jald was keeping his word; his thoughts and feelings were there for me to know.

Gaoler was not a concept he understood, and so I thought about gaolers and the early history of prisoners and gaolers. Jald was horrified. He followed the movie I was creating. I knew now how to share information with him, but the information I was sharing had flipped him out. I didn't know which way to turn.

I was thinking about what I had learned so far. If they had told it correctly, these people were one huge homogeneous society. They did not meet strangers. I on the other hand lived in a world that was far from homogeneous and strangers were an everyday reality. And strangers would be different from me in many ways. Olarians were just another group of strangers, and then some.

This relationship was getting off to an unusual beginning, yet not threatening nor in any way offensive, just a little intrusive. I smiled quietly in my mind at the novelty of allowing myself to go with the mood of my host. Something I knew I would never have tolerated from a male member of the crew and would have been uncomfortable with a female member of the crew doing it.

I also realised I had been speaking out loud and using the telepathy he was maintaining as they had agreed but this was me on this new world, it was something else and to my amazement I felt able to let my judgements go. Nothing about relating to these strange beings was going to be simple.

As usual I pushed myself just a little harder, knowing it was unusual for me to be this flexible when it came to relationships with men. Then little by little it became clear. Jald already knew what feelings I was having, what I actually liked and wanted, and he was now making available to me the same accurate, bullshit-free information about himself. He was being genuine, I knew, he was feeding me his feelings and thoughts and, perhaps for the first time in my life, I believed what I was hearing and feeling. It was, somehow, deeply comforting, a feeling I had not known, no warning bells, no feelings of caution or uncertainty. It was a feeling of safety I could not remember feeling with a man at any point in my entire life. A tear slid slowly down my face. I stopped and experienced the deep sadness I must have been holding back for a long time. This moment was as unusual as it was disturbing.

I felt as though it brought a new element into the mix. I tried to isolate it; it seemed I could no longer, with comfort, rely on my past. Now I was getting updated and accurate information about what Jald thought about me, momentarily. I knew I was getting that from him about himself as well. It was very strange and at first disturbing that he knew, accurately, what I was thinking and feeling. And that, I felt uncomfortable knowing, included about him. I was beginning to recognise how this knowledge was impacting the development of a relationship between us. This was a new learning curve, and I felt the need to master it, rapidly.

'As if to mark the moment,' Jald spoke.

I can see how this is confusing for you, but please believe me when I tell you that the idea of not knowing what your partner is thinking and feeling is equally scary to me. Unthinkable, in fact. Constantly flying blind, no idea what is happening with your partner, having to notice surface signals and make a guess. Now that's seriously frightening, Tanzin.

I could not help liking it, but it disturbed me.

'What about if I am having a fantasy about you, say a sexual fantasy?'

You already have and it was flattering. You remember! when we first made contact and then again when you were sitting in the group. Neither of us made a comment about it at the time. Remember?

I felt seriously embarrassed, briefly. Then I looked at him, heard his honest reassurance and settled down inside. This was a relationship like no other I had ever experienced. No boundaries and no private thoughts... No games and no deceits. I turned to Jald. It was at this point that I became conscious that sometimes I was speaking out loud and sometimes I was not. What brought this to my conscious awareness was a realisation that speaking out loud had become more cumbersome and not speaking out loud had become quicker and easier!

'Jald, things between people are never simple or straightforward, I don't see this relationship working. You aren't going to like some of the things I think about you, and I am probably not going to like some of your thoughts about me. If they are all going to be out in the open, known, we will quickly become bad friends and that will not be good. I am bound to not like some things Olarian, some of your personal habits, your ways, and you will know. How will this work for us?'

Trust me, Tanzin, it will. Think about this, there are 600,000+ millions of us, we all know all about each of us with whom we relate, we are almost uniformly caring and mutually supportive at all times. So, unpleasant thoughts and difficult thoughts must be able to be relatively easily worked out or we would be hopelessly dysfunctional.

'I suppose.'

I played with the thought for a moment and then for another moment and what he said made sense and I knew I was beginning to trust myself with him. People from two different solar systems, two different worlds, were making a connection. For an instant, I wondered about the others.

'Will we be staying at your place?' Jald nodded. 'How will I know where it is safe to walk or run?'

Jald was clearly confused.

How might it be unsafe?

'Violence, people not wanting strangers around.' Jald stopped.

I don't understand, Nowhere on Olar will be in any way unsafe. I could see him watching me with a rather puzzled expression. *No one will harm you anywhere on Olar!*

'What about criminals? Where are your prisons?'

Jald looked perplexed and had to ask what a criminal was. Then before I could answer I realised he had found the definition.

There are no prisoners here. No criminals, no crime, anywhere in Olaria.

I followed his thinking and began to get another inkling of the differences on this new world. Absorbing that, I enquired about shops and food and clothing. Again, it took several moments for Jald to follow, this time helped with images I was generating. He stopped again.

Tanzin, anything you want, anything at all, please just ask me or any Olarian you meet, if we are not together. Anyone will help you find a solution to anything you require.

I stopped still, just a few metres from Jald's Drifter, his small two seat traveller now coloured the colour of my hair. No criminals, no sick people, no shops, no money, no old people, no waste except from Cretia and no longer any disastrous weather events they could not manage!

CHAPTER 8

Zed & Olaria

As she turned toward me, apparently to make her invitation more personal, Olaria had an experience barely remembered from her childhood, she was feeling... shy! I suddenly got a burst of her feelings and thoughts about me, and I stared at her, slowly shaking my head from side to side, watching her closely...What was it about this man? Olaria couldn't think what she wanted to say, and she couldn't remember the last time in her long life when she had felt this way. Not since she was a child.

She was keeping me in contact with her thoughts, so I became aware she was thinking that she had already lived longer than her mother. Then I became aware she seemed to be certain I was special! I had no idea exactly what that meant or what else she was thinking because, right now, without her help, I could not see further into her. Suddenly, I realised, she did not know where to begin. Worse, she was thinking that she had never had a visitor who was not an Olarian!

I got glimpses of her thoughts, which she must have been allowing me to see. She could not comprehend how she could explain the emotional hold I seemed to have on her; of which I completely unaware. I knew she felt bound by her agreement to share her thoughts and feelings with me and being absolutely unwilling to breach her agreement, she was doing just that! And, I was thinking, I was not necessarily wildly enthusiastic about that right now!

I was captivated by her beautiful green eyes and the intense feeling of something more between us. But also, by the fact that when she had told me I was her chosen guest,

I had had a very disturbing experience. There was a pull between us that seemed to have no source, no rhyme nor reason. Just an inexplicable connection, clearly impossible.

'Oh, come on.' I muttered to myself. I felt as though I was sliding down a perfectly smooth wet wall, my hands finding nothing to grip. 'Get a grip.'

But the feeling would not go away. I felt certain it was not just me, and I desperately wanted to talk with Raille. Then what she knew about me and who I actually was came tumbling out of her mind and I was overwhelmed. Struck dumb would be not inaccurate. She was saying I was more genetically Olarian than Human and I stood a few feet from the circle that had been there for us, so inviting a few moments before, frozen now as the implications seeped in, trying my hardest to be... totally sceptical. It couldn't be true. Surely, I would have known if I wasn't entirely human! Then as more of the implications seeped in, if she was right, if this was true; what version of myself would I be taking home to Earth? Then assuming I ever got back there, certainly not the person who had been brought out here into the far reaches of space into a totally alien star system. I shook my head, but it cleared nothing. My brain felt like scrambled eggs, nothing I could do seemed to shake the confusion.

I was aware that Olaria was searching for something to say.

I hardly heard what she was saying. I was way out of my depth, flooded with disbelief. My god, my mother and father, had they known? Had they been telekinetic telepaths but no more developed than me? And had they lived their lives with this partially understood pall of anxiety hanging over them. How could this be possible? I sat on the ground and Olaria sat down close to me. Head in my hands, I stared at the ground, then looked up and watched the rest of the crew walking toward the edge of the clearing with their Olarian hosts. My mind almost paralysed, shaking my head in furious denial. But the more I thought about my life, the more the horrifying reality began to seep in. Surely it could be not true? Except for Peta on Sunstreamer, they were leaving me.

Somewhere in my mind I had heard her ask something and realised I had been chewing over a question, wondering if there was indeed a form of energy that linked all life. I was thinking of particles, separated, one part spinning one way seemingly connected to the other part spinning in harmony but thousands or even millions of miles away.

The energy that links all life.

I nodded. I was remembering stories from Earth from years ago. I was speaking their names. The words were falling out of my mind; she heard me, then I was just shaking my head in wishful disbelief, totally overwhelmed. I realised she had no idea what to do. I was experiencing her concern and distress but had no resources to help her, I could barely help myself. She saw that I simply could not clear my mind; my mother's voice was alive in my memory.

There were no mutually defined boundaries as yet, but the Olarians had made it clear indirectly, they were capable of making us their prisoners and although I didn't feel it, I knew Olaria could see that the idea had stayed with me, that I could not put it down, that it simply would not go away.

Zed, Olaria's voice in my mind cut roughly into my disturbed musings. *Please, I cannot have you feeling you are my prisoner. I hardly understand what this means. We have nothing like your dictionary definitions of prisoners on this planet.*

When I finally showed her what exactly a prisoner was—she was horrified.

You are wrong. It is not the way I want us to be. The way you are thinking about it is not a behaviour we could fully comprehend. Please, put it aside and let me know when you are ready for us to leave? You are not and will never be held prisoner here. Please believe me, it really is not something we could tolerate.

But I knew, in other ways, I was already enmeshed in the fears of my parents, and that felt like being trapped, a prisoner to their fears. I never really knew what my parents had feared, but, now, I was getting an inkling, however, I was certain they only had a fear of an unknown, albeit a real fear, probably of exposure.

Olaria was genuinely distressed. Based on our crew's experimental conversation with the aliens, I knew she was not just being polite. Yet I could detect no impatience nor uncomfortable nuance in her question and knew she had caught my last thought. I turned finally to face her. Her eyes were warm, her smile genuine and my doubts about her integrity seemed churlish, but I was on guard should I feel the ambience change. There was a lot to find out. So, I smiled carefully back at her and invited her to lead the way. She looked at me. There was as yet nothing to give their relationship traction, so she turned and pointed towards the boundary of the field a few minutes' walk away.

I frowned; I saw nothing. She continued to speak directly into my mind,

Zed, please look closely at where I am pointing.

Between us and the tree line I could barely detect a shimmer of what could have been haze.

Whatever it was, it appeared to be causing the trees behind to seem slightly blurry. She looked directly at me.

I know you are enjoying the slowly swirling colour of my clothes. I have used nearly every colour we possess in making these, please select from amongst them a colour you really like. I feel a little uncomfortable, even embarrassed and definitely surprised at myself, but when I made this outfit, I had in mind something I believed you would like, something that would impress you. Please tell me you understand.

On earth it would have been a concept, a statement I would have understood. But here? Billions of miles away, on an alien planet, it simply made no sense, the context made it totally wrong. The feeling of being out of my depth clung to me. With a conscious effort I put the unmanageable feeling aside and pointed to a slowly shifting blue, almost iridescent, apparently moving across her waist. An instant later, the shimmering haze in front of the trees had taken on a clear shape in blue. My eyebrows shot up, and I smiled.

'Okay, I see it!'

A teardrop-shaped object was clear now, just on our side of the tree line. With the addition of its new colour the trees became almost invisible. The shape was a small teardrop, and I realised it was a flying machine, in some ways similar to but very much smaller than the shuttle.

Being taller than Olaria, I looked down at her. She looked back up at me, her green eyes full of life and a tiny glint, which I decided was essentially amusement. This was confirmed as she continued to keep her word, and so her thoughts and feelings were immediately known to me. Then she smiled, and for no particular reason I noticed her teeth. Like those of all the Olarians I had met so far, they were even and white, much like my own. And the expression on her face was anything but hostile or off-putting. I felt like a loosely assembled pile of iron filings being drawn slowly toward a powerful magnet. There was nothing unpleasant about the feeling. Except, in some part of my brain, I felt, it was inappropriate and wrong. With an effort, I let the judgement go.

It's my Drifter, she said, pointing to the flying machine. She told me about them, how every Olarian learned to build these craft in their teens. Some were astonishing looking objects, hers was small, neat and functional. I could see it seated only two! There was an uneasy tension between us, and I stood still and looked at her. I knew she was feeling as inept and uncertain as did I!

He's defensive.

The thought slipped out. I looked at her with a feeling of disbelief.

You're surprised? How can you possibly expect me to trust you? This whole scenario is fraught. I have no way I can imagine that I could trust you. If our situations were reversed?

She looked at me. It would not be this way if their situations were reversed because she would know exactly what was real and what was not. The moment the thought was complete she knew what needed to happen, as it could with him, though not with the rest of the crew. She had thought; I am going to have to rely on Zed for managing the others, and immediately she realised how compromised he was probably going to feel. Although I did not understand what she was thinking, I knew I felt uncomfortable with it.

Whilst almost everything we make is based in our use of the energies that are around us, for us your Lander and Sunstreamer are astounding objects of extraordinary and barely comprehensible complexity, not made of energy, however, controlling a great deal of energy in ways that we don't yet understand. She realised he had no point of reference for the idea of making something out of energy—as she and the Olarians had no way of understanding how the Sunstreamer was constructed—nor had he any obvious awareness of the energy flowing around them.

That it was disturbing her. She planned to do something with it that involved him. *We simply think the shape we want, its size, its structure and the energies we have chosen reform themselves to conform to the image we have projected out into the world, and, when we are satisfied with it, we seal it with dark matter.* She knew she was making no sense to him at all. He needed to make something out of energy. She knew he had the capability but, as yet, not the understanding, nor belief that he could.

She thought for a moment about how their children learned and realised she knew how to help him begin. So, cautiously, knowing he was in part following her, she said, *Zed, let me help you understand how we do this. Allow me to help you construct something from pure energy.*

She was reminded he had no idea how potentially powerful he was, all that had been blocked off for what was probably his entire life so far. Why did she feel so obliged to make certain she released it? The feeling was so strong in her, it was proving irresistible.

I frowned, shook my head. On top of that she seemed to be suggesting I could actually do this, make something like this? I looked closely at her. I knew she thought I was telepathic and telekinetic like them, but nothing in my experience allowed me to believe her. My concern about being duped was strong. It was, I sensed, partly blocking her.

I felt, just the edges of an uncertainty, a sense of possibility, something intangible.

She seemed finally to realise I simply could not understand her and did something; she was thinking of me as a child! I knew she was in my head and she said as I felt her there.

These connections have lain dormant in your brain for decades. Do not worry, I have done this many times with my own and other people's children, and I really need to do it for you.

Then I realised, even as she did whatever it was, she was doing, she was thinking of me as a child! Her child! Then the thought was gone. It had felt absurd and confusing. Next moment she was giving me instructions.

Zed, on the wall beside your bed on Sunstreamer you have an image of your parents from many years ago.

I frowned; how could she know? And then I realised, somehow, they could see anywhere.

Before I could begin to let that thought gnaw at me, she said, *allow yourself to see that picture on the ground in front of us. Without really thinking about it I tried to follow her instructions and imagined I could see the picture on the ground in front of us. Now, imagine the picture is actually there exactly as you are seeing it, set into the ground, then when you have it there, look away from it, just a small distance, you will see it is still there.*

I felt like a child at a Circus Sideshow. But I did as she asked and realised the picture I had made was there in the ground, apparently, at the edge of my vision. Then it vanished. Olaria smiled.

Okay, so far so good. For a moment you saw it, didn't you?

I looked at her, feeling more than a little stupid. Nodded.

Zed, this is another world, and we know your brain can allow you to do more than you have ever been permitted to imagine. Please, just for a few moments, trust me. This is not a trick, this is a part of you, you have never been allowed to find. You are a thinking person; you know there is more than you have so far been able to see. Let me take you just one tiny step. Keep in touch with what I am thinking and feeling as I feed it to you.

She stopped; would he allow her? She was watching him, feeling his uncertainty, felt him push through his scepticism and discomfort before he turned toward her, saw him suddenly find himself connect what was happening to the fears of his mother and Diga his biological father.

'Okay.' He hoped the answer was nothing he would regret.

Zed there is another kind of energy prevalent everywhere; it acts to constraints energies you can learn to see. These active energies come from every imaginable source: from the sun to the plants. Another different type of energy is seemingly everywhere, we use it to bind other active energies, usually giving them shape. Once we have established a shape with it, we let it go. Your dictionaries call it Dark Matter. Once used it leaves us with the object, we used it to create. So, she continued, *in a way we make things by simply imagining them into existence.*

I was barely following but nodded. My parent's warnings and admonitions were with me and I was having to fight them, hard.

Alright, now recapture the picture of your parents once again. But this time, once you have it, allow your mind to imagine you can see everything there is around you. Imagine you can both look and ever so slightly look away, just allow your mind to imagine it can allow your eyes to see what is not there to see and you will notice, suddenly, the colours of all the energies and this mass around it of what you call Dark Matter. It will not actually interfere with seeing what your eyes can always see but will add a new range of images. You will, if you allow it, be able to see this Dark Matter flowing around the boundary of your image. Please give that a try. Don't overthink it, just visualise it.

I looked at her, knew there was nothing to say, did exactly what she had told me to do. In an instant the picture of my parents was there with streams of colour everywhere and through it all, massive clouds of what Olaria had called Dark Matter. I was aware that nothing was actually interfering with my ability to see what my eyes could ordinarily see. I imagined the Dark Matter flowing around the picture, holding it, and then I let go. I immediately stopped seeing all the colours but there on the ground was the picture of my parents exactly as it was beside my onboard bunk. I looked at Olaria.

'What just happened?'

Look back at the picture. Don't try too hard, just will the picture into your hands.

Feeling strange, I did exactly as she had said and felt the image almost leap into my hands. Now I could feel it, a solid thing in the frame I had imagined. I turned to Olaria.

'Tell me this is not some trick you just pulled on me.'

Zed, I give you my word; you did that. My part was just to activate a tiny part of your brain that you have never been encouraged to use, so has never developed. This is no more than a first baby step. But now you know, you really are an energy telepath, like it or not. You have a great deal to learn. So that you do not talk yourself out of believing what just happened, look out at the world around you and make the decision you made before to see just beyond your usual looking. See the energies of the world, just decide and do it, please.

Partly in fear that it would all prove to have been a dream and partly in the hope it was not, I looked out at the world as I had before, with Olaria's help. Suddenly it was there, the colours and the Dark Matter, yet everything in the field was exactly as my eyes had seen it, the Lander, the others. Then I let it go. Immediately, I knew something incredible had just begun for me. It would, I realised, alter my life and I turned to Olaria, let go the energies and shook my head. She was standing there smiling with relief and delight.

Impulsively, I reached out to her, briefly hugged her, let go suddenly feeling embarrassed and uncomfortable, apologised, but she shook her head at me, smiled and said, *Zed, I am delighted. You have no need to apologise to me, I can see how much this has affected you. All of us have been hoping you would let us open up this world for you. Many people just witnessed what you did and are absolutely delighted for you.*

I turned toward the blue object she had coloured for me, shaking my head. A realisation settling on me. I had always seen the colours in my mind, just never in the outside world.

Now, Zed, while you are looking at my Drifter, I will remove the blue, all you need do is allow just the edge of your enhanced vision come alive, you will then see it as clearly as you were seeing it when it was blue.

She looked at me, eyebrows raised, and I nodded cautiously at her. An instant later the blue had gone, and with just the smallest of intention to see, the Drifter was in clear view. I almost held my breath and then looked around the field. Sure enough, there were still two drifters parked around the perimeter. My chest felt tight. I became aware I had almost ceased to breathe. I did not want the new images to go away, I knew I was trying to hold on to them. Olaria's voice broke into this paused state.

Breathe Zed, it won't go away, ever, unless you push it back. Whenever you want to summon some energy to use and shape, you only need to think it; try.

I did, and what she said was true. I knew another door had just opened into my life.

Are you ready to come home with me?'

I wanted it all to be true. But was it? Was I really free, would I be able to go home, and if all these experiences were real, who the hell was I? Some deluded bewildered soul. That I knew was true. I knew I was certainly not the man who had stepped on to the Flight Deck of Sunstreamer only three or so days ago. This was not something written about in any manual I had ever read.

On the way to her home, she chatted to me in English out loud, practicing, and I let the gentle pleasing sound of her voice drift over me. Although there was no other sound in her Drifter I had almost no idea what she was saying. I was absorbed with what had just happened and that was clearly changing my life. I was pulled back from my reverie by the memory of her question on Sunstreamer.

Why didn't you contact us?

She must have known I was one of them from almost the earliest moments of their contact. Their brains worked in a different way to ordinary human brains, but not from mine! I was, genetically, apparently, one of them. How could this be possible? There had been no meeting of our two species before Sunstreamer arrived here. Or had there? Why had this extra part of my brain not shown up in the neural scans I had had back home? I needed Olaria to help me understand.

CHAPTER 9

Ghia and Kyuto

When I stepped out of the Lander, my attention was immediately drawn to the clothes the Olarians were wearing. So, when Tanzin began admiring them, I enthusiastically joined in, praising the impact of the amazingly colourful and unusual clothing. My tension must have been almost palpable, which was of course tied to my pregnancy and the future of my unborn daughter. I am naturally reserved and knew that I really come out of my shell only when Gerard is around, or I am exclusively with the female members of the crew. I know most of the crew have learned that behind my natural reserve I am genuinely a warm person, especially toward people I know and care about, and I'm sure it had taken only a very short time before the entire crew knew this now included all of them.

When Olaria had set up the circle and Kyuto had asked if I would be his guest. I had gone to him without hesitation, but he had known I was uncomfortable about relationships, especially with men who were not Gerard. The introductions had begun with the Olarians agreeing to remain non-telepathic, in order to better explore and understand the communication realities of the human crew. When later the Olarians had helped their guests participate in their telepathic reality, I had been at first curious and then horrified at the intrusive intimacy the experience was creating. I was of course not the only member of the crew in that category. I know Kyuto was aware of my distress and my strong negative feelings about him, about them, and about how powerless I was to change any of it. So, when I agreed to go with him to leave the crew and explore each other's worlds and we moved off toward Kyuto's Drifter, I'm sure Kyuto was significantly more aware of my confusion and distress than I and his awareness of my feelings kind of spooked me.

Ghia, I am going to try to keep you aware of all that is happening between us. I know it is at least as confusing and distressing as I found talking with you in the absence of my usual telepathic reality but can understand now how genuinely helpful operating in each other's reality is. We can stop doing this at any time. It might be best if you just ask me to stop. You should also know, as you experience me, I have been monitoring how your baby is experiencing our engagement. I held up my hand as a clear sign to stop.

'Are you telling me you are using my baby as an indicator of how we are progressing?'

Yes, she is beautiful and in excellent health.

'You have to stop. You are freaking me out. Do you know what harm you might be doing?' Kyuto smiled.

Ghia, I have been monitoring the health of babies in utero for many centuries when my skills have been needed. It is one of the reasons I asked to be your host. In my project team I am often used to help others learn about the development and growth of in utero children.

He knew I was angry, but also deeply interested in and curious about my baby.

I was totally overloaded, I simply waved my hand and said, 'Okay.'

Kyuto kept moving toward the boundary of the field in which they had landed, and I realised he was taking me somewhere and as he was keeping his part of the bargain, I knew it was his home toward which we were heading. He interrupted my thinking by pointing to the boundary of the field we were approaching when suddenly I realised I was staring at a small lander-like craft painted out in all my beautiful scarves and hats, the photos of my friends and family, my old-fashioned baby clothes and the image from the photo the crew often looked at on my console which I had reproduced on the entire South wall of my cabin (The wall she could look at from her bunk). The photograph that had been taken on my mother's sixtieth birthday. It showed our farm and the branches of the huge Oak tree and the remnants of the birthday party my family had held under its sweeping branches in all the detail of the original. There it was, in front of me, in full colour, slightly distorted in perspective but otherwise perfect. Kyuto picked up the mass of seething and intensifying emotions I as generating and accurately read my distress but had not picked up the reason for it, jumbled up in my confused emotions. I know he had at first missed my frustration and fear it was just too much, and at that moment I exploded. Kyuto's last act had been one too far or me and my restraint and caution burst, and I lost it.

'I hate that you can use me like this. You are making our position on this planet impossible. Being non-telepathic is not a disease nor a disability. I am a member of a tool culture that found its way to this planet, something you have not been capable of doing. You have taken my freedom without regard for me or any of us, and now you are using my baby to control me by showing that you can have a direct impact on her.' For a moment I stepped outside myself and could see how bad this must seem, but I was far to upset to allow that to have any impact on me so I just she kept on travelling with the feeling that was overwhelming me at this moment, something I almost certainly would never have done had I not been pregnant. 'Why do you want to hold us captive here on this planet? We did not come here with warlike intentions. We came here because you deceived us into believing this planet was uninhabited. We come here as scientists and explorers, and you are treating us as your prisoners. Do you think we really believe we are free to return home, that we could possibly trust you? This is neither a friendly nor a hospitable act. Right now, this place does not feel safe, and I do not feel in a safe place to learn, and that is definitely your doing.'

I was staring at Kyuto.

I paused as I settled down and blurted out, 'Fuck', then with a brief twinge of guilt continued smoothly, 'that was not really great, was it?'

My awareness of my outburst had just come up to meet me full frontal. To his credit, Kyuto, who was clearly uncomfortable, behaved impeccably and for myself, well, having dumped my entire anxiety state on him I fell silent. I could feel his discomfort.

Ghia this is a less than ideal way for us to begin a relationship, however, I need to thank you for your honesty, it is a value, I believe, you will come to realise underlies our entire society. And I do fully understand what you have said, and you have my word that I will take this up with the Council at our first break. They, and at this time, their organisers all heard you and a discussion is going on about how to remedy this situation you have described so vividly. I do not believe my colleagues would have any appetite for our engagement under the terms you feel may be existing here.

Kyuto's agitation was evident and helped me recognise more of the complexity in which I was involved. *I thought we had been clear that we were not intending to impede your freedom of choice. I am opening our thoughts on this to you so you can perhaps accept that there is no duplicity here whatsoever.*

Immediately, the soft sound of hundreds of voices affirmed Kyuto's words. They were warm and kindly shared and strong, so much so, I could feel their warmth and support bringing tears to my eyes.

All of you could choose to return to Sunstreamer and leave at any time and no attempt of any kind will or would be made to stop you, except we would try to persuade you of the benefits of sharing knowledge which is so important to our existence.

I momentarily felt Kyuto open my mind to the discussion of the Council 'staffers'— I could think of no other words to describe them—on the issue, and was able to hear what each had said and I knew at some deep level what I was hearing was true, but the biggest impact, the thing that convinced me was the feeling I was getting from each as they spoke and I knew what I was hearing was uncensored. The impact was fierce, especially for me, because I deeply trusted my instincts about integrity, and I felt I was being given genuine access to what was actually occurring between the staffers who supported the eight. In an instant, years of training and discipline kicked in. My mind cleared and I turned to Kyuto.

'I have to apologise. I am genuinely curious to learn about you.'

I was immediately aware Kyuto felt a huge sense of relief and I could feel his genuine warmth toward me. I knew my outburst had disturbed him.

Ghia, please do not get angrier at me, but I want to tell you; all over this planet right now, some pregnant Olarian is having an emotional outburst to her partner perhaps as strong as yours and almost certainly with much less reason.

The ferocious outburst and the interchange that followed had cleared the air. Both Kyuto and I were feeling engaged. I had stepped over an edge, honesty and duplicity were experiences I could differentiate, and I believed without reservation, Kyuto was being honest. This was the first moment I felt trust toward the Olarians and knew how much I needed to feel and believe that, if I was to learn in this seemingly familiar yet unknown world. Later I thought I would need to say as much to the crew, and I felt myself hoping that each of them might have reached a similar conclusion, but it would have to have been by different routes. Lord I hope Gerry gets to feel the way that I now do...

It had opened another door through which I was loath to walk. Was it really safe, really a good idea to let pregnant women loose in space? And whilst I was thinking it half in joke, there was just the tiniest edge of concern as I thought about the possible consequences, had I been with a less generous people. I had no straightforward way to think about it but, unpopular as it might be, I knew it needed thinking through and then I put it away for the moment.

I looked again at the picture he had put on the drifter and felt immediately sad and homesick. However, because he was keeping his side of the bargain, allowing to me to know what was happening in his head, I knew he was about to remove it. Immediately I jumped in to ask him please to leave it. Having access to his mind and his intentions was both overwhelming and satisfying, and, not without power. I loved the image on his Drifter and wanted it to stay there.

It connected the two worlds for me.

Ready to travel to my home?

'A Drifter?' The question mark hung in the air between us.

I knew Kyuto was following my thoughts on the little object in front of us and realised I wanted to know exactly how it worked. He smiled, felt for an instant on more solid ground.

We build these ourselves, Ghia. They are a pure energy creation. This one will take only two of us and we could manage about three thousand of your miles per hour if we wished. When we are young and have built our first one, we race them, helping each other find the fastest safe speed we can manage. They will actually travel a lot faster, but there comes a point when it does not feel safe.

'But how is it powered and how do you control it?' The professional Astronaut and Scientist was hooked, and Kyuto was delighted to explain.

I choose an energy source and connect it to the front of the Drifter, then whilst I am connected to the energy source, all I need to do is think where I want it to go and it will follow the path I establish in my mind. There is really no more to it than that.

No more to it than that! Really?

'That sounds both extraordinary and impossible science-fiction, rather like your beautiful and amazing clothes, which all the girls would love to be wearing.'

I knew my interest in the clothes was more over the top than I would normally have expressed, and suddenly I was sure that the mess pregnancy was making of my hormones was telling me that pregnant women should not be dumped into alien societies, in the interests of intergalactic safety.

Kyuto laughed, and the sound slid through me. It was like no laughter I had ever known. I heard the delightful tones, then felt the warmth that travelled with them, and then I experienced the strong, musical, yet masculine feel at the end. It was laughter I would always want to hear.

He seemed to be a very nice man. The thought had barely passed my consciousness when I was experiencing his emotional response and again was reconfiguring my attitude to telepathic communication. He was becoming a real person to me. I found that I could know what was happening when we spoke and that left me feeling safe.

Would you like to be fully connected to my mind as I search for, find, connect and use the energy to manage the Drifter? I nodded and suddenly I was in his mind and felt the burst of energy I nearly leaped out of my seat.

Sorry, he said I don't know how to do that without the sudden shift in energy between us.

I smiled, 'It's okay, I think I'm just going to need to adjust to stuff I have never experienced before.'

'Maybe I'm adjusting to Olar!'

Kyuto laughed, and I could feel the pleasure and delight my slowly changing emotional state was causing him. Then suddenly, I saw the incredible image he was seeing, innumerable strands of light coming from everywhere, and he seemed able to see them without his vision of the rest of the world around him changing! I watched as he selected a particular strand and thought its connection to the front of his drifter then shutting the other strands out apparently willed the Drifter to follow the track he was making in his mind. It was just being, pulled? Then followed his path of climb levelled off and accelerated.

I was breathless. It was exciting. He disconnected me from his mind but continued the telepathic connection, telling me how pleased he was I had enjoyed the little adventure, about which I knew he had been anxious. I smiled at him warmly and could feel us settling into a more comfortable relationship.

When we get home and you meet my partner Seret, I am sure she will be delighted to make an energy outfit for you and show you how to wear it. Unfortunately, we had a brief conversation about it amongst ourselves when we saw you enjoying our clothing, but we cannot see how you could get it on or off without one of us being part of that process. However, you and Seret will, I am certain, find a way. He knew I was delighted, and we moved on.

As we travelled to his home, I admired the countryside, knew he was still thinking about the discussion by all the female members of the crew of the Olarian clothes and was ready when he finally said, *So, tell me, what is it that so fascinated you all?*

'Well, you all looked pretty amazing and all of us would love to be wearing them.' Kyuto smiled.

Seret is delighted, listen.

Immediately I heard, felt, knew Seret was speaking to me, welcoming me and telling me she would be delighted to talk clothing with her!

Kyuto invited me to touch his clothes, and I leaned over to touch the material, but my hands merely slid through the energy field.

It covers my body but has no weight or substance whatsoever. And I can hear you thinking it must be a trick but it's not, it is merely an energy field, weighs nothing but can hold solid objects if I need to. May I feel your clothing?

I nodded and he reached over and touched my sleeve.

Solid, smooth. A textile, synthesised?

I looked at him, a little surprised.

We had arrived at his home. He put the little Drifter down on a small clearing a few minutes' walk from his home and as we began the short journey to his house, he continued the conversation.

The words don't mean anything to me, he said, but I am using your thoughts about them. What exactly is a textile and what synthesises it?

When I answered, I was still consciously aware of thinking my answers rather than speaking them. It still felt uncanny that he always knew what I was about to say just as I was thinking it. Even though I was fully aware of his thinking and feeling as it happened.

I had to think for a bit about how to explain about my clothes. Then I had an idea. I took him on a tour, entirely from memory, of an old knitting mill that was still running near my parents' home. Showed him the raw materials and the processing. The whole tour took about ten or fifteen minutes and I had to close my eyes sometimes to remember the things I had seen. We walked slowly as I was talking, and he was silent for the entire journey as I showed him pictures of the sheep and the shearing and the spinning and the fabricating.

Then I did the same with cotton from bush to clothes and then with one of the synthetics. He was nonplussed. He was staring at me, really still.

I could feel his mind feverishly struggling with questions. He wanted to know about the energy, electricity, the machinery, the labour, so much was incomprehensible, and I could feel his almost insatiable hunger for understanding. In the end, after several minutes of silence he said,

Almost unimaginable, and the noise! I burst out laughing. It was a pleasure, and I meant it, it had been a significant learning experience for me as well.

Promise me you will take me on more journeys like that one, he said, and that you will answer the questions you have raised.

And of course, now I had a working mechanism, I did. Finally, after another brief silence, he said,

That was brilliant, but you must know just how many questions you have raised for me and an innumerable number of others listening in. I realised I had not thought through what Kyuto could not have really understood. Factories needed a whole chapter to themselves and I had to take him slowly through the ideas underlying them and the notion that men and some women, but mostly men would leave their food-growing life and their families with all its traditions and travel to the new cities to make money and here I met another stumbling block, which, I decided, needed to be dealt with later. I tried to imagine what the Olarians would take for granted and wondered how I was going to make the leaps that would surely be involved. One of the biggest obstacles was the total absence of money or any elements of an economy in Olarian society. And that created an information, knowledge, understanding vacuum of quite gigantic dimensions. At which point we had arrived at his home and he invited me to follow him inside.

It had not been a long walk, but I could feel the energy of the plants on our walk to the house and knew it was through Kyuto's telepathic connection. I was thinking about how I was feeling so certain this was Kyuto's home. He had watched me moving through the plants and fed me his experience of them as I did so. I stopped some twenty metres short of the house to experience the strangely seductive and delightful experience of being greeted by the landscape. I was a country girl, and the messages that Kyuto was enabling me to experience from the flora around the house were deeply moving to me.

I could see that he too was absorbed by my engagement. This was something that had never entered my awareness at home. I wondered if the plants on Earth were like this and that people simply did not know.

I was being swamped by the realisation of the differences between what we and the Olarians took for granted. I followed Kyuto into a room which I imagined to be his sitting or lounge room, and we settled easily into the remarkable energy seats. And, because Kyuto continued to maintain my telepathic connection. I was constantly aware that people were connecting to him, with questions. He was continuously fielding these in order to maintain his connection to me. It was, I thought, as though he was getting Holomonitor calls almost continuously, and I could feel the tiring nature of that process.

Within seconds, Seret had said hello and welcomed me into their home. Another beautifully dressed, attractive, healthy looking woman. Surely not thirty-eight? But Ghia immediately knew Seret was telling her thirty-eight was right, but that she had been here for twenty- two hundred and fifteen years. Again, I had to work hard to accept the idea, but Seret did something for me none of the others had done.

Seret had been watching and listening in to our journey to her home, had seen the power of the picture-sound stories I had been using to explain about our clothes. Now she took me on a brief journey from her childhood in her first learning group of eight to the present, stopping at many important moments including two of her pregnancies and her meeting with Kyuto who she clearly adored.

I smiled. I had enjoyed the journey and was loving the feeling between Seret and Kyuto, and my mind returned to Gerard. I became aware that Seret was giving me something which I could, if I chose, easily give Gerard, and I let my mind feel and appreciate Seret's gift. Seret felt passionately connected to Kyuto, however, Seret was also allowing me to feel her strength and independence, yet, in her connection to Kyuto she allowed me to feel the way in which she held nothing of herself back from him, she was delightedly, and for me, almost embarrassingly, open and available to him. I could feel her gift of complete trust and passion and knew that Seret was letting me see and experience this as a gift which I could use in my life, with Gerard, if I grasped and understood the emotional experience I was being silently, discreetly and carefully offered.

This unconditional openness was being offered slowly, and only as I recognised it and acknowledged it did Seret leave more traces of it in my mind in a way I could experience, understand and use. It was an unusual gift but, I realised, uniquely Olarian.

Then I realised I knew Seret was wanting to help me understand something she felt was important, something that would help me, then I heard Seret begin to speak.

In our culture men have for the most part been dominant, it is the way we have come to want them, but they are neither superior nor unequal. Generosity and awareness are qualities we desire and expect in our men and from us on the other side is a special quality of submission and compliance men expect and mostly get from us in our sexual and intimate relationship. It also is neither inferior nor unequal, it is ours to gift. It is an entirely equitable and mutually satisfying set of expectations. It is the core of what I believe you are calling love, deep, soul-connecting mutual adoration and passion. There is no dominance or submission in our daily lives except what makes sense in any particular set of circumstances. However, for around 25% of couples, the opposite arrangement is true.

Seret smiled warmly and I knew she could feel my interest.

The women are dominant and the men willingly submissive as their gift to their partner, and that also works perfectly well. We have a very small number of couples for whom there is neither dominance nor submission in their way of relating. This also works, there is for these, we have found, a sort of swapping of roles sometimes in the same sexual engagement, they work it out as they go, and all these arrangements work when there is complete mutual agreement. I would like to show you some examples of each of these so you and Gerard can choose with clarity and confidence, which will work best for you. We have, in our Living Library, many examples of each, our children study them to establish for themselves the pattern that feels most compatible for them. They then are able to test and develop optimum pleasure and satisfaction. I was barely moving, hanging on to every word, this was a set of arrangements I was finding very satisfying to hear. Seret continued.

When this quality of willing and mutually satisfying dominance and submission is no longer present in our intimate relationships and either partner stops feeling willing and able to play their part, we explore together with our... friends (she had to search for the word) what has been lost between us and as soon as that is clear and both are together in this, we separate. We always try to understand what the full nature was of what got lost between us. There are groups that study this and have done for thousands of years. We do have quite sophisticated understandings of what happens, how and why that unique intimate connection becomes lost, that phenomena you call 'love'. Also, because of what we have learned we do not attempt to... repair— I think is your word.

—these relationships, if we think they have reached an appropriate end.

And to pick up your question I am close, even intimate, I think would be your word, with all my lovers over the millennia, even today, just without the element you feel between kyuto and me. I truly delight in being his creature, he always expresses his pleasure at my gift to him and always acts to meet me in the ways he has learned I need. Nothing between us is conditional.

Seret noticed I had temporarily ceased to be connected; that I was making a comparison between the two cultures and was filled with positive thoughts and feelings about the Olarians I was coming to know. The comparison with members of my family and friends from university and beyond was disturbing me. I was wondering if I would fall into the pattern of failed relationships that seemed almost to be the human normal?

I expressed my appreciation of Seret's story and her gift and realised that Seret was about to leave.

When you and Kyuto have finished for the day, I would love to show you how we weave the clothing you have been so generously admiring. I can make some for you. But I think you will only be able to manage it when one of us is around to put it on and take it off for you. However, I believe you will enjoy wearing it.

Ghia thanked her and Seret was gone.

She is wonderful.

Kyuto's voice caught my thought and acknowledged it as his also.

Ghia, you know much of what I am thinking as we stay connected in this Olarian way. I believe I am recognising that we seem to manage a great deal more interpersonal information than is usual for you by which I mean we are more aware of our own and each other's emotional experiences, and whilst this is helpful for us and we are able to turn it to constructive use in our relationships it does not seem the same is true for you, especially when you are together with another human person and we are not involved. Do you think that's right?

I nodded; I was feeling emotionally drained.

'I am finding the constant background of your feelings and of mine and others tiring. I think because I don't know how to process them. But more significant—' I paused for a moment, 'yes, more significant is that it begins to cloud my logical thinking, my ability to process rational thoughts; if I was aware of the emotional state of each of my colleagues on the flight deck, this would almost certainly prevent me from doing my job.'

Kyuto was watching her carefully, following her thoughts.

You know Ghia, I am beginning to wonder if our constant management of the relationships around us might be one of the reasons we have never become a manufacturing society. There are groups who make things, but they are always small groups, very small groups rarely more than sixteen people and they are so familiar with one another that they are able to suspend their relationship processing to achieve a complicated and prolonged task. But that will have taken them quite some time to perfect and that would not necessarily apply to everyone. 'Things' are almost always secondary in our society, feelings and relationship connections are of primary importance.

I looked at him, becoming aware of another unusual area of discomfort for me.

'You must be aware that I am feeling as though I am always just a bit slow, here.'

Kyuto looked at me.

Well, in a manner of speaking, you are, at the moment, because you still feel the need to form the words after you have completed the thought. In fact, because there is no need to say the words, you should, in a little while, cease verbalising and then you will not feel... slow.

Can we talk about your life on Earth for a little, please? Where you live and what happens during a normal day?

Kyuto's request was the logical way to continue, and I was up for the challenge.

I used the picture-story approach that had worked so well so far. As I thought about it, I realised it would probably be best if I just launched into it. There were clearly no protocols to guide me about how to do this.

'I hardly know where to start. You know Gerard is the father of our unborn child. I am not married to him and we do not live together, so I live alone.'

Kyuto followed carefully the picture and story information I was presenting to him.

CHAPTER 10

Zed & Olaria

Olaria was thinking about my question, 'Why did the extra area in my brain not show up on the brain scans I had experienced at home?'

The simplest explanation, you will see if you allow Kyuto to show you the map of your undeveloped areas. They lie alongside several other areas of your brain and if they were not active might well not be obvious as anything except additional tissue, however, once active they become quite clear and grow quickly and you will need to make certain you do not allow any further scans of your brain once you return home. These areas will become increasingly larger and obvious. It will take Kyuto's group some time to fully understand how your brain is like and different from ours.

Zed, as to your other question, given our races apparently have not met. I don't know, but we have a story that my father said he made up because he could not tolerate the talk of gods and such. He made up an idea he called "The Seeders".

I smiled; I liked the idea.

These incredible beings he decided must be a species far far more developed than us. He decided to believe they travelled the cosmos seeding planets with the potential for life. Some would develop and survive, some would not. We were one of the survivors; he decided. It was just his way of putting aside the horrible experiences he had seen created by those in his village who believed they were the recipients of truths from their gods, unfortunately, especially his father.

I could feel my mind trying to reach back to the efforts that must have been involved in their fledgling society.

She paused to let me muse. I stood for a moment to stretch my legs and let the ideas filter through.

His idea enabled the Original eight to avoid the pitfalls of all the god stuff and made us somehow responsible for our own lives. We have been living with it ever since, for three thousand years. He was clear with his Originals, he did not know what was and was not so, just, he chose this to be his belief they were free to go with it or not. They all chose to go with it. They had all experienced the destructive impact of the common alternative.

I wondered how the idea of the seeders had arisen for him.

Since that time, only a couple of hundred Olarians have decided he was wrong and have sought a god and a religion, and, to this day the now three or four hundred believers have created a fairly cohesive story which they all believe and they live on an island only a few hundred miles off the continent of Jeland, the other major continent on which Olarians live. They chose to live separate lives and they have refused to allow any of us to prolong their lives. They believe their god would not want that. They also, unfortunately, have diseases we are able to cure but they will not allow us to interfere in their lives in any way. So...we have very little to do with them, ever, by their explicit request. They are a quiet, meditative people, who will build nothing with energy and live in the simplest possible way. Once, more than two thousand years ago, before I was born, and before we had pretty much complete control of our weather, a severe storm destroyed their homes and crops and they allowed some of our people to provide them with food for nearly a year. They were grateful but made it clear they did not want us to interfere with them again. We keep an eye on them, but that's about it. The truth is their inflexibility as a religious group acts more to discourage the rest of us from wanting to participate in religious ideas than anything else, and, fortunately for us they do not... proselytise.

I was intrigued, but I was still reflecting on Olaria's earlier attempt to speak with me on board Sunstreamer, before I had any notion of being telepathic. She frowned and turned toward me.

Watched a single tear slide down my cheek, felt my isolation, my aloneness and a deep sadness that seemed to reach out and grip her, something she felt unable to shake off.

You realise don't you, you are fully telepathic and telekinetic? According to Kyuto, who briefly studied you and all the crew, your brain is not only like ours, but it goes further. There are almost completely inactivated or undeveloped structures we have never seen before, so it seems likely you have other abilities we know nothing about. I will help you activate your telepathic and telekinetic abilities. It seems you may be some kind of bridge between us and the Human world, or even some other species.

Just what I needed at this moment, to belong neither to the human community nor the Olarian. It was more than enough. For me it redefined traumatic. And aloneness.

When you were first in contact with us from Sunstreamer, Kyuto had the task of trying to help us understand why you had not contacted us as we had expected you would, given he had found you to be telepathic. However, he showed us that you have the structures in your brain that we have learned are the source of our telepathy and telekinesis but that with you they were inactive, only barely visible and the connections had never been made. I had assumed that if you had them, you must be using them. I was wrong. We had never seen that before. Except, we realised, that was almost certainly the experience of our Originals, our ancestors, my father and mother and their friends. The thing is, the thing that caused my parents the most pain was that, had they understood, they might have found many more possible telepaths amongst their original communities, minds that would have looked like yours but been inactive. By the time they realised, it was too late. And that is a lesson no Olarian is likely ever to forget. You will understand more when I tell you the story of my people.

What you have learned today is the first step of an immense journey. You have more capability built into your brain than any of us, we will help you take the first steps; however, you need to be in charge of that, it will take time, but some of the other things your brain can do, you will need to explore for yourself, we will help as much as we can. Thing is, from what I have just observed, your rate of learning will be far greater than our children or anything we have ever seen.

I could not take it in, what Olaria was telling me, I felt as though I was struggling to fight my way out of a room full of feathers without knowing where was the door. Years of my mother's fears and my father's cautions suddenly made sense. Olaria was watching me struggle through the new information and the feelings it was bringing up. Also, I was far from comfortable that I could trust Olaria or the Olarians. If I decided that was the way to go, I had no idea what the consequences might be. I was definitely going to "Keep my powder dry."

We will work through all this Zed, and you will fit in with us in ways that will surprise and disturb you, and there will be the question of sharing this information with your colleagues to be thought through.

However, for the moment I had more than enough to think about, and Olaria was bringing the drifter down.

The clearing was tiny. The surface seemed like a bowling green, smooth, even and lush. There were bushes and trees and a clear pathway leading away from the clearing along which Olaria took me. Everywhere I looked the gardens were luxuriant and surprising, one design was suddenly transformed into another, new colours and shapes and very different plants. It brought to mind for me botanical gardens I had wandered through with my parents as a child. I had the strangest feeling that the plants were communing with me but put it aside.

Olaria's voice broke into my reveries.

Don't dismiss them Zed, they are life, and they are trying to find a way to involve you in a very basic way. They have what you might call, mood, and they have energies, shift your attention so you see more energies, not a big jump, just open the door a little and watch them carefully.

I stopped, standing still. Everywhere around me I now saw tiny waves of energy of every colour. There seemed even to be colours I did not recognise, mixing and flowing to and from the plants, some weaving their tendril-like flow toward me as well as toward other plants. The birds and insects were manoeuvring through the visual and, I suddenly realised, the olfactory miasma. I let my attention expand outward and became transfixed. The gardens, the entire world around me, was alive with action. Everything was interconnected or was building connections, relationships I thought, and then I began to hear the sounds of the vegetation world. Olaria stood beside me, watching, delighted. I realised she was thinking it seemed like centuries since she had had so raw and intimate a connection with this world as I was making available to her today. It nearly took her breath away.

I was fascinated and for a couple of minutes was quiet, but I was aware she was speaking to others but could not hear the communication. When she returned, she realised I had been unable to follow and without thinking she activated some more of my, until now, quiescent brain. Suddenly I was flooded with sound, reaching automatically to put my hands over my ears, but to no avail. Olaria apologised and the sound diminished, and she spent several minutes helping establish a series of connections in my brain which she then saw were beginning to re-organise in exactly the way their children developed but with me at many times the rate an Olarian child would manage. She explained how I needed to gain control and was genuinely pleased to realise that I had already begun to control the flow. My brain knew exactly what to do, and I stood silent for several minutes before turning to her with a delighted smile and spoke quietly into her mind. She smiled at me and into my mind. She was surprised and delighted at the phenomenal rate at which my brain activated and assimilated new telepathic and telekinetic processes now it had begun.

I already knew she had one more issue to clear up. It had hung around without being really settled in the minds of the Olarians.

It seems that you and your crew are actually all aged between 28 and 38 years. Is that right?

I'm sorry to keep coming back to this, but truly it seems almost beyond our ability to believe.

I looked at her, nodding as I replied, *really? Have you not fully checked this out already? And why am I asking? You know and I know; it is time you accepted the reality of our youth; don't you think? And, whilst we are on that subject, let me make a final attempt to confirm. You are not our age, are you?*

She shook her head.

I really have been alive for 1825 years but, except for memories, my body is essentially 38 years old.

I stood still and looked at her again.

You are serious? I asked, *we were uncertain whether you might be jesting.*

I had missed the inference in her earlier comments.

Olaria retold me the story of her parents and their lives. When she had finished, she said,

As unbelievable as this may seem to you, the fact that a crew of eight, twenty- and thirty-year old's, have flown an extraordinarily sophisticated spaceship across multiple galaxies and arrived here is no less unbelievable to us. There will be many hundreds, perhaps thousands of discussions going on right now, questioning how people so young could have managed this feat. How you could possibly have learned all you needed to know to enable such a feat. Surely you can see how this must look to a society that considers basic education not complete until around forty. And because we now know your age is real and that you live only a short time, mostly, we heard from John, less than 120 years, we are suddenly concerned that we may be doing something very wrong in our basic education. Many people here are more than a little concerned.

I got it. And then she told me what Ghia had suggested to Kyuto. The Olarian attention to emotional relationships. Ghia had suggested that if she had to pay that much attention to the emotional states of the crew she would not be able to do her job, and we both were thinking about the way everything has a consequence.

CHAPTER 11

Ghia & Kyuto

Kyuto was hungry to know more about my life on Earth, especially about how I lived and what the world around me was like. I was only too pleased to tell him now some rapport had been established. So, a new exploration began, and I used my now clear understanding about how to tell stories from the pictures in my mind.

I own a modern cottage, way out on the edge of Greater London.

I kept the images of the journey there and the place itself as sharp as I could remember and showed him my house, where it was located on the edge of the city. For a moment I thought I had lost him, but suddenly realised I was actually talking to a huge audience. I felt embarrassed and then became aware that Kyuto was screening out the audience, so it felt to me as though the two of us were alone. I was just beginning to get used to the incredible collective openness these people had, and when Kyuto carefully brought it back to just the two of us I knew I felt alright. I kept making the pictures and wondered out loud and telepathically to him if they had cities and if they did, were they anything like the City of London.

Where I live, we think of as semi-rural, it's a little old-fashioned village with rapid aerial transit links to the city and less than an hour from my family farm. It is well serviced with schools, shops, modern medical and excellent childcare facilities. It is the place I plan to live when my baby is born.

I stopped at this point because I could feel Kyuto absorbing my story through the images I was creating as I spoke. It was a little complex, but effective.

Kyuto reproduced for me a picture of the settlements and houses in different parts of Olar and I smiled, realising that there really weren't any big cities here. For a start I had seen no shops, knew there were no factories.

We have collections of dwellings quite close to each other, like I just showed you, but nowhere is it anything really like the city or towns you have been showing me.

Kyuto was aware that he had an interesting spread of information from me and before continuing he wanted me to know he had plans for us. However, first he was curious about one thing for which he had been getting flashes of information, so he asked how I saw him, and I laughed out loud at what I was thinking about him, and he smiled but looked at me with a question mark in his eye. So, I tried to explain, *you look a bit like my image of a rock star who is also a computer nerd!*

He looked puzzled, and I led him in detail through the two characters and he laughed, and I laughed, and it was a moment of genuinely intergalactic humour.

Later when I got to report back to the crew Peta would ask, shaking her head in a kind of incredulous disbelief, how on earth I had got there and I would reply,

'Well, he is handsome in the way our rock stars often are, like all the Olarians he has a great body, his voice—in my head—is very calming and rhythmical, and his hair is darker than the others and stands up more and his face is a bit longer and he just fits my image of a really nerdy muso. But that is where the similarity ends, although I can't get that image out of my head!'

At this point I was thinking that the notion of this as a scientific enquiry was pretty bats.

I knew he had plans and told him I was happy to move on.

At my request, Kyuto showed me the flow of a normal Olarian birthing cycle. I was truly delighted, and envious. In that moment an idea was seeded in my mind. Having my baby here was not such an alien idea. The ease and non-intrusiveness of the entire situation just felt deeply wholesome. No drugs, so surgical anything just people and calm and a deeply organic process. And while right now that was just a thought, it was not a thought that was going to go away.

Kyuto suggested they take a short trip to one of the many learning centres, one which, he was letting me know, was situated less than a mile from his home.

As we walked, we talked. Kyuto asked about my education.

Well, I said, *I loved schooling, but I hated school. I was the only kid who loved their schooling. In small rural schools, like this one, way outside greater London, nearly all farm brats, you were either good at some sport or you were in a lot of trouble if you were really smart. I was unfortunately smart. So, I learned to be good at sport. My parents wanted me to get a profession and leave home and leave the farm to be run by my older brothers.*

I came into existence as a careless mistake by my parents, five years after my last brother, and for most of my childhood I was reminded of this fact. Don't get me wrong, I was loved, but not important. I don't remember a night my parents did not nit-pick each other, often over him wanting sex and that was up to the night before my dad died when a Robot-tractor went a bit nuts, ploughing a wet field and fell on him. After that, I'm sorry to say it this way Kyuto, but my life became more even and peaceful. I feel bad even saying that, but it's true. I got the scholarship mum needed me to get and went away to get a proper education. So, I was basically on my own from my fourteenth birthday.

Through this entire discussion I had kept making pictures for Kyuto.

At University I got a part time job and began to collect old things that reminded me of the farm and fell in love with old fashioned clothes. It seemed to be a way of connecting the past and the farm and compensating for the sterility of the science and engineering and the messiness of the biology and chemistry. So, I sort of became a collector of small and tasteful things.

I knew that Kyuto was surprised at the growing strength of his desire to help me. He knew I was happy to go with him to visit the centre and would be a bit relieved of the self-disclosure which I was finding stressful. I knew he had a strong desire to take me on this visit and in a very Olarian way I let him know she was really ready for a new experience. He knew I felt his enthusiasm for this journey and his hopes for me. It was enlivening, revitalising, and I was able to get those feelings that seemed to stay around the Olarians. The ridge line behind Kyuto's house took us through a wooded area where I could feel the energy of the trees and their strength and some kind of connection, I knew they had with me. She could feel how strongly they connected with Kyuto. It simply made me feel...joyous!

As we walked, Kyuto began to talk about the centre we were about to visit.

I don't know exactly what they will be doing, but I have discussed our visit with the adults there and they are looking forward to meeting you. The children are doing inside things today. We all learn the values of our world in our groups of eight. Two groups, sixteen children altogether, are here with four adults and you will see that everything is geared to helping the children absorb the values on which our entire society operates. At the end of each day the parents arrive to help make dinner, and the fifty odd people eat together in the main dining area which will become a general living area when the meal has been cleared. During the evening adults and children will play, stories will be told, and activities devised in which most people will participate. We will return to our place before dinner but I promise to bring you back here again so you can take part in the evening activities, I am hoping you might be able to do that with Gerard.

I felt grateful and smiled at him. But I felt an edge of uncertainty. School had not been a rewarding experience for me, even though I had loved it.

I am looking forward to experiencing what they actually do. Will you keep me telepathic for that experience?

Yes, I think it will help you understand how our cultures differ. Until Zed had us engage with you free of our telepathic way, I would never have thought there was any point. However, now I know the differences are extreme. When you are being telepathically connected with this many people, you will need me to modulate your experience because the children speak even faster than we do and with all sorts of abbreviations and variants some of which will later become part of our language.

Every generation does it, and it took us a while to realise it was important to let that happen.

So how do they learn? Do you have any books, is there a curriculum - I had to take Kyuto on a quite complex journey to clarify that idea - *I have so many questions, but I'll put them on hold and just experience all this.*

I could feel Kyuto's relief and smiled at him in what was becoming my understanding of the Olarian way, letting myself feel the feeling, knowing he would get it without me having to do anything, knowing he would make no judgements about it. Little by little I could feel myself trusting him and as I realised that, I knew, without any specific effort on my part, everything he was feeling or thinking and that it was safe for him to be aware of my thoughts and feelings. In this place, there was no immediate risk. I could feel myself sinking into the culture and was finding the experience satisfying.

What can you tell me of the lessons they will be leaning? I asked.

I felt Kyuto exploring my thoughts in an effort to know exactly how to answer my question.

I laughed again as I realised that my questions were sort of wrong and bridging a human education system and an Olarian one was going to involve some confusing and complex new experiences. Kyuto gave up trying to find the similarities from my memories and smiling warmly into my mind, suggested that it might be easier to speak after I had spent some time at the centre, and I agreed.

We sat on two energy cushions Kyuto created, and I was able to hear the discussion between what I thought of as the teachers and the students. I realised that the adult, who did not really like the idea of being seen as a teacher, once she understood my image of a teacher, was creating scenarios in which the group engaged, sometimes in twos and threes, sometimes in a whole group discussion, the topic seemed to be co-operation and competition, what they involved, what they meant and how they worked. It was clear that the adult had a strong position, co-operation first and foremost, especially where any others were involved, such as competition with individuals wanting to enhance their own performance. But not all the students agreed and there were some amazing disputes and challenges, and it was clear that although the adult's position was clear, the children were yet to be convinced. If this was indoctrination, it was the most flexible and easily challenged process I had ever seen or could imagine.

I turned to Kyuto. *Will they all come to agree genuinely, congruently?*

Yes. I was uncomfortable with Kyuto's answer.

So, tell me why this is not brain washing?

Kyuto examined my images of brain washing techniques on earth.

Okay, he said.

You are thinking of oppressive things, but there is no oppression intended nor, employed here. Everyone is, without undue pressure, offered the opportunity to explore both co- operative and competitive behaviours. Clearly, we believe in co-operative behaviours as a primary interpersonal act. Because it works and every child gets many opportunities to be both co-operative and competitive, sometimes for days or even weeks, but in the end without exception they all find much greater satisfaction, more options, from co-operative behaviour. We have created games to enable them to compete, however, successful competition results always in co-operation such as you will see in some of our ball games where each team tries to win, however, having more points than your opponent means both lose so the object becomes twofold, find the players who can score the most goals and swap them around until they are scoring the same number of goals on each side, and have both sides kick a high score.

They are, however, encouraged to learn to dissent and so to challenge everything, it will take more than two years for most of this group to firm up their support for co-operation, they have a lot of experiments and explorations to make before they will see the overwhelming evidence of the value of co-operation, but so far, in every area, the evidence in our world is overwhelming. And I think there is an element of what you are calling brain washing because we want everyone to get the kind of advantage that seems to be linked to the co-operative way.

I experienced a brief, if disturbing, thought. What if it was the competitive nature of humans their inability to constantly monitor emotions of those around them, that led to the development of science and mathematics and the probability of them building spacecraft and a lot else?

I knew immediately Kyuto had got it and was more than a little disturbed by it. This was not the first occasion that idea had begun to surface since Sunstreamer had disgorged her crew into the Olarian world.

Is it not this way on Earth?

I was at first embarrassed, then a bit defensive, but I stayed with it.

On Earth, competition is far more valued than co-operation. We have ball games and always, always the object is to win. To get more goals than the other team, to beat them. Fans, that means people who follow a particular team can be quite violent when their team loses and often brawls will break out between supporters of different teams, sometimes people have even been killed in the violence that follows a game.

The entire group including Kyuto was silent, looking at the images I had created with horror and confusion.

Why?

The enquiry must have come from nearly every adult and child in the room, and from innumerable others who had been listening in.

Well, we are competitive. We believe in competition as the best way to give individuals incentive to improve, to be better than others. To become leaders by demonstrating they are better than others who might want their job or their position on the team.

The group talked for about half an hour about human responses to competition and co-operation and in the end, agreed to end the conversation for the moment, but I was asked if I would be willing to come back to it. And of course, I agreed. But this discussion of competitive and co-operative values stimulated a group of the students to take me on another tack. Just before they did, I was aware that Kyuto was listening to a discussion somewhere on the planet about how the human's competitive ways may have been in part responsible for their developing the ability to find the Olarians. I was also aware of the level of distress this was generating.

I was taken aback when a group of three of the children aged probably about 17 years spoke to me.

Ghia you have been listening to us talk about what is important, it is a subject we visit regularly. Can you tell us what is important to you and to other human beings on Earth?

For a moment I was nonplussed, then I remembered Zed talking to the crew one day during a briefing about what matters. I don't remember who asked him, but I remember his answer. I remember him saying it was not an answer he had created. It was old wisdom. It was so simple that I found myself agreeing with it in its entirety and it came back to me now as I was thinking about your question.

Zed put it to us most clearly: *people need someone or something to love and my hand rested for just a moment on my belly before I continued, and usually, someone or some creature to love them, they need some way to fill in their time which is satisfying for them and they need hope, something to look forward to in the future. And in our culture, which I am still supposing is, in some ways similar to your own, he said you need to find ways to fill in the time 'till you die, and surely that is as true for you as for us, no matter how short or long your life. We might do it in different ways, and surely each individual must decide? His point was, everyone has to choose between letting someone else do their thinking for them or doing it for themselves. For some people, it's easier to let others do it for them. So, for us on Earth that tends to mean being less lonely, but that doesn't seem to be a problem you experience here.*

The next moment I was amid an extraordinary babble and could make out only fragments as everyone began talking at once. Fortunately, Kyuto came to my rescue and sorted the babble into half a dozen conversations about what I had said, and I imagined how pleased Zed would be if he could see the impact of his very simple statement. But the group hadn't finished with me yet. They had days of discussion to take from what she had said so far but they were bursting to hear me tell them about the human religions about which they had heard some of the adults talking about.

I had to tell them I was not well-informed about religion as I had myself, neither been brought up with one nor had any interest in exploring them. So, they shifted to asking what humans thought about the purpose of life. A subject they had been exploring. I remembered a conversation the crew had had during their training about the purpose of life. Again, I remembered Zed had expressed a view I had found satisfying and about which I was still considering.

I tried to remember it as Zed had said it, *I think that life has no specific purpose for any individual and so each one of us must find a purpose that suits us, a purpose for ourselves. There are also those, of whom I am not one, who believe that our purpose has been established for us before we were born. Obviously by some power or intelligence vastly superior to ourselves. That it is our job to find that purpose and fulfil it. There are many additions and variations to that theme. Sometimes I do wonder if there is some form of vastly greater developed ability that shapes the cosmos, probably for some purpose I am unable to even comprehend.*

I went on, *It seems that for Olarians the purpose of life is primarily to learn, for many humans this would not be true, if they had thought about it. Some people, such as he was thinking about, believe they were created by a god, a kind of supreme being, and that what someone who was supposed to have been in contact with him, I think they are mostly male, wrote, should be the guide for their lives, even though many people differ about the meaning of what was written or who the writer actually was. Different writers write different truths about different Gods! The worst part is that they often feel so strongly about what they think of as the truth that they will fight to the death with others who disagree with them.*

The looks of distress and repulsion and horror on the faces of some of the children disturbed me. Why are some of you looking at me with such distress and I think disgust?

Ghia, killing and fighting one another seems an awful thing to do. We would never allow it.

I thought for a moment, *I seem to remember that some of your early telepathic ancestors killed Cretians and sealed their world with an energy wall and then destroyed all the old villagers ending their society. Is that not killing and violence?*

There was a great deal of agitation and distress in the group, and I thought the adult would stop it or perhaps Kyuto, but, while neither turned a hair, I understood that discussion of Cretians was very close to a totally taboo subject and was only being allowed because I was a visitor, and I was interested. The group was asked to engage with what I had said and their feelings about it. One of the teenagers said,

That was three thousand years ago, since that time we have allowed no violence in our society.

Well, I replied, *perhaps that is because you have removed the people who would be your enemies and so being peaceful as a society is possible and relatively easy. I do not want to be critical of your gentle ways, you can look deeply into me and you will find I love them, but perhaps when everyone is the same, more or less; peace and tranquillity and harmony are easier. Especially when your education system is designed to maximise harmony. On Earth we have many tribes, cultures, countries, races. Most hold tightly to their roots and so conflict is normal.*

I took them through some of the conflicts I had seen on the nets.

The thing is, I think you also have an extraordinary advantage in being telepathic, as I am just beginning to learn. I want to return to an aspect of this way you have that has another face. Maybe, because you are so decent and caring and know almost everything about anyone with whom you associate, perhaps this has acted to shape the things you have learned and the things you have not learned, especially things that have enabled us to find you and not the other way around.

The group was silent, I was aware that a great deal of thinking was going on amongst these young people and I was aware that this discussion had spread way outside this little microcosm. Kyuto confirmed it for me.

My word Ghia, you and Zed have indeed opened a bag of worms. He smiled. I was thinking about these children and how they were learning and was again wondering what I wanted for my baby. Then it hit. I was being permitted to open Pandora's box. This was an undiscussable, on this planet, amongst this community, until now.

Why? I looked at Kyuto. *Why have you allowed me to discuss this?*

He looked at me, eyebrows raised, the edge of a gentle smile just touching his lips.

The Council felt, quite rightly I believe, that you had a right to raise the issue of The Cretians, and that, truthfully, it would be easier for you than for any of us. Not a courageous position, but practical, easy for you, incredibly complex for us!

Here in the middle of this fairyland in which I felt I had landed there were serious and hard issues to be considered, and I was gaining a healthy respect for this alien community. The truth is, I could see they were horrified when they saw the experiences I had had in my school. They had watched me recall being bullied in class as the nerdy girl and bullied in the playground even when I had done well in sport. Rural farm boys didn't like smart girls. These Olarian kids saw my memories. I was unable not to make the comparisons. Ironically, I was seriously beginning to wish I had grown up here. There was no dishonesty, and nothing was allowed to remain untidied unless it was an untidy end that would come up again and be part of an ongoing development issue. As the children spoke, I could hear their sense of belonging, of challenge, of security, their pride in their learning, their strange (for me) competition and their co-operation with other groups and their insatiable curiosity.

The parents of some joined in from different parts of the planet, as did other people who were not direct family. I wondered how such engagement, if it were ever to occur, would be received back home. It was an eye-opening hour as the children explored their learning, their emotions, their relationships. I knew I had never been involved with people who so genuinely connected to and cared for one another. I ended up in tears, with the children coming to me, holding my hand and talking reassuringly to me. A piece of me was deeply embarrassed, but a small piece. I felt extraordinary warmth and felt welcomed and safe and challenged and disturbed and satisfied and realised that for one of the few times in my life I felt safe in that place.

Later that day, as evening fell and Kyuto was suggesting they might have dinner, Seret returned and led them to a dining room with a very interesting mix of Olarian and human design. The table and chairs and the food bowls were mostly of energy format, but some had clearly been made from materials which seemed like ceramic or like treated timber. The food in the bowls on the table smelled inviting, and I knew I was hungry. Before I retired for the night, Seret promised to dress me in energy clothes in the morning and explore with me getting them on and off.

As I settled down for the night in a bed identical in every way to the one in my bedroom at home, constructed from my memory by Seret, I reflected on the most amazing and absolutely unimaginable first day of any mission I had ever known or heard about.

CHAPTER 12

The Cretian Attack

Zed

I stood at Olaria's front door. Well, it was not really a door like any I had ever seen, but it was where a front door would be if there was going to be one. She put a hand on my shoulder.

Please come in.

It felt as though the house snuggled into the garden. But we stood there, she could feel my unwillingness to cross this threshold. I looked at her, at the garden, at the Olarian sky, as beautiful a blue as home. But I did not move and right now, she could not read what I was thinking or feeling. I just stood there, jammed up unable, for this moment, to keep her at bay. I could hear the ripple of surprise from many voices at the edge, but I stepped away from her and the front of her home, onto the path up which we had just walked.

She heard me silently ask for a seat.

Zed follow my mind, and I watched as she created the seat, experienced immediately how she had done it and as she removed hers, I made one for myself. She knew I felt pleased with myself for creating it, and I sat. She joined me. We looked at one another. I could not let my feelings out. She got that. I sat in an impenetrable silence. The last hours had been too much. I felt... the pieces of me lying in tatters around me, I could not find myself, I was not there.

The crew could no longer be the people they had been. Nothing was ever going to be the same again and I was seriously missing Raille. I did not belong here. I had become... something else. I no longer belonged, anywhere. I was wracked with sadness. Sadness, utterly alone. I could find no part of myself on to which I could hold. Heartbroken, abandoned, I felt alone, I needed to find... what? Myself!

I just wanted to... disappear, go home, just where exactly was that now? As Olaria was about to speak, I vanished.

I was sitting on my bunk on Sunstreamer, tears streaming down my face. 'Move,' before the computers identified my presence on board and suddenly, I was sitting beside the Lander, alone. Then with no warning I was back with Olaria and now I had added fear to the litany. This craziness has to stop. At the edge of my awareness, I heard Olaria speaking to someone.

His brain has connected to his ability to make simultaneity jumps, he has no conscious control, no idea...

Whatever else she was saying I missed.

You've created a monster. Maybe I wasn't actually meant to be telepathic and telekinetic? Maybe I was just supposed to have the potential?

Please Zed, you are not thinking clearly.

Well, I was certain that was right. I sat in the seat Olaria had taught me to make for the tiny amount of what remained of that day and all through that night, unmoving, not a sound and... not really asleep and not in contact with Olaria, with anyone.

However, events elsewhere were not standing still.

Sunstreamer was making its second pass over the continent of Cretia, which Peta now knew to be the continent surrounded by an energy wall which was the area shown as blank on the original Probe scans. She and Harma, her host, had been in conversation as Sunstreamer began its second orbit over Cretia when the penetrating emergency warning system was activated and could be heard on every deck of the spaceship.

Yuri spoke to Peta. 'We have identified a Missile launching 3 seconds ago, it is potentially a threat to Sunstreamer. Automated Defensive System will engage in 3 seconds.'

Peta did not interrupt the spaceship's Automatic Defensive System. In that time Peta got Harma and herself into a seat at the instant Yuri activated the ADS and fastened both into their full protective harness. 'Shields are repositioned toward the missile. Missile is presently climbing through 15,000 feet and accelerating through Mach 1. Initiating a 10 second full power burn, in one second.'

'Harma Hang on.'

Peta got the words out just in time.

The pressure of the burn was immediately felt on the Bridge as Yuri instigated the defensive burn and reported 3 seconds later.

'No change in the missile trajectory, the missile is not target-responsive.'

Peta immediately took over.

'Yuri, taking over. Cut the burn at 8 seconds.'

At 8 seconds, the pressure from the acceleration ceased. Sunstreamer had outdistanced the missile, which exploded harmlessly miles away.

Tanzin and Jald had ceased their discussion when Tanzin's Ucom had alerted her to the change in Sunstreamer's navigational status.

'Lotus, give me all change co-ordinates and ADS course data.'

Lotus was pretty well exclusively devoted to the use of the Astronavigator. Her priority overrode any other allocation of the Quantum Computer's time. Right now, Lotus was feeding Tanzin and her Ucom full navigational status as it was happening. Before she began the repositioning calculations, she heard John wanting Sunstreamer to resume mapping and avoiding all lines of sight with Cretia.

She had listened carefully to the conversation between John and Peta.

Jald had watched her and had been following her thoughts from the beginning of the incident.

For an instant he was overwhelmed with the rapid set of maps and calculations with which she was engaged. He saw flashes of their solar system, of the planet tightly meshed with a series of incomprehensible calculations done at a blinding speed he could not follow. He realised this was a mind on a mission. Tanzin's grasp of his system completely stunned him and the Living Library observer responsible for following her thoughts. Neither Jald nor her observer could believe the complexity and the speed with which she completed the visual and mathematical calculations that Peta was watching flow down the Holo screen directly into Lotus.

Peta was not disconcerted, she had seen this before, the instant before John had given them the silent instruction to exit the Olarian system Tanzin had done just such a set of calculations, and Peta knew it was being done by a brilliant fully integrated navigational genius. Tanzin simply did not make mistakes in generating these kinds of instructions, nor the equations underpinning them.

In less than thirty seconds the Holo stream ceased, the Holo screen glowed green, and Peta knew she could instigate and complete the repositioning. Her hands moved smoothly with her verbal instructions to the computers, and five seconds after Tanzin's navigational instructions ended their flow off the Holo screen, Sunstreamer was accelerating into its new orbit. Minutes passed as it repositioned and slowed and settled into the new orbit with barely any disturbance to Harma or Peta. There would be no more sightings of Cretia.

Jald and Peta's host and the two observers could barely believe the complexity and ease of the actions of the two crew members following the simple instructions from their Captain. None of the crew seemed to have experienced any disturbance at the events to which they had been party and none of the Olarians who had been involved were immediately able to grasp how John's simple request had been translated into a seamless instantaneous repositioning of the huge spacecraft. The Olarians were impressed with the efficient and effective capability of their visitors. No longer were they unclear that these eight people had been able to bring this extraordinary vessel to their planet. This had been a further introduction to a technological world way beyond their experience. Slowly, the significance of the Cretian bomb and their Surface to Air Missile sank in.

'Was there any evidence of further missile activity before we lost contact with the site?' The question from Peta to the Computers. The words were hardly out of her mouth when Yuri reported that there had been no evidence of further missile launches. Without a crew request the computers had widened their scan to fifty miles around the launch site and collected all the data on the site. Peta instructed Yuri to send all the operational data to the Captain's UCOM and to copy in the entire crew.

Peta turned to the seat into which she had almost thrown Harma, her host.

'Harma, I need to apologise for throwing you into the seat, but the acceleration can be dangerous if you are not strapped in, although the Sunstreamer's Human Safety Monitors would have ensured you were not damaged as they got you into a seat.'

Harma was smiling at her. I'm okay Peta. *That was impressive, however, had you asked I could easily have destroyed the missile shortly after its launch.*

She turned back to examine the computer records of the area within fifty kilometres of the launch site for any sign of further launch activity. No pre-launch activity was detected, and Sunstreamer was already well outside the range of the energy-sealed territory. However, there was evidence of multiple other launch sites around the live one from which the missile had been launched.

Harma had willingly taken a backseat, but his comment to Peta had not gone unnoticed.

'What if there had been another missile launch?' She asked.

I would have terminated its flight many hundreds of thousands of feet below you, you have my word.

Peta looked at him. This was not some macho boast, and this was confirmed 30 seconds later when Yuri reported that, in spite of the fact that the shields would have been adequate a completely new layer of shielding had been in place right on the extreme edge of the Sunstreamer's shields. Shielding of unknown origin and type.

Peta turned to Harma, and found herself using the telepathic link between them, *That was you, wasn't it?*

Yes.

He replied, I could not possibly have allowed anything to happen to you or your amazing vessel. However, had I known how extraordinarily competent you, your navigator and your computers were, I would have been much less concerned.

Yuri again reported in.

'There were no other active missile sites within at least a fifty-mile radius of the original launch site. None that showed any sign of activity, but there were multiple life form heat sources in that area.'

Peta turned to Harma, leaving all her hailing channels open.

Your actions would have saved us, wouldn't they?

I would like to claim that I could have been helpful, however, your shields were more than adequate for the power of the projectile.

In that moment a bond was formed between Peta and Harma that would bind them together, how was not yet clear. Peta was impressed, and that in itself was no small feat.

The entire crew, excluding me, had been listening in, together, they shortly realised, with a large section of the entire Olarian world!

As Peta had slid quietly into her chair. Yuri continued, 'The missile was approximately thirty metres in length, accelerating to just over Mach one on a tight intercept course with us. However, it would only just have reached our outer shields at the extreme limit of its climb. The rocket propulsion system was of a primitive type not known to us and the explosive warhead was of an unknown type, but, without the shields, and if it could have reached us, it might well have been sufficient to seriously damage the outer hull.'

Peta added an instruction to the computers.

'Yuri pull up your scan of the launch site and do a detailed analysis of the whole area around it. Search for and mark out like weapon patterns and any signs of activity. Collate all data on the weapon and split the shields between the planet and space.'

The computers built a full three-dimensional image of the missile and provided a full analysis of its construction, fuel, payload and engine characteristics. Tanzin's orbit would make Sunstreamer invisible to anyone on the surface within the energy wall surrounding Cretia. Peta turned to Harma.

His hand was up, and he was clearly in conversation with someone. It turned out to be the Council. Finally, he spoke to Peta.

My apologies I was speaking with the Council. We seem to have stirred up; how would you describe it? A hornet's nest.

Harma was clearly very pleased to have been involved in the incident and was very pleased to have participated with Peta in the adventure.

Having noticed the area from which the missile had been launched, he went back to discussion with the Council. Peta tapped her communicator.

'Captain, you will have received all that data from the commencement of the incident?'

'Yes, Number one.'

'The missile was fired from an area approximately thirty-five kilometres from an earlier Atomic explosion and in terms of safety for the people at the missile site that would have been way too close. The relatively small atomic bomb seems to have been placed against the wall. It was activated ninety seconds after the launch.'

They both heard the simultaneous response of the Council, *The Cretians!*

The Captain's final message to the crew was simple. 'Well done, Number One. We will have a full debrief in the morning.'

In the early hours of the morning, I got up and followed my morning meditation ritual and then I turned to Olaria who had, it turned out, left herself sitting watching me nearly all night, dividing her attention between me and an emergency meeting of the Council.

I think I'm back! But I feel disgusting, I need clean clothes and a shower.

She realised how uncomfortable I was feeling about my clothes and without pausing said, *Zed, please step out of all your clothes.*

I raised my eyebrows. *You want me naked?*

Yes, please.

I held my breath for a moment then realised I was being absurd. I was not uncomfortable being naked, usually. But in front of Olaria who I was finding sexually attractive, that was another matter. She looked at me. I was already hard and erect and deeply embarrassed.

Zed don't go there! I just want to help you with washing and the cleaning of your clothes.

I wondered how I had got hung up on clothes and nakedness?

In a second, she was standing before me stark naked—my god; she was beautiful,

I just want you naked and being naked is so natural in our world I am seeking to make you comfortable, not sexual. 38-year-olds may not have perfect skin in our world, but this one did, and she was nearly 1900 years old. I could not stop staring. *Zed,* she said, *your thoughts are very flattering, and I am truly delighted you find me so beautiful and desirable, and I know you are erect and aroused but for now we ought to make this about the practicality of cleaning your clothes, which I can do with ease if you will let me, if you will for a moment think of me as being helpful rather than sexually provocative. I promise you when that is an appropriate thing for us to be doing it will not just be about attractive naked bodies. But I do like the look of you. Very much.*

And I could feel the warmth and the desire and the control she was exerting to stay focused on the task. She paused. *I know you understand.*

And I did... she suspended all my clothes in the air. She asked me to activate my ability to see energy and to watch which energies she used, and I watched how to hold the garments stationary in the air. I watched as she moved the energy down through the clothes, essentially giving them an energy wash. There was a slow flickering of light from the neck of my shirt to the soles of my shoes, and then she asked me to bring the clothes back into my hand. They were fresh and clean and smelled just like the day I first took them from their packets. I bathed. I would normally have had a shower but the temptation of the bath she had replicated from my memory won and I sat there luxuriating and when I was finished, stood up and used Olaria's brilliant and simple drying machine!

I was entirely ready to proceed with the day. A new piece of the process of managing energy had been added to my slowly growing repertoire. I dried myself in a single pass of energy and I dressed and joined Olaria. I caught my breath as I watched her dress in her exquisite energy wear.

You know, I may have become useless to you? Now I am really no longer me.

But she was unfazed.

No Zed, they know you as who you are and much has occurred since you sat in the seat outside the entrance to my house. A great deal has changed outside of you as well! So, it is not only you who has changed and as soon as you adjust to who you have become everything will fall into place. You know, for certain now, you are no prisoner on this world of ours. This could be your home and you must know by now that I am willing to be fully available to you, it is something I want and when it happens it will be because both of us want it.

I looked at her, turned slightly to rest my hands on the back of one of her chairs, this was not a conversation that fit anywhere else in my life. I was trying to sort my feelings as she continued.

But I know that is not yet. You have changed, but you are a product of your world and will always be.

I looked around, still trying to get my bearings, finally turning back to face her.

Your friend will certainly come to fully understand.

I pictured Raille in my mind and was able to see his smile. I relaxed a little.

Your crew members, well, they will find you as you present yourself. We know you cannot be one of us. You are becoming simply an enhanced version of the person you have always been. All of us need you to be who you are and who you always have been. She had paused and I focussed in on her again. She seemed just a bit uncomfortable for a moment, I imagined.

There has been a crisis whilst you were away. I told John you were exhausted and deeply asleep, and he agreed you were not needed at that moment and I should leave you sleep. Last night as Sunstreamer passed over Cretia, they fired what he called a Surface to Air Missile at Sunstreamer. Peta was able to ensure no damage was done, Harma reported all that had occurred. But there are consequences. Very significant consequences. Also, the Cretians exploded an atomic bomb against the energy wall with no significant effect. Please listen on your Holo before you contact John.

For a moment I wondered what on Earth had been going on whilst I was off with the fairies, and I had a nasty twinge of guilt. I activated my message bank and heard the event replayed.

'Missile launch.'

Yuri speaking calmly to Peta. I listened to the details of the event, realising that I had slept peacefully through it all. After the event the evening had settled down, but not for the Olarian Council who had realistically anticipated getting no sleep that night. In 3000 years, no Council of eight had ever sat down to discuss and consider the Cretians. I had slept on and now, in the morning I had a brief engagement with John who reassured me, had I been needed he would have asked for me to be woken. I told him I was looking forward to the morning debrief.

CHAPTER 13

First Crew Meeting

Zed

When Ghia returned next day with Kyuto to the field in which the Lander rested, she thanked him, aware, as she checked what state she was in, that her feelings toward him no longer contained any hostility, nor any feelings of fear. A day, she thought, can be a long time in a relationship.

Day one of their mission time had passed. She stood for a moment before moving toward the Lander. Were the others in a similar state? She needed to know. Where had their experiences taken them? Usually on a mission like this they would be together, she would know. But not this time.

She had spent an hour with Seret and had worn an energy dress and with Seret's help got it on and off, however; she realised she could not really wear it, except for times she was with an Olarian woman. Sadly, she could not initially manage its movement. She was, she became aware, the last to arrive. The rest were now assembled in the circle in which they had first met the Olarians. In their absence, Olaria had recreated the circle of seats and each member of the crew had returned automatically to the seat they had occupied during the introductions the previous day. It felt strange to be there without the Olarians, even more so because the crew knew their hosts were telepathically present with them. One by one the crew realised, none of the seats were wet, in spite of the rainstorm that had lasted for nearly 30 minutes earlier that morning. They noticed a dome almost invisible, now existed over the circle, protecting it from the rain. Nothing on Olar was really quite like home.

The agreement I had made with the crew was simple. When they returned to meet together, each would share their experiences. On the surface it was a simple request, but unsurprisingly, the experiences the crew had had, had for the most part been extreme. No one returned at the end of the first day unscathed, unexposed, unchanged. So, whilst I had anticipated, the sharing of their stories would bind the group together in novel ways, even I was unprepared for the mélange and the power of the events so far. Their hosts, these powerful, kind, honest people, had woven a web of connection and caring unprecedented in their lives. Almost certainly unprecedented in Space Fleet history. Probably more accurate to say in human history.

John had shared with his host, some of the horror of his father's behaviour toward him as a ten-year-old child. His father, a giant of a man from Barbados intended to, "make him a man". The severe beltings he had received every morning for a month of his thirteenth year had left scars that were still unhealed and had helped shape his extreme abhorrence of violence. He remembered telling her, but as he retold it to the crew, he realised he hardly remembered why. Had she influenced him? When he finished, Gerard and Raille both shared things about their family's attitude toward them and violence, but John was really no longer hearing them. Even the knowledge that this information would go no further than this crew was appalling for him. He went very quiet.

Ghia shared her lonely and isolating school history and her irrelevance as the final child in a farming family of 3 boys and a much older sister who had been made responsible for her until she left home as a precocious 14-year-old to go to an advanced education institution to which she had won a scholarship.

She had shared her journey with Kyuto, adding, 'Kyuto struggled with my isolation from my family, my emotional untidiness and my need for control alongside my ability to be a party animal yet really quite shy and introverted. This sad combination added to my lack of self-confidence and my inability to manage it—which of course most of you don't get to see—. I found it really hard to talk about that. You all see me as competent, thank goodness, but he dug into my behaviour and found what really only Gerard and Zed know; I keep people at a distance because I don't think of myself as very likeable!'

She shook her head, rolled her eyes and found her hands giving herself a hug.

She was looking at Gerard. 'Lord, this is embarrassing. Kyuto also seemed to feel uncomfortable about my pregnancy, not that I was pregnant but that my plans for the future felt, he said, cold, and made him feel sad. He said it made little sense to him that the more successful I became, the lonelier and emptier my life might seem. He found it difficult to imagine having my baby alone and putting it into childcare so I could go on working! It was, he thought, getting more and more difficult to see how money did anything except create distress and problems in our lives. I didn't feel like disagreeing with him.'

Everyone turned to look at Gerard on Watch Duty today, so on the Holomonitor. He was looking both somewhat bewildered but also pleased, if a little sad, nevertheless he was smiling. Ghia was honouring their connection.

'Kyuto acknowledged getting my drift. So, I explained to him that whilst marriage had become pretty archaic and that fewer than 30% of our world's population still did it, I really liked the idea and wanted Gerard and I to get married.'

Some of the crew who were not looking totally lost in her story clapped with enthusiasm! I was delighted, rarely had I seen a crew become so involved with one another's private lives and I looked meaningfully at John who was in his turn looking not just a little bewildered but as the whole experience began to sink in he was quickly becoming angry and definitely frustrated, this was not appropriate behaviour for an SFC mission crew and he desperately wanted it to stop. But he was sitting here with Aliens who were in his head, in everyone's head!

His crew were sharing personal stories, including himself, and he knew this was inappropriate and unprofessional, I could see that he was feeling like an angry child wanting to stamp his feet; he seemed to me to feel trapped in the spaghetti-like intertwining of relationships and connections. He wanted this to stop. For the discussions to be professional and finally he spoke in the grip of his anger and frustration.

'This has to stop! It's just as well that everything we have just said is not on record.

Nevertheless, this is simply wrong. This is not how an Explorer crew is supposed to behave.

He was almost spluttering with anger, distress and frustration.

Dead silence greeted his outburst. No one knew what to do, and all eyes turned to me. This was my job! I brought Olaria immediately into my awareness.

To her, telepathically, *Bring everyone, now, please!* In an instant the 8 members of the Council were in their seats, John's anger had not abated and the Olarians were silent, all looking at, and the Olarians into, me, then back to John.

'John, look around, listen! The 7 people you brought on a mission are now, in a manner of speaking, more than six hundred million plus eight. We cannot be the eight-person mission crew you brought here. We cannot act as though we are simply an Explorer crew with a vessel from Space Fleet Command. We cannot do that. We decided to meet an Alien society, we cannot act as if we are doing something else. This mission has, to use an old and sexist piece of colloquial jargon which I confess nevertheless appeals to me "gone tits up" we need to grapple clearly with what this mission has become, by our choice. We chose not to return home and leave this problem to someone possibly more suited to it! And you will forgive me for saying, I believe we are the ideal crew for managing this strange and absolutely undocumented new task.'

Then I went silent, and the silence hung over the fourteen people sitting in a shelter no human had ever seen before. I looked at and into the thirteen people in the circle and the two on Sunstreamer and returned my gaze to the Captain.

'John, this became too much when you shared with us the beatings your father gave you to make you a man. That was a horrendous experience to have and even more distressing for you to share with your crew and these alien people. But your shocking experiences also helped shape you. Nearly every person on your crew has been damaged by parents and a society that does not nourish us. But it is not that way here. There can be no lies here and we frankly do not know how to handle that and,' I paused, 'I apologise in advance for what I am going to say, but... all of us had better bloody-well learn fast.'

Peta, Raille, Elise, Tanzin and Ghia breathed a sigh of relief and silently to themselves, and the listening Olarians,

'Thank god.' However, John was not there yet, and Gerard felt confused. He needed Ghia to settle him down, but she was a distance away.

'I don't know how we are going to carry this off when we get home, but we sure as hell won't be able to do it without you. This is unprecedented, but for heaven's sake, we're space travellers, an Explorer crew. If we can't do this, then we are all in the wrong jobs!'

John was staring at me. Floating between anger and relief. Silence hung like a blanket over the 14 of us on the ground. No one moved, everyone was watching John.

Now even Gerard, who had been focussed on Ghia, realised she was onboard, turned to watch John. Not a breath of wind disturbed the quiet of this tense scene. Time seemed to be standing still until John, looking squarely at me, slowly nodded his head.

'Thank heaven you're here,' he said, and then again, 'thank heaven you're here.' As everyone took a collective breath, he turned to everyone, gently shaking his head. 'My apologies to you all. I think, until Zed said that I had genuinely forgotten what it really means to be an Explorer in space.'

A sigh of relief went around the group before each of the crew reclaimed themselves and realised what I had said.

'This was just the beginning!'

And that, I decided, was also a good sign. Ghia looked at me, 'Zed?'

I just smiled and nodded 'Go on.'

So, she continued with her story of the day. She was clearly struggling to maintain her equilibrium as she told of her sharing with Kyuto; and Tanzin, with whom she was probably closest, got up from her place in the circle and came to sit beside her, in a seat Olaria had clearly created instantly, for the purpose.

Ghia smiled gratefully at her for the gesture. 'I think,' Ghia added, 'Kyuto felt some distress as he followed the images I was creating of the future. I guess if you don't die and you do not have to suffer any pain because you can control it from the time you are about twelve and if you are always able to be healthy, then a species like us must be hard to comprehend. When I described in images how I imagined the rest of my life, he was... gobsmacked.'

There were chuckles and smiles around the group, but the mood was not light.

Ghia paused. She was looking at the group and finished by telling them about the Child Development Centre she had visited, 'and I want to say, his little centre was like a fairyland to me. He has promised to take me back there, and I want to hold him to that. (Everyone felt a smile they knew was Kyuto) I was introduced to the sixteen children and the adults looking after them. During the few hours I was there, the children often checked up on how I was feeling, and it was a strange but not unpleasant experience. One thing struck me and attached itself, I still can't let it go. The teachers—they don't like being called that, but Kyuto couldn't find an English word for their concept—encouraged every child to explore and understand their feelings and those of every other person around them, including the adults!

'Also, how they were expressed and to use what they learned with the others, especially those to whom they were most attracted! When this was being discussed I tried to imagine my own teachers even talking to me about love and life and intimacies, including sex! What a joke! They were also being encouraged to explore every curiosity they had and are given unrestricted access to the Knowledge Holders, total access! They are also constantly encouraged to think about things they are looking forward to that day, tomorrow or further into the future. I thought it was amazing how the teachers spent seriously long times with every child; so structured and deliberate, I just wished I had grown up here!' She finished by saying, 'Gerard, our child could do worse than to be trapped in this world, and perhaps even with me.'

The entire crew seemed to be holding its breath. Gerard was pale and appeared to be speechless. It was as if all of them could feel her sense of security about her child here in this world. The group was silent and absorbed.

Raille said, 'Ghia, my experiences are in no way identical to yours, but even in a very large and competitive secondary school I constantly felt bullied and abused for being too smart. It was not pleasant. I was truly relieved to get to Uni. where my abilities were no longer a liability. Your story resonates with me. And, as we sit here now, sharing experiences in ways that would not have been possible only two days ago, I suspect that all of us are being seduced into this very strange yet very intimate Olarian society.'

I had observed Gerard following Ghia's story closely. It seemed her revelations had primed his desire to share some of his story with the crew, most of whom were watching him on the Holomonitor and were evidently surprised but pleased when he volunteered to share some of the story he had shared with his host.

'This is just a short piece but probably reveals some very disturbing pieces of my life that only today have I recognised as shaping much of who I have become. And I am telling you all this because after John spoke, I realised his story was, in some important ways, reminiscent of my own.

I grew up in Chechnya but my family thought of itself as Russian, and I was one of three children, I was the eldest. My father was a chronic violent alcoholic and when inebriated would beat both my mother and us children. One night when I was ten, he came home and beat me and my mother. It must have been the last straw for her because when he was gathering his breath for his next assault, my mother picked up a heavy iron frypan and knocked him unconscious. She would not allow him up until she had extracted his word there would be no more violence in the home unless he wanted her to kill him, which she would do if he laid another hand on her or any of the children. For some reason after that eventful night my mother encouraged me to follow my natural curiosity about engines which had become an obsession that was to stay with me for the rest of my life, and eventually to Caltech.

'It had,' he said, 'followed me into the military and then eventually into SFC.'

The other significant incident which heavily influenced me, unbeknown to me, I learned when my host asked me how I had become so obsessed with my desire to be with Ghia.

He blushed, I feel really embarrassed telling this story, but it seems to have been at the core of a big piece of my adult life. Its significance I only found yesterday, twenty years later!

'I was twelve years old, I had been creeping down to the kitchen for a late snack one night, when, passing my parents' bedroom where the door happened to be slightly ajar, I heard my father speaking gently to my mother and her moaning and calling out in pleasure. At the time, I had no understanding of what I had heard. However, yesterday as I was trying to tell Gret what it was that so totally connected me to Ghia I suddenly realised, and I apologise for telling this Gee, but you did say I should not be secretive about it. The sounds Ghia makes when we make love are the sounds my mother was making that night. And I have had no awareness of this until yesterday. And it doesn't change anything between Ghia and me. But it was one hell of an insight. It was the first time I realised I could be gentle with a woman.'

There was absolute silence in the group, it was as if no one was even breathing. The insight from Gerard was truly astonishing to every member of the crew. Me not excepted. Moments passed, and at first it seemed, no one knew what to say, until Ghia simply said, 'Thank you, Gerry.'

If he had been on the ground, I think the group might have actually physically hugged him! It was an astonishing revelation, and he felt the warmth that was being passed on by the Olarians.

Tanzin seemed to be moved by Gerard's comments and now looked somewhat anxiously around the group. Her slightly furrowed brow suggested caution. From the telepathic sharing everyone knew she was thinking, these were the people with whom she worked, they relied on her absolutely as she did on them, how could she share the intimate details she had found it easy to share with Jald, an Alien, a stranger. But whatever feelings were circulating through her, above these she felt a powerful urge to trust them in the way they were presently trusting her. It was a big step when she began.

'There are only girls in my family, I have no memory of my father who, my mother told us, left when I was one-year-old. My mother was an Internationally acclaimed Cellist. Each of my three elder sisters are talented musicians, the entire family except me.' The crew looked at her in some surprise. They knew she was currently one of the two top Astronavigators in the world, more trusted in space circles than almost anyone else in the world. Yet now, she was telling them about her talented musical family as though she was a failure!

Tanzin continued, not fully grasping the meaning of the expressions on the faces of her colleagues; then suddenly feeling them. 'As a result, although I was never badly treated, I felt isolated from my family, the black sheep, and from the rest of the world. Except when I was learning and mixing with bright and talented people, fellow students or instructors. Within a year of finishing school, I topped my University year in physics, maths of several kinds, and astronomy, but my family were neither interested nor impressed, even when I graduated top of my year, did a master's degree and then a Doctoral Degree in Astrophysics and joined Space Fleet Command's Astronavigation School. It was as if I had been born for it, but for them it was insignificant. I was not a musician. Since beginning University, I have had no contact with my sisters or my mother. I am afraid I might never have contact with them again. I really am the black sheep of my family and it still hurts.'

Tears were sliding down her face. She was touched and surprised when Gerard shared with her his alienation from his family and clearly understood how her experiences in her family were for her now. To the continuing surprise of the group, it was Raille who also understood. His parents also brilliant academics in their fields had given him no sense of his worth until he had become free of them and found his place in University, where his interest in the natural world around him and an astonishing talent for languages had changed his life. He too had had no contact with his parents for almost ten years.

As each of the eight crew told their story, someone would connect with their experience and a great deal of sadness, tears, and many warm connections were shared in this strange space on a field on a distant planet in a fashion that would have been unthinkable only days before. None of these experiences were part of the normal engagement of members of Space Fleet Command, and for them to be shared amongst elite members of the Explorer Group was novel and was clearly going to be consequential.

As the crew reported back one by one, there were many deeply personal stories from their past which they had shared with their Olarian hosts and now, by their agreement with me, shared amongst themselves. Some if not all the shared experiences showed how deeply they were involved and helped explain the depth of their connection to their Olarian hosts. I included real stories about my life, but not about what I had learned from the Olarians.

Before they moved, Ghia asked, 'Did anyone, other than me, ask their hosts to speak out loud in Olarian?'

Raille replied, the sole response to Ghia's question, and, not really to anyone's surprise, he could now speak several words of Olarian with an Olarian accent.

And, his host said, he will learn to speak it beautifully! He is amazing and I have rarely enjoyed someone's company so completely!

It was on that note that the learnings from the group so far, ended. The meeting was not on record, that was my contracted deal with SFC, it had brought a heap of hostility from my colleagues, which I mostly ignored. However, my agreement about the right of crews to share personal information that could not be used in any way by the organisation, except by me in my engagement with them, had been a deal breaker for my joining SFC. Given the situation we were in at the moment, decisions about the strength of bonds between the crew as well as between the crew and the Olarians was front of mind for my involvement in planning for our future.

CHAPTER 14

A Glitch from Jeland (The second Olarian Continent).

While the crew were still meeting at the lander site, the Olarian council had returned to its meeting room and a small crisis was being created by Sjiss, a Jelander (the other major continent on which the Olarians lived), over the concerns of a number of Jelander's relating to the impact of the human crew on their lives. Essentially, it was less the crew than the fact that they had stirred the Cretian hornet's nest. Sjiss was speaking to the Council.

The lives of the Earth people as we have seen them are truly abhorrent to us. They are violent, warlike and cruel. Their society seems to be sick. Now, as a result of their overflying Cretia, we have a crisis looming with the Cretians, something unknown to us for 3000 years. We would like the Council to ask them to leave and not return.

Olaria and the Council had returned to their meeting room. She was focussed now on Sjiss; she understood his fears, however, she knew he was aware of her desire to have a child with Zed. Every Olarian had been able to be party to the discussions that had occurred both with Zed, but more particularly by the Council of 8. Was he suggesting he did not approve? She quickly determined he was not. He apologised to her for not having fully considered her wishes, however, was firm in his desire to see the humans leave.

What aspect of the human presence most concerns you? Olaria asked. *These are people who have travelled the universe in ways we strongly desire to emulate. Are you suggesting we should not learn from them in order to be enabled to do the same?*

Sjiss was briefly nonplussed. He had not thought through his own and his colleagues' concerns.

He looked at Olaria and the members of the Council.

It is true I may not have thought this through, fully. However, it is also true that the human race is potentially very dangerous to us. They are also responsible for establishing hostilities between us and the Cretians. A scenario for which we have no desire to be embroiled.

Olaria was aware that Sjiss did not fully grasp the significance of what the crew had learned about the Cretians. She wanted me to be available to the Council and asked Sjiss if he would object to her bringing the Human Crew into the conversation; gently reminding him, they were invited guests of the Olarian people and had already contributed a not insignificant degree of new learning to them. Furthermore, she had gone on, they seem to have a better grasp of the Cretians than do we. Especially, I would like you to meet Zed and be willing to ask him, face to face.

He is, you are aware, probably as genetically Olarian as you, but born on another world, which, in itself is pretty interesting. Are you agreeable?

It would have been considerably more than churlish for Sjiss to refuse. It would also have been culturally unlikely he would have considered not meeting her request. So, Olaria joined the crew in their meeting and made her request.

'How,' John asked, 'will we get to this meeting?'

Your hosts will join me in a moment, if you are agreeable, and will take you to our meeting in a simultaneity jump with them.

There was silence in the group. I have already taken Zed on such a journey and he can reassure you it is both safe and exciting.

The crew turned to me.

'It is true, a simultaneity jump is an amazing experience.'

We will keep the Sunstreamer connected to us and so, if you are agreeable, we will ask his host to bring Gerard, currently duty officer, back to us with a simultaneity jump so he will not miss out.

On board Sunstreamer, Gerard smiled at his host, who nodded to him and an agreement was reached. The crew made the jump. There was a brief discussion to allow the excitement and the novelty to be shared before the meeting with Sjiss continued.

Before we begin, a discussion about your concerns and your request, it was Kyuto speaking, we would like you to also review our personal engagement with these humans, one at a time, so you can perhaps remind yourself, or simply refresh your memory about each of them.

There followed a brief review by each of the eight hosts of their experiences with their human guests.

None of that is new to me. I am certain you all know. I am not for a moment wishing to suggest the eight we have, are not interesting, intelligent, educated and, in their way, impressive, however, they bring danger and frightening change with them. Cuckoos, I think they would be, if I have understood that bird.

Several of the crew smiled.

Sjiss was clearly hostile and frustrated. The intensity of his tirade disturbed Olaria and for the first time on Olar, I felt as though I was in a combative space, unlike anything I had experienced so far. It was clear that Sjiss was infuriated by the presence of the human crew and finally asked; *how can you bring them into this discussion? This is an exclusively Olarian concern!*

The crew were getting the entire telepathic communication, and each looked at Olaria, then each of the members of the Council with whom they were at least familiar. The members of the Council were, for the first time since they had arrived, generating frustration and what seemed to be a frustrated anger! I was unable to contain my surprise.

Sjiss, I cannot believe what I am hearing here. And I apologise sincerely for our presence. Are you telling us you want us to go and never return after we have just found one another? You do not want us here?

Sjiss was almost halted in his tracks. His thoughts were hostile, his intent clear. His frustration at Olaria's action left him almost silenced, but not quite.

I don't know what to say to you, Zed. We have never had to deal with others in our entire lives, not for thousands of years. You are the most disturbing thing that has ever happened here since the meteorite whose trajectory we had to adjust to ensure our survival, and that was more than a thousand years ago.

It was evident he had more to say but that the crew's presence was impeding him. What I had said, angered, disturbed and generally interrupted his presentation to the Council and in human terms, it threw a spanner in the works. To me he sounded both confused and very angry. This was a side to the Olarian civilisation I had so far not seen and the frown and disturbed energy he brought to the chamber impacted them all.

I believe you ought to think carefully about what you are doing here and might consider including us in your deliberations, this really is no longer only your lives and culture that are at stake. You have also disturbed us, created hope we did not previously feel.

'Bloody hell.' John's interjection was almost explosive, and he raised his eyebrows and looked at Ghia and Tanzin, shaking his head. 'Lord, you've got me saying it now! We were just beginning to be able to think about what we should be learning here!'

And it was clear that Ghia's desire to have the Olarians help with her pregnancy was now influencing him. John's eyebrows were drawn tightly down, and his shaking head made it clear that he was no longer confident he had made a good decision about returning to engage with this powerful and complex society. This was not, I could see, what John believed he had signed up for. Then John caught himself and shaking his head, apologised to the group.

'My motives were no longer simple. I was wondering what I would do without Olaria's help.'

And none of the others had any idea, now, what was motivating me.

Olaria interrupted the flow of her meeting.

We are talking about our human guests. We have chosen to ask them to stay and not to return home when we had the opportunity. Like them, this is the first opportunity we have ever had to meet others who live in the cosmos. Are you seriously asking them to go away and not return? Are we so conceited, so stultified, so stodgy and afraid that we are not willing to explore something as momentous as another sentient life form who can speak, with whom we have mutual understanding and who clearly are exceptional in that they can come to us whilst we cannot go to them? I am including our human friends in this outburst because I want them to know what is going on here and how afraid we are of novelty and innovation and the unknown. They have travelled across unknown vistas of space to find us, no matter what their motivation. We need not to lose our slender connection to them. She stopped.

The voices from thousands of miles away were for this moment silent, stilled by her impassioned outburst. The crew were silent, and no sound emerged from the spaceship sitting overhead.

Olaria was clearly not a person to be pushed too far. She was universally respected and the very fact of her defending the human intervention, and the fact, known by all the Olarians, that she wished to bear a child fathered by me was a very definite incentive for Sjiss to allow her some leeway in this discussion. Tensions were high, as were the stakes. This much hostility was extreme for an Olarian.

Olaria looked at Sjiss. *Would you please reiterate your objection to the human presence on Olar so they understand how they are involved? Whilst you are doing so, I should remind you that the Council are feeding, telepathically, all the emotional and other comments, selectively, to them, so as not to overload them, but so they are genuinely equal participants in this discussion They too are going to have to live with and be accountable to their organisation for their decision to accept our offer to stay and share learning with us.*

Sjiss was clearly uncomfortable with the presence of the crew. However, Olarian manners were impeccable. He knew they had a right, at some level, to be party to the concerns of the Olarians he represented. So, without hesitation, he repeated what he had said to the Council. The crew were unsurprisingly disturbed. The issue of them being prisoners had been in an instant totally washed away. Now they knew getting home was not an issue, but now at a time and in a manner they did not want. Also, not in a way that was likely to give them a warm reception back on Earth. One that would test the wisdom of their choice to return through the wormhole when they could have, and probably should have, returned to base.

With all this in mind, I made my own reading of the nature of this event. Fear, anxiety, guilt and an indescribably unconscious lack of understanding of the nature of the brink on which they were standing was moving Sjiss and others to behave like the proverbial Ostrich. A lot of Olarians were studying me. I was keeping my thoughts separate and pretty much unreadable, but with a great deal of difficulty. I knew what I wanted to say, but not yet exactly how to frame it. Then it hit me.

I know you play gambling games, and you use what we call dice, 6 or sometimes more sided, each with a number. And if you do not telekinetically manipulate them, you do not know what the final score will be. Well, I would like to suggest that you are playing a game of dice with the survival of your planet.

I paused, watching the impact on Sjiss.

When it was clear Sjiss had got it, was upset, and concerned, I continued; *your understandably powerful desire to avoid any contact or engagement with the Cretians, neighbours and entitled citizens of this planet, is, right now, placing their future and yours at risk. Their ability to build and explode atomic weapons could poison your planet for more thousands of years than you may wish to live. Poison the soil, the air and make some of your world uninhabitable to them and you. Although, I don't know if you have the ability to clean the poisonous atomic waste, whilst you procrastinate and point, not inappropriately at us, they could be rendering parts of your planet into atomic wastelands, entirely without your awareness.*

I stood still and focussed my attention firmly on Sjiss, emphasising my point.

This horror may not cease at the borders of the wall you have created. Your deep desire to follow the directions your parents, your Originals, gave you, could, I apologise for pointing out to you, quite likely to be the cause of the death of your world. Not something I believe they would have wanted. Not how they would have wanted their behaviour to be understood.

Your anger at our disturbing your Cretian neighbours may possibly be the trigger for actions that will save your world. We do not yet fully understand you. But, we do understand your attitude to the Cretians and we believe you simply lack the necessary information and awareness of the technology with which they are experimenting to look after either them or yourselves.

I shook my head, running a hand through my hair.

That is really all I have to say. What you do with this information is of course, entirely up to you. I can assure you that, if you send us home without understanding the dangers to your planet, we will probably never return. We know the effect of the poisonous destruction with which the Cretians are playing, and we will not put ourselves at risk by returning to its effects, especially as we are unsure that you, even with your extraordinary abilities, will be able to clean up the atomic waste.

It wasn't only the Olarians who were taken aback at my harsh and brutal verbal assault. The crew were collectively cringing. Yet, Olaria was looking at me with admiration and passion which was not going un-noticed. Then, one by one, the others of the eight began an acknowledgement, and from somewhere inside recognised and affirmed the meaning of what I was saying. They had all seen the footage of Hiroshima and Chernobyl and the development on Earth of atomic weapons which we had shown them after the

Cretian attack. A virtual pall of silence descended on the meeting. How far, John wondered, was too far, here?

The pursuing engagement grew in number and volume from every corner of the planet. The Council seemed calm and as I explored them, I saw they recognised the essential accuracy of my devastating broadside on their response to the Originals' message about the Cretians. They were increasingly confident, could the Originals have foreseen the consequences of their message to

future generations they would have issued a very different message. I was certain a myopic lack of curiousity would never have been their intent.

Olaria was certain I was right, and one by one the Council grasped the significance of what I had said. They realised, I had knowledge they did not, and was quite possibly, correct. They had chosen not to notice what was going on under their noses. They were still cleaning up the detritus of the Cretian way of life. They knew they had to take responsibility for stopping it, incidentally they also knew they had no idea how. Courage, honesty and intelligence were qualities they could both recognise and value. I was exhibiting these in the interests of all and at no small risk to myself and my crew.

The time was passing; however, the mission was five days and some of that was now gone. Nothing was going to move too far forward until this issue was sorted. Olaria suggested the crew might want to sit this meeting out, they knew she believed the outcome was inevitable and suggested we go back to our planning, promising she and the Council would return as soon as it was resolved.

Back at our landing site, before the crew got down to the task of planning out the next steps in their exploration of Olarian life, they needed to share their feelings about the simultaneity jump. By midday the crew had got as far as it could without help from their hosts and the Olarians had reached agreement. They needed to deal with the Cretians in some new way, yet to be determined. They were hoping for help from Raille and I.

The Council showed Sjiss the Living Libraries copy of the Hiroshima and other Atomic destructive experiences we had shown them. He finally recognised the danger his intervention could have on the future of the Olarians, apologised to the Council and requested Olaria permit him to make the Jeland group's apologies to the crew, especially to me. They clearly had acted in haste, inadvisably and inappropriately and he and his like-minded colleagues were no longer holding a desire for the humans to be asked to return to Earth, they were holding a strong desire for our help. He was disturbed, Olaria was pleased, and Sjiss joined the eight at the Lander meeting space. The Olarians had begun referring to it as Human Haven.

Olaria asked John if he was willing to welcome Sjiss to their meeting.

He was, and Sjiss spoke briefly to the crew.

I owe you an apology, to you especially Zed. We are afraid. I am afraid. No disruption to our social world has occurred before your arrival to our planet. The truth is rather than face the trauma of something so unknown, I and some of my fellow Olarians would feel safer if you were not here and we had never met you. However, that is both imprudent and absurd and as you have inadvertently been responsible for giving us contact with the Cretians, I think it is safe to say we wish we did not have to face the very real difficulties associated with this circumstance.

Sjiss had been agitated during his presentation, his shoulders and upper body had been in almost continuous motion, squirming I thought. But now he had settled down.

I can only speak for myself and a substantial number of Jelanders, but Olaria has reminded me what this tantrum I was throwing was actually about, and I am quite clear my feelings and thoughts about you were not useful, friendly, nor appropriate. I apologise unreservedly and would ask that one of your hosts please bring you all to visit us on Jeland before you leave us at the end of this brief mission. Allow us to provide you with an excellent Jeland meal and share with you our concerns and seek ways to deal with some of the issues connected to learning about one another.

I would like to say to you all that I believe we do need your help. We will be responsible for turning our attitude and our behaviour around, we need to take a lesson in courage from Jard and his Council of eight and hope that when it comes to dealing with the Cretians you may feel willing to actually help us.

With that he said his farewells and disappeared. A smile appeared on the lips of the crew as they heard Raille looking intensely at his friend as he whistled a few bars of an old song "...and another one bites the dust." John was wondering how this mission might have been without my presence and not for the first time looked at me with a wry smile and a certain degree of relief.

CHAPTER 15

Zed & Olaria

Zed

On our return to Olaria's place, as the evening of our second, not inconsequential day, turned slowly into night, I asked; *Should I assume the Cretians have never attempted to destroy the wall before yesterday?*

Olaria looked at me, more disturbed and uncomfortable than I had so far seen her. The events of the previous evening with the Cretians had upset her more than the issue with the Jellanders and more than I had realised. Meeting eight aliens had been an extraordinary event; however, it had been, in part, anticipated. The Cretian attack on the spaceship was something entirely unexpected, and it was evident the engagement with Sjiss had resulted in her feeling well out of her comfort zone.

I'd like to say we have had almost no problems with the Cretians 'till now, not for thousands of years. Not 'till your arrival. However, that would be entirely untrue. There have been many attempts to get under or more recently over it. We had to bury it another few hundred feet and raise it many thousands of feet since they learned to fly. But through all this we never thought of ourselves as being involved with them! I know, I am beginning to realise it that sounds... pathetic!

Olaria was moving around, it felt as though she was in fact berating herself and so in a fashion her comments looked and felt a little like a soliloquy.

We have pretended they were none of our concern and steadfastly put them out of our minds and got on with our ordinary lives. Well, now we have come to a place where we cannot easily continue to bury our heads in the sand primarily because you and now the Cretians are forcing us to change. The Council are finally aware, ignoring our problems is not a good idea. Thing is, no one in our world wants to speak with the Cretians at all. Even now, even after the meeting with Sjiss, some of the Council would like to draw a line under these events and move on without engaging with the Cretian issue any further.

She looked at me, knew from what she could see and feel in my mind that I was frustrated. But truth is, I was hardly hiding it. My efforts to appear calm and at peace were unsuccessful, I was gripping the table edge so hard I was surprised my fingers did not simply slip through it.

Their blindness and their resistance to engaging with the Cretians could cost them dearly. The last two days had disturbed my life, my inner world was in chaos, I could no longer return home to my world, to who I was, to my life, all that had changed the moment I reproduced that picture of my parents and brought it into my hand. I was already well on the way to becoming someone else! And the Olarians wanted me to sire a baby with Olaria. Earlier in our discussions Olaria had been very clear with me, she was drawn to me, had been from the beginning. As they had learned how genetically advanced, I was, her desire to bear a child with me had been shared and at the time I had been surprised, probably amazed and a little disturbed would be more accurate.

Now reflecting on my reality, I realised, I knew, sex with her would be extraordinary, but parenthood, I felt myself baulk at that.

Raille grounded me, had done since we met at ANU, where we were both instructors in mixed martial arts. We liked each other. We had travelled nearly every vacation, fought in competitions together as a tag team and built a deep level of mutual trust. Two loners, more than able to hold our own, anywhere. But and it was an enormous but, now I was keeping something back from him and it was seriously eating at me. More disturbing than the thought of the relationship I might be entering into with Olaria. I needed to share what was happening to me or my relationship with my only friend might well end up in tatters. That felt even more disturbing than Olaria. If I did not fess up to him, that relationship, my only real friend, would be in tatters. My honesty with him was being put to the test, dare I share with him everything, dare I not share with him everything? Culture is all the small prejudices and beliefs and ways we each do everything. We crash our intimate relationships because they are an exemplar of culture clash, mainly gender and history. I shook my head hard, but nothing settled into a new and proper place.

However, the Cretians were something I understood, not them specifically, but them as a hostile alien reality, familiar territory. Not to the Olarians!

Olaria, let's explore this a little.

Olaria's eyebrows shot up, but as she scanned me, her feelings slowly shifted. I was generating a calm and a confidence she did not quite understand, and my obvious grasp of the situation had the effect of calming her and she quickly realised she needed to trust me.

Olaria, I apologise in advance, but I think you need to know that on Earth people behave badly all the time. We have got used to it. If the Cretians are about to become a problem, then you need to get on top of it, quickly, and stop it getting out of hand. There is nothing they could do you could not stop, if you had a mind to, if you had the will, however, if they are messing with Nuclear Weapons you need to act fast. Your biggest problem is going to be yourselves and the cocoon of positivity you have built into your learning and your culture, and your head in the sand attitude toward your warlike neighbours. Your total lack of cultural awareness. I'm really sorry to be the one saying this, but you need to understand. The universe we know is not populated by people who have created so constructive and care-taking a culture as have you. Clearly the Cretians have not. And, the chances are, they are not going to let you fix them, even if you could. They probably do not think of themselves as in need of a fix. That's the thing about cultures. Yours included. You need new perspectives that will enable you to maintain your integrity. The Cretians are on a powerful destructive path and you will wear the consequences if you do not act. They could poison your world for thousands of years.

Olaria was wide-eyed, I was in her mind as deeply as I could penetrate, knew she was exploring me, knew how frustrated she was feeling. This was an experience for which she had no precedent. Suddenly I felt her relax. She realised this situation was neither frightening nor an immediate crisis in my mind. So, having decided to trust me, she now watched and listened. I felt the change, felt our relationship begin to change and knew this was going to be more than simply a consequential event.

Olaria, maybe we can help you. This is something we understand. The kind of technological development that lies behind these events is part of the reason we could find you here in this system, possibly millions or billions of light years from our home.

For perhaps the first time, for some inexplicable reason, I felt quietly and calmly in my element. I felt on solid ground.

The situation arose when Sunstreamer's orbit took it over Cretian territory for the second time. They may have believed Sunstreamer was Olarian and picked it up visually on its first pass over their territory, any electronic scanning and Sunstreamer's computers would have known, so they must have got a visual sighting. Now, all that is clear to us is that the Surface to Air Missile was intended to damage or destroy Sunstreamer in the absence of any information about those aboard her. The atomic explosion on the other hand was not aimed at us but at the Energy wall and so was unlikely to have been an expression of hostility toward us unless they thought us was in fact you, Olarians. Have I have missed something, or do you think I am in some way mistaken?

Olaria was looking intently at me with earnest and eager anticipation, I could feel her exploring my thoughts. I then heard her discussing my explanation with the other members of the Council and within a few minutes my analysis had been checked with several other crew members and the other members of the Council and Olaria turned toward me. As well as the look of concern on her face, she was smiling, pleased that I had been able to follow her conversations with the Council. Her expression was almost comedic. She was apologetic yet not contrite.

She was generating a powerful emotion I was beginning to recognise as her intense distress.

My apologies, I understand that what you are telling me is true, but what exactly do you mean, 'does it foreshadow?' In three thousand years this is unprecedented.

I thought for a moment, realised the Olarians had no idea what to do. They seemed unable to access the cultural response that had been Jard's and the Originals, that seemed to have been buried in some place they no longer wanted to revisit. Also, they had no prior experience of hostility in their own lifetimes on which they could draw. Change was impacting the entire crew in ways none of us had ever imagined. Every one of us had been disturbed in this alien reality. The Olarians were also in just such an emotional space. All our lives have been disturbed, but we were more familiar with difference and change and we had never before known what others thought or felt.

So, time for me to regroup.

Well, to begin with it suggests that the Cretians are toolmakers like us approximately at the stage of development we were at about one hundred and fifty years ago. It suggests that you need to think very carefully about the height to which you have built the wall, because before too long they will likely be able to lob a terrifyingly powerful and dirty explosive device over that wall and into your territory. It suggests that they are engaged in nuclear fission and atomics and are in the process of creating weapons of very considerable power. And please, Olaria, understand that, so far as I can see, we have had no part in these activities. Our presence may have been noticed by their astronomers and perhaps the timing of the attack on our vessel and maybe the timing of the attack on the wall have been related to the time Sunstreamer's orbit took it over their territory. At present there is no way to know if they are aware of us as space travellers or merely imagine Sunstreamer belongs to you. Does this help?

Whilst we may be curious about the Cretians, we are unarmed and unable to communicate with them so we will certainly will not be making contact with them. It seems our presence here may have awoken a sleeping dragon.

I had to pause for a moment whilst Olaria found Dragon in the English dictionary they were using, and she smiled.

I want to add that there is a synchronicity about the timing of our arrival here and these events on your world that stretches my belief in chance.

Olaria was looking at me with a new expression. She spoke; *are you able and would you be willing to help us with this?*

Olaria, I can't answer you right now. That is not my call. But...possibly.

The impact of the role reversal staggered me for a moment.

Zed, I was still thinking you had been the cause of this enormous breach in our engagement with the Cretians. However, I understand that although it was Sunstreamer that provoked the missile; we are in part responsible. We put you in the position of overflying Cretia and, that was not the case with the explosion you refer to as both nuclear and atomic and is something which we would like to understand. Your presence here may of course be unknown to the Cretians who may have supposed the Spaceship was ours as you suggest, in which case the implications of that are disturbing but understandable. We would never fly over Cretian territory, we have never.

Olaria had been sitting quietly until she had realised exactly where her thoughts were taking her. Now she stood and began to move around, engaging in seemingly inconsequential little tasks. It was as though her agitation needed expression and, in a few moments, she ceased moving around and focussed again on me.

My apologies for my behaviour, it is clear that we have been so isolated in our own world that we have failed to consider that the Cretians might be becoming a problem, although cleaning up the atmospheric and river water waste from their world has become an increasing problem which we simply manage, because we can. Our position with regards to them has always been to neither acknowledge nor think about them at all except at the one-day meetings we have with their Senior Administrative Body every fifty years.

The next not being due for at least two decades. These are meetings we have been holding since the wall was built 3000 years ago because they form part of the agreement my father and the original council negotiated with the Cretians. However, those early Cretians died, and many generations have passed since then and the Cretians today barely know us or we them for that matter.

What would you like to do now?

I looked expectantly at Olaria and listened in to her. There was limited time left of day three, yet I knew we needed to share many more things about ourselves and our worlds and that was finally what we did. However, it had become apparent, Olaria needed more understanding and reassurance.

Our world is being shaken up, millions of people want to know what we are going to do about the Cretians and what we are going to do about you. Many of us are unable to separate out all the elements of this situation: you, the Cretians and ourselves.

You're telling me you may want us to go, to return home before the end of our five days?

Zed, I don't know what I'm telling you, to be honest. Very little has changed in our world over the past 3000 years except for things we have instigated, especially today when we have been believing we can manage pretty well everything, until now.

I was following her mood. She had been agitated earlier but she was evidently beginning to put the pieces together. From time to time, she had moved closer to me, sat with me for short periods then got up to move, more or less in sync with her changing thoughts. Her face had maintained a frown and it was evident her distress was barely diminishing. I wanted to change that for her. So, I picked up the theme.

We are undeniably responsible for your disquiet, and I am wondering if you would rather that we had not found you, and perhaps you wish you had simply blocked our Probe's ability to see anything on your planet. However, it is too late for that.

She looked at me, she was radiating a low but nearly continuous level of distress. But she needed to say more, so she began.

Yes. Although we pretty much expected you, without knowing really when you would arrive or how we were going to manage your presence here, even what you would look like, especially after the tiny probe. Although, even as I say it, I know that sounds bad. I don't mean it in a pejorative way. People are more or less accepting of your presence and especially of you personally. You are of enormous importance to us, you know that. But the recent behaviour of the Cretians is completely unexpected. The last twenty-four hours have emphasised to us how resistant to change we really are and how, in some ways, we are really unprepared for the future and lack any readily available resources for engaging constructively with them.

And she stopped. She was scanning me very carefully, so I continued cautiously.

You and the Council want me to father a child with you? And you will be factoring that into your engagement with us? Olaria answered with a smile, a nod, and a strong emotional warmth that flowed through every pore in my body.

You know it. I want you to feel it. This is from 700 million Olarians and me personally. So, in the way that you and your crew think, you are the most important thing to have happened to us in 3000 years. And that is an opinion shared by our entire population but especially, by me.

I continued looking closely into Olaria's mind, now aware of the complex set of emotions she was experiencing. She added, remembering my question from much earlier. *The radio message you received from the Cretians, it was really very simple, it was a kind of jeering "see how you like this" message. I am not able to escape the fact that I have also known since the moment we met that I wanted an intimate relationship with you.*

She moved closer and I could feel the warmth and substance of her.

You do know that I want to have a child with you! Is that definite and specific enough about how big an impact you have already had on our world and especially on me?

She moved closer to me and I could feel her looking into me and nothing about it was unpleasant or disturbing, it was, I was feeling, quite - and I had an uncomfortable moment as I thought about the word that had leapt into my mind; *delicious!*

I stood immobile, it was not that I was unaware, it was the feeling of intimacy and connection the simple statement was creating on my body.

It is many centuries since I have felt this way. And I am of course speaking about the value of such a child to our world, but I am also speaking of a strange deeply subjective relationship I wish to share with you. I want you to have an experience with me you will remember for the rest of your life. I want you to know pleasure that will fill you with delight and satisfaction, does that make it any clearer to you?

This is personal beyond the desire for a child more advanced than us. Yet, not, I think, exactly what you would call love, and I'm sorry that I can't further explain. I think, you also feel intensely interested in me personally and sexually, is that not so?

I could not have answered but I was certain my mind was feeding her and my body's response unmistakeable. She had probed as deeply into my feelings as she could go and needed my confirmation, which she got. I could feel the urgency in her.

I want this to be information, not seduction. Believe me, I do want to seduce you, but I want this experience to be more than an opportunity to create a new generation and I know I am not saying this well. My feelings toward you are strong and I feel obliged, for the moment, to keep them out of the way.

I looked at her partly in disbelief and partly in recognition of a truth I could barely accept. I had known, almost from the beginning, I had been feeling an intense emotional connection with Olaria. Since I had been able to reach into her mind, I had known about us as an intimate couple. It was too quick, and like her I needed to get my bearings.

I want to create a relationship with you that is intimate, loving and fully sexual and I want us to have a child together. Although I believe we will be what I think you would call lovers, and you will want that, however, I believe we will not be in love and that saddens me. A young human and an ancient Olarian are, you must admit, an odd couple! You are a beautiful man. You are one of us as well as an Earthman. Does what I have said disturb you, shock you, can we please have at least a small discussion about this, although I think you are not yet ready to have such a relationship with me?

I stared at her, my emotions churning. Perhaps incredulity was top of my list of words for the moment. I began to try and find a way through this Alice in Wonderland experience. I did indeed feel as though I might have fallen down the rabbit hole.

I thought, I am not ready for this. I am a crew member on an exploratory voyage. What the hell is happening to me? I live in an unexceptional but comfortable apartment in Canberra, Australia, Earth! My clothes are in a wardrobe behind a sliding door in my bedroom. This... this is unreal.

I found myself trying to get a firmer grip on my reality. Thinking through an ordinary day. Of course, I was not thinking about Olaria who was watching and listening carefully as I inadvertently took her on a journey through my ordinary life. Aware suddenly that she was quietly and respectfully asking me to do that. I saw myself lifting my Kimono from an old-fashioned cup-hook on the back of my bedroom door. I love that Kimono; it was the last birthday gift my mother gave me before she died. I don't want to think about that. It's unusual, soft, made from something that feels like fur. I go out on to my balcony to meditate, 20 minutes exactly before my Holo buzzes quietly and alerts me to return to the world around me. I get into my running gear and go for a five K run. I meet Raille and we talk and joke a little and as we leave, we give one another a hug. Then I return to my apartment, get into my work gear and a high-speed transport takes me to wherever I am working today. What in heavens' name am I doing here? It was supposed to be my last trip for the year. Just an ordinary investigatory trip for 11 days whilst I kept an eye on the crew.

I slipped out of my disturbed reminiscence.

Maybe this is just a dream.

The thought kind of nestled snugly at the edge of my mind until...

I opened my eyes, and that other world was still there, and I was staring into the most beautiful green eyes I had ever seen. They were alive and she was smiling, and I knew the smile was genuinely pleasure at seeing me, then I realised it was more. It was a passion, a desire, an admiration it was also loving! I could feel her inside me, it was ridiculous but the feeling from my body was not. This woman, who had been around since there had not even been bicycles around on earth, was looking at me with an emotion that I could not possibly share, yet that was precisely what I was doing.

She was attractive to look at. She was emotionally warm and desirable. She was easy to connect with and was clearly warm and loving and she was, I had to acknowledge, after a very careful but thorough exploration, attracted to me. Perhaps in the first instance because of my genetics. I felt confused and so we agreed to create a way to come to really understand one another and for the next two hours we spoke of intimate and personal things that would never be the subject of a discussion between people except perhaps deeply trusting lovers. The effect was fully satisfying, and we slowly began to get a sense of the worlds in which we lived, especially our emotional worlds. Not a conversation I had ever had. The closest being with Raille or my own consulting therapist.

In one respect, I realised the Olarians were not like us. Although their understanding and insight into one another was potentially continuous, and far more intimate than ours, Olaria felt the need to stress that they were not a colony like some of their insects but individuals; however, they recognised a need human could not possibly emulate. Almost from the beginning, they recognised the need for an unshakeable set of values.

We have groups all over this continent and Jeland who spend their time exploring the implications of different values on the operation of our society. Occasionally we systematically adjust what we teach our children and then what we as adults believe about some specific issue. You have stimulated an enormous amount of discussion about change, culture and cultural difference, material culture and much more, things we have not considered except briefly for centuries. Things for which we have no meaningful memories. I saw some of your colleagues wondering what it could possibly be like thinking you would live forever. We do not know whether there is a forever. Many, many thousands of our people choose to die. Usually before they reach three or four hundred.

At around that point, a certain malaise hits most of us and it triggers thinking about the purpose of life. Some decide not to go on. If they do, death is absolutely painless and instantaneous, so it is not feared, we have no idea whether there is anything after death or it is simply an end. We do, however, generally believe the force that is our life somehow moves on and all the significant learning of any individual is already stored in the living library.

Olaria stopped. She was looking at me, watching me assimilate the information and process it, and she realised that my most difficult task was going to be about what I felt able to share with the rest of the crew.

A sadness slipped over her and feeling the change I turned to her.

Olaria, it's true I do feel a little like this is Pandora's box and we have lifted the lid.

She smiled as I remembered the story for her.

However, as I begin to understand just a little of what this might mean, what you have done is to open a door to more about who I really am. For this I am grateful. That it will almost certainly mean the end of my life as I have known it is just beginning to seep in. Where it will lead is, for now, completely unclear. However, I know I am going to need your help.

And, in that moment, knew I would get it. She prepared us a meal which I both appreciated and enjoyed.

I reflected on how I might describe my feelings about today: intimacy with an alien who could easily be mistaken for a human, connecting telepathically with a society that seemed to meet my best expectations for a quality of life in which I could believe.

A day in which my past experience had been of minimal help. I felt as though everything was new, expanded or changed even in relation to what had previously felt familiar. Right now, the next step was not clear.

Day two had been another long day for me and for all the crew. After the meeting at the Lander, we had agreed to continue learning with our hosts and that had been how we planned to spend day three. I looked into Olaria, knowing I could feel her in my mind, and we took stock of ourselves in the moments that followed, then without a word agreed it was time to sleep. We were both aware of the obvious, the presence of Sunstreamer and her crew was having a massive disturbing impact on the entire Olarian society. Time to end day two and Olaria asked me to think about my bathroom and bedroom at home. Then, as I thought through the rooms in my apartment starting with the bathroom and a wonderful old clawfoot bath, she created it, then had me recreate it, she did the same for my bedroom and now I had learned how easy replicating physical reality was turning out to be. I was surprised at myself about how reluctant I was to let her go. Finally, we parted and sent warmth and pleasure and satisfaction to each other in a truly Olarian way. She was confident I would have no trouble in recreating my bedroom and we said goodnight. The unique ingenuity of the energy world surrounded and beguiled me. After a long and indulgent bath and no more than ten minutes after I had dried myself which had taken only seconds, I had re-created my bedroom and within minutes, was sound asleep. It had again been a deeply interesting if disturbing day.

CHAPTER 16
Day three on Olar, Zed & Olaria

Zed

I awoke as always shortly after dawn broke and let my mind drift gently over my second day on Olar. I was overloaded with the mixture of personal information and life on the planet, everything I had shared with Olaria and the crew. Slipping on the Kimono she had helped me create, a weightless energy garment which encased me easily and comfortably, I walked out into Olaria's garden. I sat at the edge of an energy wall surrounding the small garden.

I felt the plants greet me, at least that was how I experienced the energy they directed toward me and I tried to respond with similar friendly energy, then sitting quietly, legs folded, began the meditation that would bring me into the day. There was a moment I was aware Olaria had entered my mind, but immediately she left, and I sat up when the alarm on my Ucom informed me twenty minutes had passed. I repeated the gestalt ritual with which I ended my meditation and entered the new day. "If you die, you are dead and have no further part in the proceedings. Until then, the past is the past, the present the present, and the future yet to be experienced." Then I was fully awake.

Telepathically, Olaria welcomed me to this new day. At first, I had thought, being welcomed by a voice in my mind would be weird, that was my first thought as I heard her good morning. However, because she could send feelings of any kind when she communicated, the greeting heard and felt in the absence of anybody being present was simultaneously informative and deeply satisfying, especially as the feeling was a mixture of caring and affection.

I stood still for several seconds savouring the experience. Then, having absorbed the experience I tried sending a message back to her with my feelings attached and immediately knew she had got it.

'Good one Zed,' I said to myself, and I went inside, dressed, and using the Olarian way cleaned my uniform and clothes. As I moved to her kitchen, I felt the full warmth of her welcoming smile. What a wonderful experience to have each day and I determined to use it with her and in the future of my life.

I reflected for a moment on the things I was beginning to understand. Being telepathic does not mean knowing everything in a person's mind. It was necessary for me to be thinking about something for her to know what was in my mind. Unconscious was as unconscious to a telepath as it was to anyone else! Any thought brought to the fore was available to anyone in contact with you, any dream can be picked up by anyone in connection with you. There were several things I needed to understand. One of the interesting bits of understanding that was just reaching me was about the edges of relationships. Telepathically she could experience me dreaming, if she was paying attention to me at that moment and I had learned that was true for me with her, however, it would only happen if the timing was right! Sometimes I was finding myself just knowing something but at other times I needed her to tell me and sometimes I needed to know to ask!

A very subtle shift in Olaria's appearance both physical and emotional told me she had been following my small transformations and explorations and I became aware at the same moment that we both knew we were together in a potentially better place this morning. The warmth, depth and strength of her relief and pleasure surprised and nearly overwhelmed me. It was tangible energy and touched emotional experiences from different memories, and I was pulled without intentional thought into this somewhat confusing moment. This strange, powerful, beautiful woman was having a disconcerting impact on my otherwise disciplined, ordered life.

I had watched her enhance her appearance and thought, shapeshifting was the Sci-Fi equivalent. But it was more like she had added an emotional component to her appearance, and I couldn't really define it.

Simultaneously, my mind was warning me to be wary. Don't run before you can walk. It was a voice from my mother and my first supervising therapist. My intuitions had leapt ahead of me and I wondered, should I draw them in or trust them? Olaria was watching me with obvious pleasure, and I felt her smile. Try trusting them, I thought, and she laughed.

Please do, Zed, no harm will come to you here.

She had done so much in a short time with nuance, small changes in emotional energy which I understood, and which had had so large an impact on me, I needed to understand. I knew intuitively how to make those changes, now I had to learn to feed them out directly to the person with whom I was speaking so, I turned to Olaria and shared both my remaining uncertainty and my growing comfort and warm connection. The move proved effective, and I could feel her settling down with us and then understood, her reply and her smile, her changed appearance and the waves of gentle emotions flowing from her enhanced my connection with her.

A part of my mind was working hard to translate the consequences of this new learning. I wondered if there were actually words for it. It was somehow a pastiche of emotions and ideas, except, I could not and would not usually have been able to say explicitly which feelings and ideas had melded together to form the experience. I decided to leave it for now, I mean, to whom was I ever going to have to explain it? Then I had a guilty thought, Raille.

I became aware of Olaria's need to take the issue of our arrival and the Cretian event further and could hear, now, some of the comment coming in from all over Olar and shut it out as I turned to her. She began, *the council has a problem that I believe you understand. We feel individually morally bound and collectively ethically required to not press ourselves forward into any kind of engagement with the Cretians. We have confirmed they cannot breach the wall. We have decided to increase its height above the ground to some miles above the altitude reached by their missile.*

We have enough to deal with in the relationship between ourselves. I replied. *It seems to me that you have a very complex set of decisions to make about your future with the Cretians. If we can get to really understand each other, as we must, then it will be a moment to discuss any part we might legitimately play in the future of your relationship with the Cretians. Right now, I would feel really arrogant and inappropriate to be suggesting ways you might deal with them.*

I thought about the situation, fully aware that Olaria and unknown other Olarians were deeply connected to my every shift of thought and feeling. Were embarrassingly involved in the intimacy between Olaria and I. I felt momentarily unable to be in any way emotionally close to Olaria, to pursue a deep personal relationship whilst being watched by an audience of people I have never seen, never met! Everything in my personal history was working to obstruct the development of this connection. Simultaneously, I knew that this had to be made to work for us, there was some aspect of our connection, some emotional caring or even loving contact that must be there between us all the time that I did not experience, did not understand. So, I just looked at her,

How can I do this? I don't know these people who are listening in to us, I have no feeling that they will not abuse my privacy. I realised immediately that was wrong, will maybe be making negative judgements about me that will leave me demeaning myself even in the absence of knowing who they are and what are the issues.

It was a voice from someone, a woman, and immediately backed up by a man, that slid the next piece into place. They both spoke, so I listened to the two of them without trying to separate them.

Zed, in some non-physical way we do not understand, you have been brought here. Although this is the wrong way to say it and I do not mean it in the impersonal way this will sound; you are the most significant biological event in recent Olarian history, and neither of us wish to embarrass you with that. Your crew are, by our standards, decent life forms, none clash too strongly with our feeling of harmony in life.

When any of us are with you or with you and Olaria who is universally respected, admired and loved by pretty much all 600 or 700 million individuals on this world it is not a small thing for us to be wanting you to feel absolutely safe with us. There is no way any of us would consider allowing anything harmful to occur to any of you as we are slowly coming to understand you. This adventure that includes us all is hugely important in ways we have yet to understand in the life of our world and we would like to believe, in the life of your world. We have studied your language as best we can, we are certain we do not believe in chance.

Somewhere in some Cosmos, some Universe, our meeting makes sense, may even have been intended, planned. For all of us, two things will remain true so long as you are genuinely engaged with our reality. You and Olaria seem certain to bear a child who will be a step beyond us. Possibly beyond all of us. You, although you do not yet fully grasp it, are already more complex and powerful than us, you merely need to learn to activate some parts of your brain for the next step to occur. But, equally important, all eight of you from your planet Earth will, we hope, make deep and open and supported connections with enough of our people for you all to feel genuinely part of us.

We are afraid of your world. It has violence and values we can barely comprehend, and this is only with the little you have allowed us to share with you; we are hoping you will share much more. We do know that you have a strong point you make when you remind us that we have removed all our potential enemies. That thought and its implications are seriously disturbing us.

Very slowly, gently, in some manner I did not know how to describe, I felt myself inhabited by something like, caring, concern and goodwill rolled together. The feeling was coming, I realised, from huge numbers of people whose existence I had never experienced but who were instinctively and without expectation supporting me. It is not something I would ever have imagined possible. I tried to find some frame of reference for it and thought that it might be like the feeling that a football player in a Grand Final had when the entire crowd in a gigantic stadium was standing, shouting his name and praising his incredible effort at kicking the winning goal after the siren. Now this was no experience I had ever had, but it was the nearest I could vaguely imagine, as being something like the experience I was feeling at this moment. It was a high of an extraordinary kind.

Olaria was speaking to me again. Speaking about the relationships their children and young people created together.

By the time they are sixteen, seventeen or eighteen they know pretty well everything there is to know about one another. In their 8's and 16's and of course the adults who look after them and all the parents. These relationships are intimate relationships, often sex is involved, pregnancy is easily controlled and there are no unplanned children, so the pleasures and skills of sex and intimacy are taught to all and practiced by all. The experience you had a little while ago from an unknown number of people listening in to and experiencing your reality is reproduced in a myriad of ways for every child. Each young person as they enter their sexual maturity has already watched and experienced many people engaging in sexual behaviour, mutual pleasure and satisfaction, which for us includes what each was thinking and feeling from beginning to end and afterward. They all try out the experiences they have witnessed and in which subjectively they have participated.

Their lives include endless numbers of intimate relationship explorations, some of which are more satisfying than others and each chooses to enrich their lives with journeys that help them find their particular preferences and ways of understanding the connections they are having with others both sexually and non-sexually; everything is experienced and explored, and the adults around them help and support and clarify and expand the richness of all of these learning experiences.

Olaria suggested I might like to watch one or more of the sexual experiences that are stored in the living library and seen by every teenager during the course of the development. She thought it might help me come to understand how Olarian intimacy might be the same or different to its human equivalent. It turned out all of the crew were being led to this experience at the same time so we could talk about it and we and the Olarians could learn about our sexual preferences and attitudes.

I was unsure exactly what I was being invited to do, and Olaria explained it by saying that it looked like a much more informative and richer version of what you seem to call pornographic movies.

I hesitated.

Zed, if we are to have a really satisfying sexual relationship, I believe it would be more than helpful if you permitted yourself to see how our children learn about sex and agree to see if the information helps us learn about our different expectations and ways of getting and giving pleasure. This is just a thing to learn like any other, in our world.

The more I thought about what she was saying, the more I realised that this domain of education was seriously lacking on Earth and what she was offering might be a huge jump in understanding for me. I agreed to see one of their experiences. She wanted me to first see two eighteen-year-olds who were in love and who had learned but not experienced sex before for themselves, make use of their learning to enrich their relationship. She wanted me to understand how their learning had enriched their first experience. The memories were stored in the living library the first one is Gral with Jeriss, and they were both 18 years old.

Ready?

Remember, you will experience this as yourself watching these experiences as an Olarian would, so you will have the telepathic awareness which we are making available to each of your crew who have all agreed to experience it, all with a little caution. It is very raw and intense and at the end of just the one, you will probably feel quite drained, but you will have learned a little about how sexual education happens for our children and you should be able to reproduce what you experienced.

I wondered what I was signing up for. Like most of the people with whom I had grown up, I had watched some porn on the Holos and never felt very satisfied with it. The actors were always gorgeous looking women usually with very large, enhanced breasts and men who seemed to maintain an erection forever, no matter what was going on. Sometimes they were a couple who were making some money from being professional porn stars. However, after a few experiences that had been often impressive, I had avoided them. The ones I had seen were almost all lacking in complexity and genuine passion.

It must be more than 15 years since I have had anything to do with sex that was not with a woman with whom I was starting a relationship. My experiences had never been impressive, more often than not, fast and high impact and after an explosive orgasm on my part I had always tried to make sure my partner also had a satisfying orgasm. Pathetic really, but I guess reproductively effective, although all my partners had been on contraceptives. I had also learned that what I wanted and what I expected and the actual sexual experiences that I always looked forward to; were miles apart. So, with some trepidation, I settled down in Olaria's lounge room—it was a room not wholly unlike what might be found in a human home and I registered that sitting places were sitting places at home or out amongst the stars—to learn. This felt as though it would be pretty raw and would be almost devoid of normal emotion for me. However, I understood I would experience some of the genuine emotion of the young couple, which was leaving me feeling that I may well make some very invidious comparisons that might not help my morale. Olaria assured me this is not how these experiences turned out.

Nearly all the Olarian women I had met were very attractive to look at and had nice bodies, so when I found myself being drifted into a memory, I had never had it felt a little strange.

Gral was a handsome and well-built young man for 18 and Jeriss was also a very attractive 18-year-old, she had a well-developed body. The memory begins with the couple meeting after, and I'm guessing here, they had been learning and it is early afternoon. They are in no hurry, I can feel their emotional states, excitement, anticipation.

Below their conscious attention, both know they are being observed, but that is the norm for their experience in almost all their learning.

I think they are walking to a nearby park, but then I see it is high up overlooking a rather lush valley with some animals grazing in the near distance. Jeriss turns to Gral and pulls him to her. Gral is feeling incredibly excited and horney yet they both remain dressed. She kisses him with passion, and they lick and kiss, I can feel them tasting each other and loving the flavour and the intimacy of it, I can hear/feel the soft moans of pleasure and anticipation, Jeriss cannot keep her hands off him, she clearly thinks he is a beautiful man and from his passionate lust-filled response he clearly feels the same way about her. There is something delicious about them, I can feel it through my entire body and all their intimate connections seem to linger.

I have a momentary feeling of embarrassment and discomfort, I am a voyeur, this is wrong, inappropriate. Then I don't know if it is Olaria or one of the many Olarian observers or someone else telling me to just experience the couple, enjoy them and although it feels wrong to be looking on from... somewhere.... I settle down again, without consciously realising the picture I am seeing is not an event happening now, but one that has happened some time ago. I think I was pulling myself out of the memory, except I was pulled back into it as it continued. Jeriss is leading this engagement, she grasps his hair and pull his face to her neck where he licks and kisses her and she moans quietly with pleasure, absorbed by the sensations and when he kisses his way up her throat, she takes his mouth and their kissing becomes stronger and deeper, nothing is held back.

As he looks into her eyes, I can feel the delight and the hunger and passion. I am no longer getting any twinges of embarrassment for them, I am now drawn deep into the relationship, I find myself identifying with Gral but sometimes I experience the feelings of Jeriss and it is quite extraordinary, something I have never felt before. I let that go as he looks at her with a gentle question in his eyes. She smiles and I hear her murmur, yes please, and holding her hands he steps just a little away from her and makes a small movement with his head and both are naked, their energy garments have disappeared. He is rock hard, and she looks down at him and something between anxiety, desire and pride can be seen in her eyes. He is unquestioningly aroused. Without a sound, she creates a surface, a soft one onto which she falls to her knees and with incredible gentleness sucks him deeply into her mouth and his hiss of excruciating pleasure acts to encourage her further. But then I am surprised a little to see him withdraw himself from her gently and slide down on his own knees and kiss her again and this time suck her tongue, tasting himself on her. They hold one another, sliding their hands over one another's bodies murmuring words I do not understand but I am in no doubt what they are expressing.

He lifts her gently off the ground and lays her on her back and I can see the dazzling smile she is giving him as he moves toward her neck kissing and licking and then slowly down to her breasts which he feels, squeezing gently with his hands before applying his tongue to one nipple sucking and I am aware of the feeling of increasing sensory pleasure and excitement and notice her breasts swell slightly and her nipples harden and he very gently nips one and she squeals in just a touch of pain and pleasure and he slowly licks across to the other breast repeating his engagement and then slowly licks and kisses his way down to her now widely spread legs. I hear him whisper to her, telepathically, Jeriss clasp your hands behind your head and don't let go 'till I say... Is that all- right? And I feel her delighted, yes. She obeys him without comment and with a soft but excited smile as he slides his tongue down to her clitoris and slowly moves it around barely touching the sensitive head and she moans deliciously. He is encouraged to slide his tongue down further and taste her slipping gently inside and then returning to her clitoris.

I remained watching for the next 45 minutes, totally mesmerised and not until I had seen both of them have multiple orgasms and continue their endless passionate sensory caring for one another did I find myself again feeling embarrassed but now I realised these two eighteen-year-olds were more sophisticated, more interpersonally sensitive and more able to control themselves than anyone I had ever seen or ever been. I had observed sexual behaviour I had never thought to try, never actually understood. I was thinking, 'a woman's vagina is an extraordinarily interesting and complex sense organ. Why have I never used what I have learned about it? So many things to think about, to try...

I slowly came back to my daytime self to find Olaria looking at me from a seat not too far distant from me and promising me I would learn and have the opportunity to practice these and many other experiences when we became lovers. And she smiled as she could see I was ready to move across the room and begin.

Not now Zed, although you should not presume you are the only person in this room with salacious and passionate loving and lusting thoughts!

I wondered when and why I felt so certain it was when and not if!

And, for a moment, she opened her mind to the feelings she was experiencing as she looked at me and I was totally delighted at the wash of loving feelings and lusts that she was sharing with me. I knew then I wanted more of her than she felt able to share at this moment, and I knew she would be available to meet my equally strong feelings for her. Inappropriate as that seemed, I hoped this might become a part of our relationship. And I was wondering about having children, and Olaria picked up my question.

When someone is approaching a time when they would like a child, they just let their group know and the information is finally brought to the Council and any issues are raised, dealt with and timing confirmed. The choice is, of course, theirs. There is rarely a sense of urgency and we have only a very small group of people who cannot bear children and some who do not wish to.

By the time our eights are reaching the last decade of their organised education, they will probably have decided about which of the planetary learning and development activity groups to which they wish to belong. When life has no necessary end, some things take on great importance, they are, it turns out, exactly the things you have said to your crew and that really interests us: having something to study and learn where tasks and people are involved, things to look forward to, that really means, hope, values shared and others to love and be loved by.

There is no isolation, nor extreme loneliness here, not like you were showing me. No one has taken their own life unnecessarily in over 2000 years. We all set our own goals and engage with however many others we need in order to get new lines of study and development going. I think perhaps I should stop. I could carry on about our lives and our world endlessly and that is without all the things that interest me, to which I am sure we will return.

I wanted more of Olaria's personal story. I could have listened to her talk for many hours, knowing I was at best merely scratching the surface.

'There is so much I want to know about you and your feelings, your relationships, how you spend your normal days and what growing up was like.'

Olaria allowed a stream of emotional energy to slide from her to me. There are simply no words to describe what it felt like to share this kind of intimacy. She knew I wanted to hear more so she added a little more information for me for the next few hours.

Alright, I was born in Tall Trees Valley where my parents and the originals all lived for most of their lives in The Big House they had built there. It was always called The Big House even though it was at least six dwellings by the time I was born and at least thirty-six members of my family, several generations including brothers and sisters, lived with us. As I told you, the valley is truly beautiful. I promise to take you there. Over the millennia all of the original big trees have died, and others have replaced them. I remember my father talking about the fires that used to burn in the mountains, how it took them nearly a century to have the knowledge and skill and power to control them. It took even more time for them to learn how important the fires were for the rejuvenation of some of the trees in remote areas in the mountains.

As children there were eight groups of us in the Valley, eight groups of eight. Our education was partly organised by my parents, who at the time, although I did not know it, were thinking that the world which they had been partly responsible for creating was getting too complex for them.

When I was sixteen, I fell hopelessly in love with a cousin, we were lovers for nearly six months before I realised that I was already looking for someone different. In fact, I was over that kind of intimacy for what turned out to be nearly the next three years.

Olaria paused, *why are you shocked? Oh... a close relative. Well, we are encouraged to have any kind of intimate and sexual relationships we wish, so long as we do not want any children to be born in that relationship.*

I digested that slowly, realising that the human prohibition was about passing on unhelpful genetic characteristics which of course did not apply here at all. Then I realised I had picked up judgements about people who did that sort of thing and I surprised myself at my narrow-mindedness! I got it and put my outraged judgemental feelings back where they belonged. If there was no likelihood of having children what actual problem did intimacy with a close relative pose? None.

Olaria smiled, *you know, don't you, that you just experienced jealousy along with your abhorrence?*

I looked at her and inside myself and knew it was true and regretted the feelings of abhorrence.

We do not choose those to whom we are attracted, and I feel genuinely pleased that you feel that way about me, and, if you scan me carefully, you will find that your feelings of attraction are reciprocated, regardless of the rightness of it, or otherwise, remembering we are aliens from different worlds!

I knew she was right. I was feeling a deep attraction alongside the thought, two alien creatures! We looked at one another and smiled. It was an unlikely scenario, yet I was unable to release myself from the feeling, it was wrong: perhaps especially because of the complicating circumstances of our relationship and a growing gnawing concern for the way I was going to manage his relationships with the rest of the crew. However, I consciously put that aside for the moment.

Olaria continued.

The thing that all of us were encouraged to do as children was play with energy, explore it, experiment, ask questions, try things that interested us. Learn, learn, learn. Nothing was out of bounds, and there was continuous loving support for curiosity, exploration, desire to know and find out stuff, any stuff. I think that is probably the most basic experience I had as a child, try anything, ask anything, study, explore, learn and especially learn about dissenting and how to use it.

You do realise, don't you, you have forced us to look at ourselves from outside in some genuinely new ways and we are loving it. In three days, you have energised our learning journeys by forcing us to take new perspectives. We have never had to face nor experience, outsiders.

Whilst my parents were the most important two people in my life, they were also larger than life. My mum and dad created our society when they found out how to stop us ageing. I also was influenced by this, by the way other kids and other adults treated them and me to a certain extent. But, in the end, knowledge and learning and disturbing our understanding of anything were the messages I learned as a child. Loving and caring for others, sex and sensuality, intimacy far beyond what we know about each other was another strong element in my growing up. So, I always felt that I should build relationships and understand myself and get closer to other people. And truth be told, I think that is the core of me.

I got how it was for Olaria and her people. I knew she wanted some important piece of my story, and I would give her that, but when it was all boiled down, what the hell was I going to say to the crew when I described my first few days with Olaria?

CHAPTER 17

Day Three on Olar, Zed & Olaria

Zed

I am 38 years old, on a planet billions of miles, probably billions of light years from my home and about to tell my personal history to a woman born before the country in which I grew up even existed on a map of our modern world and listened in to by some unknown number of people I have never seen nor heard before! It feels very creepy.

I was born in a Country called Australia, the sixth largest continent on our world but with a tiny population of around 50 million people in a world with more than seventeen billion of us. My father had come to Australia as an immigrant from another continent and a country called Portugal. He met my mother while they were both studying and teaching at the Australian National University.

Here I had to stop and make pictures and fill in some backstory.

She had come from another continent and a little town call Dolgoprudny in Russia. My father died in a freak motorbike accident when I was five years old. Five years passed during which my mother sent me to a boarding school which I did not enjoy. During that time my mother married Brian, who became my stepfather, and I got a little sister Marlette. Is this alright?

Oh yes, each time you tell me names you make pictures of the places and the people, so I am meeting them as you speak, and you remember the scenes! It is excellent.

Okay then. We lived in Canberra, which is the National Capital, I thought for a few moments about the city and the ANU where I had studied. *My mother was very tidy and organised, and since you told me, she was I think a little telepathic herself and was terrified that I was also and that I would give myself away and get into a lot of trouble!* Olaria was frowning, but she watched me think it through and got a picture of what my mother had feared. *My mother insisted that as well as study I had to learn a musical instrument which is my miniature harp.*

She stopped me for a moment and asked if I would show her and, in my mind, I played a small piece. She was entranced.

Did you bring it?

Of course, it is a miniature and I never go anywhere without it.

Will you play it for me?

I promised I would. It was aboard the lander with the rest of my gear.

I also had to learn a martial art and become proficient at it and of course I had to study. Somehow, that was part of who she thought we were.

Olaria followed my life through the pictures in my mind as I spoke, and for her this was a rich journey. I watched her and wondered at this moment how much of my life was being shared around the planet.

Olaria's gentle laugh pulled my attention back to her.

You can check that! Many, many thousands of my people are deeply absorbed in your life and many want to actually meet and touch you! And no small number are very smart, interesting and attractive women! So, do not feel alone, I could not even begin to tell you how many of our people are entranced with all of you as they are learning about your lives. Use your telepathic mind and see and hear them, and say hello, they will be delighted as you will see.

I did as she suggested and in moments, I was engaged with people all over Olar and Olaria had to gently suggest I say, thank you to them for the moment. I smiled and as I did so I looked in at her and realised, in truth, I was not the only one to show some jealousy, and I was delighted, I laughed, and she clearly loved the feeling between us.

She added, *however, most of the time only two members of our communications group are actually with us in this conversation, Ceil and Schra, they are relaying to others. So that you have a sense of this I am going to help you open a pathway to them, you can do this, if you follow me using your telepathic mind.*

And following her, I stretched through the pathways she had begun to open and quickly found myself "face to face" as if I was with them.

I need to warn you that although you have the mind to be able to do this, as you have just begun to use it, I am still keeping the Olarian world at a distance from you. When I reduce my blocking them, you will almost certainly feel overwhelmed. That is the easiest way I can think to describe this experience until you become familiar with it, at least for the first few minutes. I will let them in, then manipulate the pathways in your brain to give you greater control. Once I've done that you will quickly be able to shut them out whilst you attempt to feel your way into fully controlling this communication process. Are you ready?

I looked at Olaria, knowing from her earlier work with me, pretty much what she meant. Nevertheless, I was hungry and willing to explore. She opened the channel, and I was at first unaware of any change, then I heard Ceil and Schra say:

Hello, we are really pleased to speak directly with you, we have been enjoying your conversation with Olaria, thank you.

I put my hands up to my ears and Olaria realised I was a little bemused. She thanked Ceil and Schra and looked at me with an eyebrow raised.

There are many people who would be interested to speak with you. Until your last little experiment, I have had to let people know they cannot yet speak with you telepathically. They can, however, always monitor how you are feeling, the emotional messages you generate are not controlled fully by your conscious mind and so simply exist for anyone connecting to you to be aware of. Over time we learn to modulate these signals, however, any incongruity, that is, any discord, discrepancy between what you are feeling and the emotion you would like people to receive is always recognisable. What you call, duplicity, simply cannot happen here.

Perhaps the simplest way to explain is what I have noticed with your Ucoms. You can accept an incoming request or not, and you can receive a written message and read it or ignore it. I think you will find this is a close approximation of how we manage contact with others. So, with telepathic incoming contact requests you can learn to filter them, and you will, I promise you. In fact, even as we speak, I can see that your rate of developed control is very high already.

I sat back, astounded.

Those voices, these people, Ceil and Schra, where are they? They are from all over the planet. Ceil and Schra are only a few hundred of your miles away. Distance is no barrier unless there is serious solar energy distortion and then one of our work groups who monitor planetary energy communications will retransmit or modulate all the transmissions. I'm trying to use your words. It's not really quite like that for us!

I nodded, just pleased for the moment to be able to create the quiet.

Tanzin has been telling Jald about your TV and Holo's so all of you are like Soapy Stars; did I get that right?

I burst out laughing.

Before I continue, could we spend a little time with you helping me understand how telepathy actually works between you?

About an hour later I had got the gist of the telepathic process and Olaria had me practice over and over how to establish and the maintain connection with all the telepathic pathways I could use. It had been a tiring day, I had shared some of my life and my early life with my parents and I could easily have called it a day, however, I had agreed to a late afternoon crew meeting.

Olaria had taken me on some complex journeys, and I was as full of information as I could manage.

CHAPTER 18

The Cretians Again

Zed

At our late afternoon meeting of the crew on day 3, Gerard made it known that he was not finished with the discussion of the Olarian relationship with the Cretians.

'Why did the Olarians not pay attention to the Cretians and what was going on in Cretia. It was, head in the sand, Ostrich-like behaviour, and made no sense for an obviously intelligent society?'

I realised Gerard trusted clear technical logic, things he could follow. Superstitions bothered him. He was, I thought, a creature absolutely optimised for technology and people rarely made sense to him.

So, I looked at Gerard.

'Gerard, perhaps if I explain it as I understand.'

Gerard nodded, he was, as always, open to an explanation that made sense to him.

'I agree at first, it does not seem to make much sense. However, this decision was not made on the basis of common sense, any more than your decision to be with Ghia was based on any sort of common sensical information.'

Gerard frowned as he processed the idea.

'Are you saying it was some sort of intuitive emotional thing?' I shook my head.

'Yes, and no. When the Original eight defeated the Cretians, it was after years of being harassed and attacked in their settlement and of having their children killed. The victory was sweet, but they felt the need to protect all future generations from ever having to deal with the pain involved at the loss of their children, so important for the survival of this new community. They wanted future generations to be permanently free of the violent warlike Cretians.

The behaviour of future generations respected this intention and respected the desire of the revered Originals for future generations never to have to have anything to do with the Cretians again except on the occasions of the 50-year meeting which had been the final condition of the treaty the Originals made the Cretians sign. And by the time the very first meeting had taken place it was evident that it was already a meaningless obligatory ritual. The current Olarian society has no enemies and no desire to have anything to do with the Cretians. It never seems to have occurred to them this might become dangerous. So blind-yes, not wise-yes. But I think, in the circumstances, understandable.'

Gerard acknowledged the explanation.

'But it has had pretty unhelpful consequences.'

I agreed, adding; 'I believe it can't realistically be our problem.'

Peta was unhappy with that. 'That's all very well Zed, but if we had not overflown Cretia, this would not have happened. We are to some extent responsible. I don't know what obligation we ought to think we have here, but I can't think of it as, none. I would like to hear from our hosts.'

Olaria, who was present with the other hosts, picked up the thread.

We have discussed this issue, as you would imagine. At first, we felt annoyed with you for causing this crisis. Then we realised, not only was this inappropriate, but, actually, your understanding of what was probably happening in Cretia might be absolutely critical to our lives over the coming decades and we have been inappropriately blinded by our obsession to not feel any degree of responsibility for what was going on there. We think there is no doubt you are, to some extent, but not entirely responsible for stirring up a... hornet's nest?

Peta was nodding, 'an accurate metaphor.'

We asked you to continue scanning our world, so we are certainly involved. However, this is clearly our problem, not yours. We have not taken responsibility for even noticing and analysing the ever-changing constituents of the air and water that we cleanse from Cretia. But we have no idea how to engage with this. We have no experience to guide us except the measures taken by our Originals and we would like not to take that path. The truth is, I think we may feel totally unable to. So, we have decided to ask if you believe you can help us. And, if you believe you can, will you?

With that, a silence descended, seeming to envelop the fourteen on the ground and by Raille and his host on Sunstreamer. I decided to break the silence.

'I know something about managing situations like this, on Earth. But the ethics and practice of social change on another planet in another galaxy is not something about which I think I feel qualified to speak.'

This time John's laughter caught the group by surprise.

'Please forgive me, but on that subject, I do feel able to speak. I believe there exists no known exemplars of this situation in SFC records, so far as I know, and probably could not be. For, if there had been another alien experience someone would have to know, I do not believe it could have been totally hidden. And, given I believe there has almost certainly never been a situation like this on the human record, this would surely be the place to begin one! Zed, if we were back home, you would know how to engage with this problem?'

'Yes, I would.'

I replied, 'however, we are certainly talking about many months, maybe years. We are here for a few days! This would involve a miracle beyond my wildest fantasy.'

John looked around at the crew, finishing up with me and an open question mark as his expression.

I was shaking my head. 'Shit John, I don't know! If you want to leave me here for the next 12 months, maybe I could have something going when you return. I don't hold a known skill set for Interplanetary Social Change programs.'

There was an amused chuckle from some of the group. Raille suggested a Ouija board. I shrugged my shoulders and suggested that as the Human History Holos were being recorded by the Living Library, the group wait to see what ultimate impact the Human History Holos had on the Olarian society. And whilst not ignoring the issue it was agreed to move on just for the moment.

CHAPTER 19

Mission Parameters (Crew Meeting Continued morning day 4)

Zed

'I'm just thinking out loud.' John lowered his head and frowned at nothing in particular, produced a wry smile and shook his head slowly from side to side began to speak in measured tones.

He was speaking, seemingly, from the schematic he had built over the months of preparation for this mission. It had appeared one morning during the final week of preparation on his Holo screen and contained everything that had been discussed. It was an amazing diagram, at first it looked to be a chaotic mess, however, as he talked the crew through it, everyone had seen, it contained every major decision the crew had made.

Now he had transferred it to the large Holo screen from the Lander and we could see all the pieces.

'You all helped create this visual summary of our entire planning discussions. I'd like everyone to look at it and ask themselves the question. Given our hosts have asked for our computer scan data and analysis, which we have unconditionally agreed to make available to them, as soon as they are completed, is there anything else on this summary of all our data collection plans that we might usefully do that would benefit our hosts as well as ourselves? The data cannot be what we would have collected to assess the viability of the planet for human habitation, although that was our mission profile. We intended to arrive here at or around midday Greenwich mean time and spend the next 24-36 hours orbiting, mapping, and then decide about locations for specimen collection. Well, that plan got shot to hell. We have already blown several days from our schedule and the real question is, what part, if any, of the entire data collection profile, might be useful to the Olarians?'

Everyone had been so absorbed with managing their relationship with their Olarian hosts no one, except apparently, me, had been concerned over their mission parameters. John wanted to know what the crew thought they ought to do about it. He was going to have to accept responsibility for what they did and did not bring back.

'That's a pretty vexed question, Skipper.' Tanzin was frowning and looking intently at him. 'We seem collectively comfortable with the idea we will leave as planned. I am looking at your extraordinary diagram, which I just love, but I believe the computer scans are pretty well it. The big question for me is, how are we going to convince our debriefers it was not realistic to collect the data we had planned and which the organisation approved, and how will SCF deal with us once the Power players get their hands on the data, we bring home, assuming they believe us, which I am imagining they eventually probably will? I mean, who the hell would concoct a story like this that can not only be checked against each of us separately, but can be verified by a three-day journey? And, we have been living on the planet for three days and we are all well which suggests apart from marginal uncertainties—due to lack of specific information—the planet is habitable to the Olarians and seems to meet all the obvious markers we use for environmental safety regarding humans.'

However, I knew as I looked around the faces of the crew, no one was imagining the debrief was going to end well for any of us. It seemed absurd, sitting in this beautiful place, however SFC was an organisation with powerful controlling political and economic interests and a single mission crew were small fry amongst those interests. I looked around the crew, I now knew far too much for my peace of mind.

'I know this is on record, but I am going to say, I do not feel confident I am going to be okay. Or that any of us will.'

The group became silent. I remembered I had begun this conversation soon after we had met the Olarians and Olaria had made the conversation telepathic, ending with the idea that we ought to carry it on later, when we had been here a while. I was thinking, day four, might be the time...

'So,' John continued the thought on, 'for the record, is there anything from our list that we ought to do?'

It only took a few minutes before it was clear there was no science from our data collecting plans that anyone believed ought to be salvaged. There was complete agreement that the primary task was building a working relationship with the Olarians. And, figuring out what we were going to present to the debriefing team, when we returned home. John and I both noted no one was thinking "if" we return, but "when". I listened to an old jingle that was playing in my mind. "What a difference a day makes...!".

John's voice disturbed my reverie. 'Thoughts? I find it difficult to believe I am having this conversation, but we know at a functional level we can live here, the Olarians assure us, without any danger to our lives or our health. Our final conclusion must surely be, "This planet is not suitable for human habitation."'

No one even believed any longer that tangible data collection was appropriate, were uncomfortable discussing it, except, it turned out, me.

'Bear with me, again,'

I began, 'please, and try to keep an open mind. And, to our Olarian audience, please try to be a little patient with us. You have impacted us pretty intensely since we got here, and you are in part responsible for what I am about to raise.'

Now I definitely had the full attention of the crew, and I knew I had a pretty big and not entirely easy audience from around the Olarian world. 'Well, so far, I have really loved almost everything about this world. Except it is, to me, very closed and I don't really mean myopic. However, our Olarian hosts have created a beautiful society with which I have fallen in love. I can go anywhere here and have no fear of being set upon, of having to deal with unpleasantness. I can be pretty confident of the values that operate around me and so can nearly always have an idea how to act without offending. I see some nods and some expressions of disbelief. Well, here is my question to you and to our hosts.

If a party of young humans was to come and live on this planet under the tutelage and... supervision, management—I don't know what the right concept at the moment is—of some Olarian adults, maybe groups of 8, if they were of the right age, might they not in say five or ten years, be able to become genuinely constructive leaders for the establishment of our new planets.

Surely, they would have with a better chance of a healthy future than what we are doing now; sending 20–25-year-olds who have already been socialised in the greedy, power seeking, disingenuous society of their home planet?'

Elise, Gerard and John were looking at me with sheer disbelief written over their faces. The rest were frowning but seemed to wait, maybe for another punchline. I was holding back the incredible Olarian telepathic amazement at my proposition, a homogeneous society in which our presence, eight humans, was already causing waves of distress.

'Allow me to travel a little distance with this thought. If the Olarian world is planning to build a relationship with our human world on Earth, might such an arrangement not fit the learning needs of the Olarian people in an environment where they have control? Might this not be a mutually constructive learning opportunity?'

It was the beginning of an idea that was seeping through my mind. My thoughts included some opportunities that involved the Cretians and the Olarians and... Humans! The mere idea of a technological society with trading and money at its core and with seemingly very poor interpersonal management, living on their planet was not flying well. My proposal was literally shocking. However, the crew did not, as yet, know this.

John was looking at me with concern.

'Zed, can we put that on the back burner for the moment, just hearing you propose that has made my skin crawl. Would you object to us exploring—apart from what our hosts may already have in mind—what else might be on our agenda?'

I nodded.

'Sure.' And John moved on.

Telepathically I dropped a comment to Olaria, *as always, there is just so much space for my kind of craziness.* I saw her smile and felt her slowly dawning recognition of just how far ahead I was thinking in terms of how some interplanetary relationships might be worked out.

CHAPTER 20

Day Four Late Morning

Once our meeting was done, day 4 was spent with the crew travelling with their hosts to projects and activities all over the planet. The extent of the projects included weather mapping and management, deep ocean management and living in underwater homes projects, energy explorations at several quite different levels, education, health, geologic explorations, the list went on and it took the crew hours to catalogue and share just a fraction of the Olarian projects and cultural activities; the growing of food and its distribution was fascinating, and on and on it went.

By late in the evening of day 4, an exhausted crew called it a night and the Olarians who had been with them through the day and evening were more than happy to call it a day and take their guests home after a final crew debrief.

During the day, each of the crew had spent an hour or so experiencing the sexual and emotionally intense education to which young Olarians were subject. It was not like pornography. It was far deeper emotionally and the intimacy and openness far greater than any of the crew had ever experienced. For some it was way too deep, intense, intimate and embarrassing, however, the discussions that formed part of that learning experience, took the learning into domains of intimacy far beyond everybody's previous experience. Everyone was left with seriously new knowledge and understanding they were going to take time to process and assimilate.

The crew debrief at 'human haven' at the end of a long day was substantially different from any we had had so far. There were things to talk about which some of us could not discuss. In the end, the sexual experiences were left with our hosts! This was a domain none of us felt open to talk through as a result of this first in-depth experience. Every one of us was further out of our comfort zone than with any other experience we had had,

There were no words for what was involved in this depth of emotional learning. What we had all learned was going to resonate with us for the rest of our lives. The implications, the downstream consequences, would not finish any time soon, and would not likely, sadly, turn up in the crew debrief. Perhaps the greatest immediate consequence was the intimacy that was experienced between the Olarians and the eight of us.

At this stage in the lives of the crew, no sexual experiences had been part of their experience on this tour of duty, certainly not with each other and so far, not with the Olarians. However, most, except Raille and perhaps John, had moved close. The change in the relationship between Ghia and Gerard was absolutely clear to the rest of the crew. This aspect of their learning was going to have to simmer slowly, and for most, quietly, however, there was no question, this was the highest impact experience in a journey of high-impact experiences. I imagined the group was ready to call it a day, but I was mistaken. I did my routine ending to their meetings.

'Does anyone have issues to discuss that need to be addressed now and that will move us on?'

I was unprepared for what happened next.

Gerard said, 'Yes. There is a small matter I would like to raise. Zed, I feel uncomfortable about having a telepath amongst us, truthfully, I feel a bit vulnerable. Would you be willing to deal with this?'

There was no way such a request could be sidestepped, and I knew it had been an intermittent concern for several of the crew. One aspect of this issue was that the Olarians were sharing the emotional reality of the crew allowing each member to understand the emotional reality of the rest, except, they were relaying limited emotional information about me to protect me and they were extremely uncomfortable about it, but recognised my life might be compromised back on Earth if the full extent of my telepathic and telekinetic capabilities were known.

'You have all known me for some time. Learning that I am telepathic should really be no surprise, I mean if any one of us was going to be a bit telepathic you'd think it would be your shrink. And truly, not a bit surprise, I have always wondered how I seem to know so much about all the people around me. And it really is a suitable and useful one for a shrink.' Some chuckles from around the group were reassuring.

'So, you already know what kind of an oddball I am, and I have not changed. I am what I have always been, very tuned in to the people around me. All that has changed is that now I understand a bit more of how and why, and that is a big plus for me and in fact for all of us. Is there anything about that Gerard that does not sit well with you? Or is there anything that anyone thinks needs to be added or dealt with still about my capabilities? I guess I should add, does anyone feel they need to question my loyalties?'

That, interestingly enough, was not where anyone wished to go. Tanzin asked,

'Does this mean you can now read our thoughts and feelings?'

I lied. 'I don't think my abilities extend that far, certainly at the moment not much more than always. However, being telepathic and being me and being here is disturbing my self-confidence. I apologise in advance for this, but I really need to hear from all of you a clear and honest acknowledgement of me as one of you. This telepathic stuff is shaking me up more than a little. The alternative is way too disturbing for me.'

They needed me, they knew, but they also did actually trust me. If I needed them to acknowledge me, they were without exception willing to give me that. And one by one they did exactly that. Gerard was the last and his beautifully crafted comment sealed it.

'You have my genuine seal of approval, Zed. You are an odd one, but I'm damned glad you are one of our odd ones.'

The affirmations from the crew settled me, even given the lie I had felt obliged to tell and I smiled my thanks to them. Finally, I felt able, at last, to swallow the lingering threads of my brief disturbing identity crisis. They needed me as much as I needed them. It was time to move on.

However, I was aware I had understated what I could do and what I almost certainly would be able to do in the future. I also knew I could not safely reveal what my abilities might become, it would not be reasonable to expect them to conceal these for the rest of their lives to protect me and I had already accepted I had to live with this deceit.

My thoughts returned quickly to the meeting, knowing my concerns would have to wait.

CHAPTER 21

Consequences and Options day 5

It was the morning of the last day. There was a lot to do.

The Biomedical Officer, Elise, was officer of the watch. She could be seen on the Holo as we took our places in the circle. John looked around, I could see he was wondering where exactly he should start, reflecting that, on more than one previous occasion, sitting in this beautiful field, we had been involved in a difficult discussion with the Olarians about our future. He knew we had not resolved anything about how we were going to face our future, the one that involved us returning home, and we were now at a point where we must decide.

We could not afford to return home without having thought through the situation that would exist on our return. Our decisions would inevitably impact the Olarians as well as ourselves. John also knew we were not the same people who had arrived here only a few days ago.

So he began, 'I need to hear from everyone about our return to earth. This has been a wild ride and I'm not confident I am on top of this mission-ending.' John looked at me. Another factor had now been added to all our meetings.

The Olarians, having learned the boundaries of the crew's ability to handle emotional and informational data, now maintained our telepathic awareness even when they were not available. The extraordinary value of this process inevitably speeded up all discussions, simplified them, and clarified many things that would normally get in the way. As individuals and as a crew, we were going to miss this once intrusive behaviour. This morning seven of the crew were sitting together and there was a strong undertow of disturbance amongst us, and it had no clear focus, but John needed some closure, I could feel his concern.

Telepathically and aloud, I spoke the feeling I knew everyone was experiencing.

'We are not the people who left home just eight days ago. Sometimes when I think about where we are, I try to imagine this is a science fiction story someone wrote and I'm just reading it.

Because this is a very touchy point with us and in all honesty, I believe that none of us really believe that the politics of SFC has not caused a massive secret like this to have been hidden by the organisation once before without anyone of the crews ever knowing-I will say it again- but so far as we know we are the first to have relationships with an alien race. Sometimes during these last few days, I have felt like Alice in Wonderland. Thanks to our hosts, I know I am not alone. '

I looked around the group, the expressions on the faces and the information the Olarians were making available to us enabled all of us to know this was true. 'We're all changed, is the fact of the matter, and the last few days is only the beginning. We have barely scratched the surface of how significant this event is going to turn out to be for us and for the world and frankly, I don't know what our responsibilities ought to be. I think I know what they probably are, but I'm not sure it's very smart to pursue them. Sometimes John, I think, we ought to simply settle into Moon Orbit and report in. I really don't know whether our version of events will even sound credible to our debriefers. It probably wouldn't sound credible to me.'

John's face was showing his tension. I felt I needed to make sure we all had a similar understanding.

'As I said on the record, earlier in our visit, Space Fleet Command Debriefers could easily ease us aside, have our information filtered through the power brokers at SFC and have us held separately incommunicado until they sorted how they wanted the information used and they could send a Battlecruiser to this place and we would be indirectly responsible for the lives of 50 or more people and heaven only knows what kind of stellar disaster. John, I feel more confused about our responsibilities than at any other time in my life. I know this has to be weighing on your mind. In the end, this will rest with you. In some ways, although I think it's stupid, I feel responsible for what happens next. You know, right now I have this picture of us sitting here, in this beautiful field, a black and white photo of a group of ancient space travellers who found the first sentient life in the universe, sitting there wondering what they were supposed to do with it. At moments like these I really envy the Olarians. They know a kind of inner security I can only imagine.'

We were sitting in the clearing, which could well become the anchor point for stories and myths that would be connected to us for the rest of our lives, maybe for all time. John looked around.

'Olaria?'

And we became sixteen. The Council had occupied their seats between us in the circle, ones always left for them.

We appreciate your invitation and your way of summoning us.

Olaria smiled, and although the crew knew these words spoken by a human would have carried a supercilious overtone, yet none was present nor intended here.

It is more than a century since anyone has done that, and with you it is a pleasant feeling of inclusion. We were talking before about your organisational responsibilities, which I believe we still don't fully understand.

Olaria was looking at John. John nodded, understanding her request.

The nub of it is, I am not sure we fully understand what they are either. During various training programs and briefings, we've had a lot of discussions about this situation happening, but I don't think anyone ever really took it seriously. I feel pretty confident no one has painted out this specific scenario. Now it's here and we are in the thick of it, I think we are going to have to make it up as we go.

Raille picked up John's thread. *Look, I know this is a wee bit off, but I have some real doubts about what might happen to us when we return with this yarn about an alien race living on Omega5Z3 even with all the Holos we have made here.*

There were smiles around the group, and the tension dropped just for a moment. Raille was popular and one of the more philosophically minded thinkers in the crew. Everyone knew that when pressed, he could encapsulate the details of an issue succinctly and clearly and that he was an optimist, and it was reassuring to see him smile.

Here's my take on our options. Our hosts have made it clear we are under no duress of any kind with respect to our return home and in spite of the many times we have had doubts about that I think finally all of us believe this or else the Olarians will undoubtedly become Hollywood royalty. So, the only outcome we need, at one level, is that all sixteen of us can live with the plan we agree to. And I do not imagine anyone would disagree that it must take account of the interests of both our worlds.

We all knew there was complete agreement with what he was saying. 'This means that whilst we are a human crew, we are also, the sixteen of us, part of something much larger, something I believe, as yet we don't fully understand. The fact of our similarity, galaxies apart, must speak to the likelihood of that. Anyone religious would speak of God's plan. The Olarians might speak of the Seeders' plan. As a committed atheist I simply don't know whose plan it might be and I don't want to support a competition about who is right when at best it is a speculation, free from what we think of as substantive data. I have talked with my host and others yesterday about their defensive capabilities and I believe the Olarians can look after themselves, here on their world, with respect to any Space Fleet intentions to visit here in the near future. However, I am not equally convinced the eight of us can necessarily look after ourselves on our return to Earth, in the light of the pressures we will experience when we are debriefed by our own Space Fleet debriefers and the host of other people who will want a piece of us. In fact, I am inclined to believe our return will be cloaked in secrecy, at least for a short time, whilst various players with a variety of vested interests try and figure out how to make the most of the situation, we have brought them. And I for one, am not looking forward to the kind of stresses to which I am confident we will be subjected.

At first there was silence, then several people spoke but quietened as Elise, our Biomedical Officer, who would normally have held back, took the floor from her perspective way up on Sunstreamer's deck.

I am as certain as I can be, Raille, that you're right and although I normally accept the processes through which we are debriefed, I don't feel all will go well with us this time, because we are involved here in things so far beyond our pay grade, I think we will be quickly separated and carried along in a process over which we will have very little, or possibly even, no control. I've been thinking about this a lot, as I know have most of us. Several times I've wished we eight were Olarian and could telepathically communicate with one another. In a somewhat negative part of my mind, I have wished that we could persuade our hosts to give Zed a pepped up and empowered use of his telepathic capabilities, so he could be our constant interacting communication link. More than this, I have a disquieting feeling that some of our comments, especially Zed's, and some of our decisions about telepathic activity may not go down well.

The looks of amazement and delight on the faces around the group drew smiles from several of the Olarians as well as the crew. This was as uncharacteristic of Elise as anyone could imagine.

What she did not know, and what I was keeping to myself for the moment, was that I had learned enough to be able to do this but felt exposing this might be risky for me. This note of ambivalence and really tricky duality hung around me, and with the Olarians sharing the crew's thoughts I needed to keep any thoughts about this deep in the background, although I was reasonably confident the Olarians would not share these and Olaria quietly reassured me.

Bravo you. Tanzin's smile spoke volumes.

A few of the crew had seen that smile the day she cracked the trickiest simulator problem in the fleet's try this if you can, a suite of supposedly impossible navigation problems. She was beginning to feel the possibility of a complex situation over which we may well be able to gain some control.

From his perspective, Raille was imagining something wonderful. He focussed closely on me.

Zed, something is bothering you. He was right.

Just listen to us, we are amongst the most senior officers in the operational fleet, yet we are sitting here at some level feeling that we are likely to be impotent when we return with the most amazing news ever to reach Earth. But don't get me wrong, I actually think Elise might be right! Vested interests about which we are almost certainly unaware are likely to be in play behind the scenes and this may well mean, if we get separated, we will become merely pawns in a much bigger game of which we know little. Collectively we might have a better chance. Isn't that what all of us are thinking, imagining, isn't being separated and isolated what we are afraid of and trying to avoid?

We have changed, but the question needs to be asked. Are we being absurd? Every one of us knows debriefings are secretive at the best of times. Some of us had first-hand experience of the horrendous debriefs that followed the discovery of the first resettlement planet, and all of us have heard the stories and rumours. There were nearly battles over who would own the mineral rights and challenges to several of the crew over the data they brought home. Our biggest vulnerability will, ironically, be the absence of any world press, no outsiders, until we have been fully medically tested and fully debriefed by Space Fleet Command.

John responded. *Zed, I know how inappropriate and unlike me this is, but, I think, given all of our experience, you are right. We need to work this problem and find a way to take us beyond this log jam.*

Okay, Raille said, *if given our seniority, experience, and knowledge of the system, we believe what we are saying, then we need a new strategy if we don't want to be steamrollered. We need to think way outside the box. We have been working with our hosts on some pretty way-out ideas over the past days, perhaps it is time to apply those creative processes to our very real problems here.*

'We-e-ll...'

Peta and I had begun speaking at the same time.

I quickly jumped in, *you first Peta.*

Okay, thank you Zed. My first thought is that we would be in a very different position if we had a real alien on board with us.

I smiled, *Peta, you're suggesting that if we were to take one of the Council back with us, assuming they were even willing to consider such a step, we might be able to build a quite different plan? If they agreed, we would need to give them a genuine assurance that we could and would return them to Olar.*

The entire crew turned to Olaria.

We have been discussing this as you have been speaking, she said; *there is no question I ought probably be the traveller. However, I need to say that I do not believe I will necessarily be able to be away, alone, for more than a very short period of time before my life could be in jeopardy. I, like my colleagues, rely on skills and actions of others and knowledge of the energy systems of our world to remain in good health. I would be loath to put that at risk without some certainty about my return. I do not want to die on Earth or anywhere away from here.*

The crew turned back to look at each other. No one was willing to consider any action that might result in Olaria's premature death.

I think, said Raille, *maybe Olaria does not need to travel alone to Earth, maybe, for her safety and health at least two Olarians should make the journey if they were willing. They could probably look after one another and provide genuine support which we, with however much genuine good will, could not. And we are probably not taking this discussion far and wide enough.*

Most of the crew were intensely focussed and involved, there was little agitation but a great deal of investment in the discussion, some of the group were walking around the outside of the chairs, it was evident how much tension the group was holding.

We are all of a mind that our return alone is very likely to have some unsatisfactory outcomes. I know that as members of our organisation we have, in a way, little right to make this judgement. However, this may have happened to an explorer crew before, and they may have been vanished in the interests of big business or... I know this sounds paranoid, but am I the only one holding this thought? Isn't this what you always infer, Zed, when you say, "so far as we know," when speaking about us as being the first to experience an alien life?

I agreed, it was the thought in my mind. Seven others were sitting very still and their body language leaving no doubt that the thought was shared, however unprofessional this seemed.

New ground was being broken. Everyone knew we were on record here that we had all been speaking out loud as well as telepathically, as had become the habit, and it was not only me who was finding this a little disconcerting. Raille continued; *so, we may need to rewrite the rule book on this. If Zed and I are to come back here to play a role in assisting with the Cretian situation, as they have indicated they would like, then probably most of you will need to return here with us. Does anyone think that's wrong? And is that even an idea anyone thinks we should consider?*

At first there were stunned expressions around the group and then slowly the possibilities took hold. It took some time for the issue to be talked through and agreement reached that while only four or five crew might be needed to manage the Sunstreamer, everyone wanted to return to be part of this, our shared explorations had no more than scratched the surface of the information that each of our cultures might share. How this would finally benefit either of us was a complete unknown at this point. Although most seemed especially concerned about Ghia, she turned out not to be a problem.

Gerard and I have talked this over, in another context, she said.

I would be really pleased to have our daughter here, if the Olarians were willing to look after us.

Silence fell over the group. The crew all turned to look at our hosts. They were clearly in conversation and the crew sat quietly before being made party to their discussion, with the exception of myself, who was now able to fully participate in the Councils telepathic discussions. However, on this occasion I was simply listening in, an experience about which I was only slowly beginning to feel comfortable. The crew listened as each of them put their arguments for and against. Finally, with no exceptions, the Council affirmed their willingness to support Ghia and Gerard's request.

They did indicate their belief this ought only be a part of a much more comprehensive plan, and with that there was general agreement. It emerged that they were referring to Ghia's health and the health of all of us.

It was Jald who made the observation before he made the next extension to our thinking. His off-the-cuff comment was simply that a partner travelling with Olaria, a very experienced member of the Health group, could map the energies and confirm what they needed for the maintenance of their health.

Jald continued; *this is a rather presumptuous suggestion, but suppose we take a larger view. Suppose that we consider the next twelve months as a making-contact period between our worlds. This could be proposed so that by mutual agreement, but especially because we propose it, that we feel confident in having our first learning about each other exclusively through the Sunstreamer's crew. That we will be responsible for helping you to gain as deep and complete an understanding of Olarian History and life as is possible in a year. That the crew do their utmost to do the same for us, and that at the end of that time we will arrange with the crew a meeting at a mutually agreed place where we could negotiate the next phase for exploration of our mutual interests. I realise your authorities may want a very different group of people to be the emissaries and contacts for this year. That needs to be put out of reach of any negotiation. If you want this to be your position.*

The crew were at first a bit overwhelmed, realising SFC and many others would not see them as the appropriate people to undertake this task.

It was Ghia's host, Kyuto who put the thought into words.

We are the spokespeople for our planet. If our representative makes this crew our point of first contact, and we hold firmly to this position, will this not constitute a defining position, if we were to insist?

The Council were clearly in agreement and I realised the Olarians had millennia of stability, they valued homogeneity and stability and were seriously ill-prepared for an engagement with a new group of strangers to whom they would feel a need to build strong trusting relationships. The Olarians were sitting quietly, still. Most of the crew were sitting almost on the edge of their chairs and were far from still or restful. These were decisions which were well outside the usual purview of their rank and responsibilities. They also realised that this crew had one irreplaceable quality, me, who was a telekinetic telepath with potential greater than was possessed by any individual on their planet. Greater than they had ever seen and with whom they did not wish to lose contact. It was as though this crew had a secret weapon, one of which the crew were unaware. The Olarians were more inclined to support a return that included me than almost any other option that could be put on the table.

I picked up Kyuto's thread, *if an Olarian is coming with us, we need a credible reason and a plan for their return. The Council have given us a head start when they discussed the possibility of Raille and I helping them with the Cretians.' I turned to Olaria. 'The first inkling of a crisis with the Cretians was the day they attacked Sunstreamer and attempted to breach the wall?*

Yes. It's true we discussed the possibility of involving you in our problem with the Cretians and wondered if, in return, we might offer to assist Earth if we have non-mineral resources, the Earth could use.

The seeds of a possibility were being sown because it was not only the Olarians who wished to continue their relationship with this crew, but members of the crew also trusted and now had genuine relationships with members of the Council. We paused, most of us needed some quiet time to reflect on what was being proposed.

45 minutes later everyone had returned, and we agreed to continue our conversation. Looking around at the faces of the crew, Peta asked; *Does anyone remember ever discussing their return to Earth and the debrief, before this mission? I think not only is this an extraordinary situation, but I haven't felt confident you—she looked directly at Olaria—would allow us to return. I don't feel that now, so I am okay about having this discussion, partly because you want something from us and of course I am referring to Zed's particular knowledge and skill set.*

She looked around the group, and there was no disagreement.

Olaria looked directly at Peta, nodded and with the gentlest of smiles on her lips said; *After we had recovered from the shock of the Cretian actions and our leap to the desire to blame you, I think everything began to change between us. Remember, this is as new to us as it is to you. None of us has ever had to deal with different people before you arrived. When Zed told me about his work with other cultures, we were collectively astonished and curious. We have never thought about building a relationship with the Cretians, ever, not at any time over the last 3000 years.*

The crew were now sufficiently familiar with the Olarians and their abilities to be certain they could be of value to Earth; the Olarians knew it was more likely that I could help create a workable solution with the Cretians than any Olarian. A human with experience of cross-cultural realities would be a significant asset for them, that it was me, they saw as a huge bonus. I can't even pretend I was not extraordinarily embarrassed, but I kept my mouth firmly shut. So, a plan began to hatch between the crew and the Olarians. An unlikely alliance was being created from what had once been a mist of mistrust and uncertainty. The crew knew enough to trust the Olarians and that was genuinely reciprocated. As Olaria needed to be the one to travel back to Earth with Sunstreamer, everyone turned to look at her. She raised her eyebrows, frowned, shut her eyes tight and then ever so slowly turned to look at me. She seemed to be looking through me as she spoke.

I think I can see a way this might work.

The Olarians knew she was thinking much more complex thoughts about my development, and I managed to grasp a significant proportion of her thoughts. She looked at the other members of the Council, nodded slowly and turned toward John.

But it was Jald who spoke. *We need your help. Given what you have told us, I believe we may be able to help with solutions to some of the problems that sent you to find another home. We could offer at the end of our year with you to help with one of the problems in your world. And, and I say this with caution because it is not a subject on which there has been any real discussion, it may well turn out that it will be important for both of us to negotiate some appropriate kind of relationship with the Cretians.*

Your existence and arrival here has meant that we need to re-evaluate our entire relationship with them, and I don't know where that is going to lead any of us, I know we feel quite nervous about this, especially about engaging with your organisational and political world. A year will give us time to manage our side of this, especially with your help. But it will also give you the opportunity to decide about how your world wishes to relate to the Cretians. And I know Zed is hatching an extraordinarily disturbing, but, we think, maybe equally creative plan about a human cohort being socialised by us! Which we find almost unbelievably uncomfortable.

It was a touchy place, but, given the Cretians had shown a definite hostility toward Sunstreamer, and so, indirectly, the crew, it seemed a not inappropriate way to proceed through very delicate territory. Everyone was aware the Cretians might not even know of the existence of the humans/aliens. And, whilst everyone was becoming energised by the scenario being built around their return, at the moment, no one wanted to go adventuring with my imaginings.

John took up Jald's theme. *During a year on Olar we could be helping you with the Cretians, and perhaps with Olaria's or your help we could travel to some of the more distant star systems and use both your and our abilities to build maps and explore. A journey Space Fleet Command would surely be excited to have done whilst other work was going on here. But the initial difficulty will be in getting back to Earth and not being trapped by powerful players about whose motives we are perhaps unjustifiably calling into question.*

Raille had been exploring some of the boundaries of this idea. *On our world we know that most negative and dysfunctional and criminal activities work best if they are kept secret and in the dark, and your culture here is, further evidence of the truth of that idea. If we take Olaria and a companion back with us and force the world to engage with her in plain view of the world press, giving them no choice about secrecy—a pattern of behaviour we have seen work brilliantly here—then we might have a chance at this. A Companion would allow both of them to be safer and together could provide valuable mutual support.*

The Council members agreed. Olaria was pleased. One eyebrow raised; Gerard's host looked at me.

We know Olaria must be one of the travellers. None of us have the range of powers and competencies she possesses, and she could easily hide the Sunstreamer from your scanning observation devices if you can let her know exactly what kind of signals these transmit before you exit the final Instantaneous Transit Zone.

Several members of the crew looked sceptical. Everyone was looking at Olaria. Olaria looked at the crew, focussing finally on Peta,

Could you describe for me the kind of scanning that is used? I can show you what I mean, could you use one of the devices in the Lander to bring the Sunstreamer into view.

Peta looked toward John, who simply nodded his agreement. Peta gave Olaria a brief and clear description of the essential parameters of the scanning currently in use. Olaria sat still, listening, and finally while Peta gave her a significant number of images and illustrations, she was nodding her understanding. She said, *just to show that for us it is reasonably simple, keep watching the picture. I will cloak the Sunstreamer from your sight by simply re-arranging the energy around it.*

In a second, Sunstreamer was no longer visible on the monitor and then a few seconds passed and Olaria brought it back into view. There was silence. The crew knew she was able to draw from sources in the universe they did not comprehend. Even so, this demonstration was astonishingly impressive.

It is not really so hard when you manage energy as we do. However, to build that ship seems as far beyond us as cloaking it is beyond you. So, to take Gret's idea one step further, I would need to meet with some of the leaders of your world, which, with the help of a companion, I could do without placing myself in any danger if I worked from the safety of the Sunstreamer. Using our ability to engage in simultaneity much as we are doing now, our physical bodies do not need to be here, but we appear to be.

We have a choice. We can be somewhere else as a projection or we can actually be there. Both processes have some minimal risks, although no one has ever been trapped elsewhere. When I first cloak Sunstreamer, I will watch for and analyse the scanning data from your Earth and Moon Base scanners and suitably protect Sunstreamer from any visibility. At most, your scanning crews will get a few seconds of a partial impression of Sunstreamer without the usual electronic identification they would expect.

She smiled and although the crew were all uncomfortable with this flagrant breach of procedure, they also smiled, none of them had ever thought to deceive the Space traffic system before this, yet here they were planning and supporting a criminal act for which they would certainly be held accountable unless they pulled this miracle off.

John needed more detail. *So, as soon as we come out of the final Instantaneous Transit Zone (Wormhole), Olaria, you will cloak Sunstreamer. We need then to proceed to moon orbit and take up a distant stationary orbit, otherwise the cloaking will be more difficult. What then?*

Well. Said Olaria, *if our future plans are to be meaningful, I need to study your planet. But I could do that from an orbit over your moon. As I said before, I think I need two or three days to enable me to assimilate the conditions on Earth and to identify and meet, with your help, the key world leaders.*

We also need, John said, *to provide a test they can give you that will put an end to their scepticism and convince them this is not a smoke and mirrors trick we are trying to pull. Could you, without knowing the exact launch co-ordinates, physically destroy an object or maybe many objects, about the size of the lander, travelling at supersonic speed from different sites on the moon or the Earth?*

Olaria smiled, *supersonic speed being...?*

Oh, sorry, John said, *our sound barrier is round about 767 miles per hour, but these small craft could easily reach two or three times that speed within a very short time after lift-off, they would probably be small weapons carriers.*

I believe so, yes. With a companion, one of us could manage the moon sites the other the earth sites.

*Then I think we might have the beginnings of a plan...*John looked at the Olarians,

Now for the big one. Do you really think you could help us with things like environmental and population problems?

Olaria said, *whilst I cannot know for certain, the time I spend exploring your planet from the Sunstreamer should enable me to be quite clear about the nature of your planet's problems and have some ideas about ways we might be able to help with them, if our help was wanted. Given what you have told me about your global businesses, we may also be able to assist them with many aspects of their mining and locating of mineral deposits, once we can travel more extensively in space.*

That is all well and good, said Gerard, *but how are you going to get Space Fleet Command to agree to free an Advanced Explorer Spacecraft and its entire crew on spec.?*

But John had been thinking about that. *We will, as always, be dumping our entire computer readings of Olar into the Space Fleet Command master computers. There will be months of work in analysing that data. The output will be very valuable to some people on the SFC Board. So, I believe Dr Khan may be able to get us critical leverage in this plan.*

A long discussion about this was needed. The Olarians especially needed a clear understanding about what use such data could be to people on earth. Could it be used to, render their planet vulnerable to attack without warning or to damage or destruction without warning. And so began hours of the two worlds talking their way through the possibilities. The legitimate fear, which the human group could not dismiss, was that weapons developed by humans in the future might be used to damage the planet if business interests came to see Olar simply as a potential resource mine.

The crew knew that this was not yet possible, but... So, the Olarians suggested a plan. It seemed practical and took account of the value systems of the two worlds. It depended on the ability of the Olarians to monitor their space up to the exit point for the Instantaneous Travel Zone, the Wormhole. Given they could do this, they were clear they had the capacity to immobilise any space vehicle exiting that zone, even at near light speed, without their agreement. They could safely halt the spacecraft and assess its military capabilities.

So, it seemed they could protect the planet. The crew would download to Space Fleet Command the full computer readouts, on condition that a document that would be known to the entire human race was drawn up. It would be shared with the entire populations of both planets. It would guarantee no threat from Earth would ever be launched against the Olarian world. Although the need for such an agreement was astonishing to the Olarians for whom political duplicity was unknown. Even their experience with the crew did not fully prepare them for the need for such a document to protect their interests. To the best of anyone's thinking, this looked like a viable path to travel. To the Olarians, agreements of this sort once verbally made were binding, not so to the politically disingenuous human world. It was made more concrete by having them think of the Cretian agreement.

Jald was looking at Olaria as a check, and she nodded.

So, I said, *the key to the success of all this, assuming everything goes to plan, will rest on Olaria being able to get the right meeting with the right people and negotiate the right agreement to enable the operation to be approved by the right authorities on Earth.*

I was watching the group and seeking confirmation of this seriously un-SFC plan was actually what everyone had in mind. I knew there were many small holes any one of which needed to be avoided to set this very iffy plan into motion. The reason it will probably work is that the world's press will ensure that the meeting with Olaria is shown live on world Television as a condition of the meeting.

I was feeling very nervous and watched each of the crew for signs of disagreement. But could see none. So, I continued; *And we will all end up healthier*

humans and probably with jobs for life as Olarian specialists! And, I would add, I believe
the key to our success as you have suggested will rest with the CEO/CIC of SFC, Dr. Miyuki
Khan. John, do you have the sense that if this plan is carried through as outlined so far,
you will feel that you have carried out your professional and personal responsibilities
satisfactorily and, as you are the only member of the crew with family on Earth, that you
clearly would like to see and be with, how do you feel about putting that off for a year?

There was silence around the group. But John had been thinking about this, one way or another, since long before this discussion took place. The possibilities that surrounded this, Olaria made clear, were ones with which she might be able to help John. She knew he would probably accept that help whilst they were in orbit if all the right things were done in an open and transparent way. But above and beyond all these details, John was concerned that his family might be used to blackmail him; threats to them might be made.

Olaria and the entire crew spent time exploring every scenario in which John's or any of their families or friends could be in danger and the ways this might be dealt with. Three solutions were explored. John's family could come to Olar; his family could be given secure protection; Olaria might be able to fashion a solution when she had seen the environment in which they lived. John thought carefully through this concern and came to believe it was unlikely that there was real danger for them and was willing to proceed. He added to the solutions the possibility that he remains behind and the Sunstreamer be given another Captain. However, that seemed only possible if one of the present crew was able to be given that position and that would have to be Peta. The final agreement was that John would choose the solution whilst they were in orbit and when the situation had resolved itself. And that was as far as they could go.

There were many loose ends, numerous issues to still be considered, and more detail of the kind of mutual interchange and learning agreements that Olaria would negotiate on everyone's behalf. Did everyone want to go ahead with this rough mud map of a plan? There were concerns, but there was unanimous agreement that this might have a serious chance of success. It offered an avenue that avoided the worst aspects of a bureaucratic entanglement inside Space Fleet Command or the United World Government conglomerate.

There were a hundred small conversations to take place and many bits to be managed before an early morning departure tomorrow, day nine since Sunstreamer's departure from moon orbit. The outline was unanimously affirmed, and departure was planned 10am Olar time tomorrow. Tonight, was planned as party night and sleep for most seemed unlikely.

Everyone was looking forward to an evening of feasting and festivities being organised by the Olarians. Some of the crew were busy on Sunstreamer, preparing.

The Olarians had insisted that as hosts they should provide the majority of the food and entertainment. The crew would provide one main course from within their own supplies or any of the resources of the planet they needed. There was to be entertainment, music by both worlds and an exhibition of art by artists from around the Olarian world. And dancing.

Olaria finally got to hear Zed play his miniature harp, and she insisted it contributed to the beauty, creativity and delight of the day for her. The crew used, to full advantage, their technology for sound and image on a huge Holographic screen rigged on the site. The Olarians brought the works, both still and mobile, of artists from all over the planet and the excitement at the energy toys and displays had us in stitches and often feeling like small, delighted children. Musical groups from everywhere. Plays from earth and performances by locals. Food beyond human imagination was served and shared.

When this day finally drew to a close nearly two thousand Olarians and the eight members of the crew had danced, sung, eaten and now had to, briefly, sleep. It was much later that the crew realised there had been a few hundreds of millions of people at that party. It was to form an annual cultural event that would long outlive the crew!

The speeches at the finale by Olaria and John were filled with satisfaction, joy, warmth and delight. The video records would become a huge moment in the history of both worlds.

Faint morning light finally brought an end and soon the crew were asleep. No one had been on board the Sunstreamer and the final sortie of the day was to return the second lander to the Sunstreamer where, for the first time, the computers had been, and would continue to be on sole active Watch.

CHAPTER 22

Moon Orbit, Earth

Departure day was emotional. In the field on which the Lander was sitting and where the crew had been meeting for what now seemed like an entire lifetime, considerably more than one thousand Olarians had physically turned up to say goodbye. The crew were standing round talking to groups all over the field, and many people were saying their farewells to Olaria. The crew had been told the entire Olarian world was watching with concern as Olaria finally said farewell and with an arm around my shoulders and one around Chand—who had been around for 2450 years and was the more senior member of Olaria's primary health group, now her companion for this journey—she walked quietly up to the lander, turned briefly to wave and then stepped inside.

It's hard to describe the extraordinary depth of emotion in that place known now by Olarians and Humans alike as Human Haven. Never in the lives of the crew had so much feeling been attached to a lander departure, but every member of the crew was in tears! It was very quietly, amazing. As the lander lifted off to meet the Sunstreamer, there was complete quiet. Raille had been, only intermittently on duty during the final onboard watch and some of the Olarians had said their goodbyes to him from the field, Human Haven, some others had made the jump to Sunstreamer to hug him and say goodbye, for now! Not least because they loved to visit the spacecraft.

The three days on the Flight Deck, as we journeyed home, were quiet and tense. What would our return actually portend? I could hardly bear to sit on the flight deck, but it was not just there, the whole ship felt tightly strung. Not least was a feeling of concern for Olaria and her companion, Chand. This was the most extraordinary deviation from any organisational procedure any of us had ever experienced. It had sounded like a great idea sitting in the Human Haven. Now we were going to enter what was arguably the most tightly controlled area of Space. There was more surveillance of the actual Orbital Space around the Earth and the Moon than anywhere in the universe.

Immediately, the Sunstreamer emerged from the final Instantaneous Transit Zone, Olaria cloaked it in an energy shield then picked up the searching energy scanners and completed the compensating invisibility shifts making it totally invisible to any scanning capabilities from either the Earth or Moon Bases which was an inconceivable feat considering the enormous speed at which Sunstreamer was travelling. The speed with which Olaria had cloaked us was fast enough not to set off a code red alarm. The scanners had picked up a flash of us and the computers would be examining it with unrelenting intensity. They had identified us, they believed, however, their hailing and increased surveillance could no longer find us, thanks to Olaria's very considerable abilities.

Every observation station was on max alert, and every vessel presently in sight of the Moon and Earth Stations was searching for us. We were decelerating as fast as we could whilst avoiding establishing any ripples in our travel corridor. The computers managing the high-intensity orbital scanners around the moon believed they might have had an image of us during the early stages of our deceleration but, if they had, they certainly lost us as we slowed to approach moon orbit.

We had set up a hue and cry but, their best efforts lost us hours out from orbit. Olaria was nearly exhausted manipulating the energy envelope that was keeping us invisible to the searching scanners. John had looked at Tanzin; *Tanzin can you plot us a visually disorienting path to high Orbit over moon base 1?*

Less than a minute later, the navigators screen was streaming a series of equations and instructions that the computers were chewing over until a few seconds more and Lotus set the screen glowing in its soft green. John issued his instructions to follow the new navigational instructions. And within a minute the Orbiting observation computer reported the anomaly had appeared too no longer be present. We knew a great deal of intense reviewing of all the sighting data would be going on and would continue until it was established what had been seen, or that whatever it was absolutely could not be determined. At which point, an extended watch would be established for all Earth and Moon orbital areas. We were going to need to be super careful. Olaria did understand.

She was impressed with the extent of the range and diligence of the protective systems. She did, however, believe she had us covered.

As we slid into moon orbit, the chatter on the communication frequency bands became intense and Olaria found herself shutting its cacophony down. Before she and her companion, Chand, engaged with the human world, they spent more than thirty minutes examining the energies available to them in this new solar system. They need not have been concerned, everything they needed was as available here as it had been in their own solar system. Olaria freed her mind from her chair in the control room and moved it out over the surface of the moon, covering the bases located in several spots around it, then over the next days concentrated on earth only 380 odd thousand miles away, spreading her consciousness slowly over the blue planet. A truly beautiful planet, which after several minutes she knew to be entirely compatible with her own life form. She quickly noticed some of the dysfunctional aspects of existence on Earth we had been sharing with her.

John was monitoring all Space Fleet channels. At the end of day one, a Battlecruiser was being prepared for a Check and Rescue mission to take all necessary steps to locate and retrieve Sunstreamer and her crew. Departure was established for three days' time. John knew the time frame was tight, but the plan was to contact the head of SFC before that time, ensuring no rescue mission was commenced.

When Olaria returned on the third day to Sunstreamer, she spoke with the crew. She communicated in that hour, a litany of disturbing observations and conclusions that would shape the thinking of the eight of us for the rest of our lives. Would ultimately contribute to changing the course of human history and the direction of the working lives of our crew. In the end it was an inevitable consequence of all we had been through. A very different future would face all of us as a result of the last 14 days. During her time Olaria had, with John's help, identified the key players: Political, Organisational, Religious, Business Leaders, Media and Space Fleet Command. At the end on the final day of the Sunstreamer's Mission return deadline John sent the following communication:

To: Commander in Chief and Chief Executive Officer Dr. Miyuki Khan, Space Fleet Command

  Moon Fleet

  From: Captain: Space Explorer Vessel Sunstreamer: John Washington

Subject: Current Status of the Explorer Vessel Sunstreamer: Extraordinary
Circumstances.

John stopped speaking to ETHEL. How to phrase the very first part of this communication so the reader would be attentive and willing to understand? The experience with the Olarians suggested that the usual politics of the organisation were not necessarily the most effective way to get desired outcomes. Duplicity and cunning no longer seemed the best way to proceed, so instead he decided on honesty and directness. He resumed speaking:

'Dr. Khan, we have made contact with an Alien Species who inhabit Omega5Z3, they call themselves Olarians. You will thus understand that our mission in its original form became impossible to carry out. Omega5Z3 is their home planet.

We are fully cognisant of the Alien Protocols. However, they have proven impossible to follow and inadequate for our circumstances. The Olarians are more powerful individually and collectively than it is easy to imagine.

Our vessel is presently holding in an Extreme Stationary Orbit over Moon Base 1. We have on board the most senior representative of the Olarian Society, a woman who goes by the name Olaria and her companion.

The Sunstreamer is presently rendered invisible by her. She has been alive 1825 years but is biologically 38 years old. This pattern of longevity results from the Olarians having learned to manage ageing. Neither the Sunstreamer nor our planet is, in our estimation, in any danger from the Olarians. Quite the contrary. And Olaria is insistent that we remain invisible to you for the moment as she awaits your response to her requests. However, please be quite clear that we have had no choice but to breach the Alien Protocols.

This race has solved many of the problems that plague us. They have done this in the complete absence of any tool culture. We are designating them, Energy Telepaths, although they are truly fully telepathic and telekinetic.

In order to return to Earth ensuring both our own and their safety, we have had to spend a significant period of the five days of the mission in orbit over Omega5Z3 (now Olar) negotiating with them. However, at no time were our lives placed in jeopardy by them and our relationship with them has been without exception respectful.

It has been necessary to bring Olaria, the Head of the Council on Olar, for her to explore Earth for herself. This was not a demand of hers or the Olarians, quite the contrary. We asked her to risk the voyage with us. She is willing to meet with an appropriately constituted group of people, which she imagines would include, Heads of State, Senior Space Fleet Command Executives, Heads of major global corporations and a wide spectrum of members of the world press, if she is convinced that you have acted in good faith. She would first like to meet you face to face.

Please treat this seemingly disrespectful request with honest consideration. Although you would not be aware of it, she already has seen and gained some understanding of you personally and is fully capable of monitoring your plans for this meeting. Her offer to meet is both a courtesy and a genuine offer of friendship. Be assured that she is actually able to monitor the thoughts and feelings of people on Earth from Sunstreamer, improbable as this may seem. The Olarians have no concept of political and bureaucratic duplicity, and Olaria wanted to ensure that I did not mislead you with respect to her ability to do this. She has already spent three days studying the planet and its peoples, which is why we have reported in three days late but short of a Search and Rescue Mission launch. That task has left her with some extremely unfortunate understandings about us. When you get to understand the Olarians, you will see how she has reached her conclusions.

I am writing this communication at her request under no duress. I am recommending that her offer be accepted. Please note that I am making these arrangements because she agrees that following our usual procedures is not a sound idea. She is capable of arranging this meeting herself. Both the Olarians and our Biomedical Officer agree that the Olarians are genetically almost identical to us!

We are assuming you will wish this meeting to occur. Please understand that we are obliged to return her to her home planet almost immediately! This means we must exit our present orbit in no more than seventy-two hours. My sincere apologies, however, this has had to be made non-negotiable. I am sorry about this but her health demands it and to get her people to agree to let her and her companion come, we had to guarantee it.

Be assured, this race has no territorial aspirations. They have no need. Their planet is in pristine condition. However, they do have a problem with which they believe we can help.

This is a delicate matter involving a second civilisation inhabiting a sealed area of the planet.

For this problem to be resolved, probably over about a year, they wish to borrow two of our officers: Our PsycHologist Dr. Zed Eko and our Vegetation Analyst and Linguist, Dr Raille Korzyst. These requests are not negotiable, they constituted a part of our agreement with the Olarians and both Officers have expressed their willingness to be voluntarily involved.

Please accept my assurances that these people could, with no real difficulty, reduce our most heavily armed and powerful Battlecruiser to space dust in an instant from so far distant from their planet that the Battlecruiser would not even be aware directly of the planet.

This said, I would like to stress that the Olarians are non-aggressive and non-territorial. Their entire civilisation is devoted to learning, which they have done with amazing effectiveness for the thousands of years of their lives.

I have said as much as I believe will be useful for you in reaching a decision, except to say that both Raille and Zed have agreed that they are willing and even enthusiastic about spending a year with the Olarians working to help solve their problem, in exchange for receiving the best education the Olarians can offer them.

In the circumstances in which we found ourselves, we have at all times attempted to remain within the Space Fleet Command Protocols in so far as they are able to take account of these unusual circumstances. They are, as we will show, in need of a comprehensive rewrite.

I tender this communication respectfully, in the hope that it will be clear that meeting the first Alien Civilisation of which we, at least, are aware, has been a valuable experience, from which I believe both civilisations will benefit.

They now, all six or seven hundred million of them, speak fluent English and, if I understand Raille, they would be capable of learning any other language spoken on Earth with ease!

Would you please respond to this message using Captains' unique Sunstreamer side channel Priority 1, in whatever way is decided, at your earliest convenience, as we are committed to returning Olaria to her home planet departing no later than three earth days from now.

Signed Respectfully: John Washington
Captain
Explorer vessel Sunstreamer

Date: 09 /10 / 2096

Ps. I am fully cognisant of the likely suspicion and distrust with which this communication will be received by some. In the interests of the human race, please do not allow this attitude to guide your decision.

PPS. If you need a test of the capacity of our guest, I suggest you arrange to have launched at least one or any number of unarmed drones at precisely 1201. This will be twelve hours exactly from the timestamp of this communication. Launch from any sites on earth or the moon and watch for their instant destruction. I offer this suggestion merely to at least give the sceptics pause. And please, ensure ALL Transport Comptrollers do NOT initiate any other launch activities during this five or ten-minute period.

_____

(Dr. Khan, please contact me using our secure Holo side-channel to confirm details of this and other arrangements.)

You do not get to be CIC of the world's most powerful conglomerate organisation without exceptional qualities of intelligence, knowledge, judgement and an intuitive grasp of risk management, not to forget, extensive deep political connections. Miyuki Khan had been Space Fleet Command's Commander in Chief for eight years before which she had been in very senior positions in most key roles in the Command. She had very strong family connections with some of the largest and most powerful Organisations both Military and Civilian on the planet, and she knew her way around Big Business and Big Government and had close relationships with some of the most significant figures in the world Media. Her family had over the last three generations become a Global Dynasty known and respected on every continent.

So, John's request neither disturbed nor seriously challenged her, but it definitely excited her curiosity and interest, more than any event she could remember. She knew immediately that today was a day she would never forget, and it had only just begun.

Miyuki sat quietly in her office, thinking through the implications of John's communication before contacting him. She knew this was probably the single most significant event in the history of Space travel and was perhaps the most significant event in the history of humanity, maybe since creation. Whatever and whenever that had actually been. She knew this was a time for incredibly careful thought and action. She had an alien, an immensely powerful alien apparently, stationary in one of her Explorer vessels somewhere above her. Apparently, a friendly and... She did of course have to find out and she did have to look after her crew but knew her responsibilities went far beyond these.

'John, Dr. Khan.' Her voice and image through the Holo. A brief silence, then; 'Dr. Khan, many thanks for contacting me so promptly, I think we need to talk.' Sitting beside John in his cabin was a very attractive young woman Miyuki had never seen before.

My pleasure also, Olaria said, *I visited you during the last three days whilst I was travelling around your planet. You were not aware of me. I visited several members of your family, Heads of State, Heads of Industry and Government, and I took a long and careful look at many thousands of your living areas, city and rural and I examined your atmosphere oceans and sub-surface structures.*

Olaria watched Miyuki and followed her thoughts and emotions as she shared this information, surprise and very carefully modulated interest. *John has kindly suggested, and I do mean suggested, that this brief engagement should be between you and I initially to set up some ground rules for a more comprehensive meeting which we do urgently need to have.*

It took Miyuki a moment to realise that Olaria was not using the auditory channel on the Holo. Miyuki was hearing her, directly in her head. You are correct, Olaria said without Miyuki speaking. *My audible communication with you is telepathic, My English is getting better, but still not quite fluent enough for a truly complex conversation.*

Miyuki smoothed her mind and said, 'Thank you for that information, Olaria. How can I be most helpful here?'

John spoke. 'I believe Ma'am, we need you to set up the test I suggested. I think it will establish for all the key players an unambiguous reason for our guest to be taken seriously as military capability and power are key influence levers in our world. Ma'am, this is very difficult and uncomfortable for me because of our relationship. However, none of us could think of any other realistic way to do this. It is a situation without precedent. If you were willing to set up with the necessary authorities, the test I have suggested, then the discussions that must take place for a satisfactory outcome to this extraordinary situation will, I believe, become possible. Do you agree?'

Miyuki was silent for a moment, Olaria watched her process her anxiety and her concerns until she had reached what was really an inevitable conclusion.

'I think you are right. With all my reservations, I understand that this is a sound method of establishing your credibility Olaria and as soon as the test is done, I would like to meet with you here in my office if you think that appropriate.'

Olaria did. At this point there was really no more to be said, well, that was of course untrue, there was a great deal more to be said, but once Olaria's credibility was established amongst the powerful players involved in setting it up, the next step would be a mere formality.

'I will, as you have suggested, John, set the test up for exactly 12 hours from the timestamp on your message. I look forward Olaria to meeting with you. John, we will need to talk more later.'

'Yes Ma'am.'

The Holomonitor went dead.

12 unarmed drones were launched at precisely 1201 from sites all over the planet and the moon. At 1201, and a period between 5 and 30 seconds, every drone was reduced to dust.

The meeting took place one hour later.

Dr. Miyuki Khan's office was appropriately set up for the present Commander in Chief Space Fleet Command. She sat in her office, facing the figure of Olaria who had simply appeared in one of her visitors' chairs. That it was precisely on time for their scheduled meeting did not make the sudden appearance less disturbing. The two very senior and powerful women looked at one another. Carefully. Miyuki in her late 40s was dressed in a tailored white shirt and tailored Space Fleet Command pants. Olaria looking her 38 years, wore her traditional garb, shimmering energy wear, the colours and patterns of which subtlety changed, constantly, but barely perceptibly.

My apology for creating surprise, and for arriving unannounced, she said. However, your security people seemed a little jumpy and I had no desire to create any sort of situation, before we met. May I also thank you, for agreeing to see me.

Miyuki quickly collected herself, calmed her feeling of surprise and smiled welcomingly at Olaria.

'That was an impressive entrance!' She smiled. 'Very impressive! But just a little disconcerting. My apology for being startled, however, in my entire life, I have never seen anyone just appear like that, in a chair.'

This was a novel situation for both. The stakes were high. For a moment they looked at one another. There was, however, a difference; unlike Miyuki, Olaria knew all Miyuki was thinking and feeling, so had an accurate, clear and as it happened, respectful impression of her hostess. And, although Miyuki had been clearly briefed on this aspect of her guest, its full and comprehensive consequences had really not yet sunk in.

Olaria was also aware of how their distinct realities were impacting this strange and unprecedented meeting. She said, *I feel the need to remind you, although I know you have been briefed, I do constantly see and hear what you are thinking and feeling; it is the nature of my people. As you are aware, I am speaking directly into your mind, I might still have a little difficulty carrying on this conversation with spoken language. This does of course mean that your automatic recording devices only hear you although your cameras will see both of us.*

There was a delicious sense of subtle testing in their postures as each watched.

Am I being clear Dr. Khan?

'Please call me Miyuki.'

Certainly, I understand Miyuki that you are seeking a position of advantage from which to manage this meeting. May I suggest, this might not be the most advantageous strategy here?

Miyuki frowned, her hand still hovering over the security alert button recessed into the top edge of her desk. She had not moved it from the instant she had been startled and automatically reached for it.

It would probably be best if you did not actually press it. Olaria's voice, very gently, inside her head.

Of course, Olaria was right, Miyuki was aware. The scene confronting someone entering the room would be considerably more than weird.

Miyuki's hand stilled and moved slowly away to rest gently on her desktop. She had seen the destruction this creature could wreak simultaneously on the dozen drones, whilst herself, on board Sunstreamer. She showed just the tiniest brief sign of a frown as she processed this unusual situation.

'It seems,' she said, 'As though you have the advantage here.'

Olaria continued watching her, listening-in and thinking. *Miyuki, it is not my intention to play the game of one-upmanship with you, I think that is what Zed called it. I need your help and we need to get along. We have far too short a time in which to achieve this. However, I want to persuade you that we may be able to mutually benefit one another, you and I and my world and yours. Zed and John Washington both agree that you are probably the key figure in making this possible. They believe that if I can persuade you, you can make it happen. Zed assured me I would find you interesting and more than capable of assessing the situation my presence here would create. His assessments have so far seemed remarkably, 'spot on', I believe, is your phrase.*

'Olaria, they have perhaps more faith in me than is deserved. However, I believe I can help, and I understand your time frame is very tight. Correct me if I am wrong. You want me to allow the Sunstreamer and her crew to return with you to Olar (Omega5Z3) first to return you, and I will have no hesitation in cutting orders for that journey. However, you wish them to stay for a period of approximately a year to assist you in dealing with a problem that has to do with another race who also inhabit your world.'

Miyuki smiled, and Olaria saw immediately she liked and trusted Zed.

I would really like your willing co-operation in the proposal I want to put to your world, but, if you feel, for whatever reasons, you will not support it, I am quite willing to simply have the Sunstreamer return me home and it then return here. In which case I think we probably need, for the present, to keep our worlds at arm's length, which seems to me a less than desirable outcome.

Olaria watched her carefully, assessing the exact impact of her message and the intent of Miyuki. She noticed Miyuki was struggling with a lifetime of competitive experiences that were not win/win experiences. She was pleased with the wealth of value dilemmas Zed had known would be inherent in this situation especially for Miyuki. Otherwise, Miyuki's behaviour would have seemed unhealthy, and she realised that in fact she believed it was, although it was clearly a necessity in this environment, and she felt sad.

Miyuki was looking at her intently. 'You know what I am thinking don't you?'

Yes.

'My god I am really struggling to know how I can deal with you. My whole life has been a struggle and hiding many of my thoughts and feelings has been an absolute necessity for me to succeed. You have scythed through that in an instant and I feel I must apologise, but I am finding you more than disconcerting, quite frightening in fact, but also exciting and refreshing!'

Her honest confusion and her intelligence and capability were opening a chink in the destructive negativity and resistance that permeated the politics of this enormous and powerful bureaucracy.

Olaria had got under her skin. Zed had been a small piece of the leverage. Miyuki felt strong and positive feelings toward Zed, Olaria could feel them. Leverage she was quite willing to use if it would lead to co-operation.

'Correct me if I am wrong but you are actually capable of totally destroying us, aren't you?' Miyuki's voice was a little tense and had an edge of disquiet.

Yes... and No..., that is not something I could consider because of the values that hold me and my society together. I say this, knowing as I do, that you are now considering how you might take advantage of what you are evaluating as a weakness in my position. I think you might be wise to consider me in some other way than as an opponent to be bested. I have not come here to compete with you. I would like you to consider that I am not weak and vulnerable because I will not act in a savage and destructive way toward you in order to achieve my ends, which, in this instance, are actually to build an interesting and mutually beneficial relationship with your world.

Olaria could see Miyuki's mind churning through ideas, seeking some way to manage this situation. Then she seemed to get it, suddenly. Play along. However, before she spoke Olaria intervened.

Please Miyuki, playing along, what you call duplicity and deception cannot work to bring mutual benefit to our relationship, nor solve the issues and problems that beset our worlds, and I believe probably, all worlds, however many there may be... Would it help you if we brought Zed into this meeting?

Miyuki looked at her with a mixture of bewildered amazement. This was power of a kind she actually could not yet grasp. So, in desperation,

'Yes'.

Then please excuse me for a moment whilst I talk with him, I will need to project him here. You should know, the whole crew of your Sunstreamer have been listening in on this conversation.

Please! Olaria held up her hand, I understand your feelings about privacy and the significance of your position, but these do not exist in my world, our society is substantively, open, there is virtually no privacy, as it is thought of as destructive, unpleasant, and avoidable, for the most part experienced as divisive, and I think your word might be corrosive. I cannot, in the time we have, help you understand why this is so, however, if you could stretch your credulity a little and consider that we have made the lack of privacy a quality of value to everyone, this would I believe, help. Also, I am not in any way attempting to undermine your authority nor your position, but this is an unusual circumstance and calls for unusual acts. I feel sure, on that you will agree.

Miyuki nodded, Olaria could feel her struggle. *Miyuki, I know this is being thrown at you in far too large chunks, but we have no time and no real options here if we are to be successful. You may rest assured that your crew will never use what they hear here to embarrass you in any way, you have my complete assurance in this. I need you to use your more than impressive intelligence to reframe your engagement with my value system. The crew have had some days to adjust to this.*

Miyuki stopped thinking for a moment and accessed her feelings, she was teetering on being overwhelmed. But you do not get to be in so senior a position in so enormous and powerful and competitive an organisation without being also possessed of courage and flexibility.

'Please,' she said, 'Get Zed...'

And Olaria was gone. Miyuki sat still, soothing her tensions, using her meditative routine to ease the tensions from her mind and body. Two minutes passed. She had left instructions she was not to be disturbed, however, a tiny red sensor in her desk was telling her there was an urgent message for her when she was available.

Before she could reply to it, Olaria and Zed were sitting in her office. She nearly leapt out of her chair, then settled as the warm smile from Zed connected her back to reassuring known reality and they exchanged a brief and connected greeting. Zed's attitude was friendly and appropriately respectful, Miyuki's status feathers were not ruffled. Then Olaria spoke.

First, yes, I have brought a projection of Zed, not his actual body! Also, I know you are concerned with your message, if I may, they wish to inform you they believe they have located Sunstreamer and wish to know what they should do about it. Extremely clever, they analysed the discrepancy between returning scanner signals in terms of variation and have located the probable spot the Sunstreamer is stationed. They are correct, that was a very elegant process they used, I had not thought of that when I cloaked her. Please ask your people not to attempt to reach her, I have cloaked the ship in an energy field that might result in someone being harmed if they try and penetrate it and I prefer not to be responsible for that.

Miyuki looked at Zed. 'It would be best,' he said.

Olaria paused in the midst of their conversation. Five to ten seconds passed before she spoke again; *I have just taken action to prevent a swarm of heavily armed small flying vessels, whose trajectory was clearly designed to take them to Sunstreamer, from reaching their target.*

She put the flight visually on Miyuki's screen.

I've frozen them, she said, *I do not want to harm them, but this is outrageous behaviour.*

'You're dead right it is!'

Miyuki was enraged. She punched a button on her comms. unit. 'This is White Pegasus give me Triple A priority to Black Hawk.'

A second later, Air Marshall Gregory McGleish's face appeared on her screen.

'McGleish are you a complete idiot? On what authority have you launched Dark Knight Attack Wing to intercept my Explorer vessel. Get them back NOW! You have maybe 30 to 40 seconds to issue return instructions before you could be responsible for the total destruction of the entire wing. Have you forgotten what happened to the drones yesterday? Apart from losing 100 of your topflight crew, you will lose several billion dollars' worth of assets and possibly be responsible for starting an intergalactic war with a friendly and intelligent new species quite capable of wiping us off the map. Do you need me to be any clearer? Your wing is currently being held captive at 130,000 feet do you understand?' Miyuki gave him about 5 seconds to reply. He began a blustering challenge. but Miyuki cut him off; 'Gregory take a look at your interceptors' current flight profile.' 5 more seconds passed.

'My god what's going on?'

'Our visitor, who picked up your insane behaviour, has kindly refrained from rendering the entire wing a cloud of space dust, are you reading me?'

He was. 'But...'

'Gregory recall them NOW you have 20 seconds to have them turned around and heading back to their base or you may possibly lose them all. Go. Whilst I hold.'

Olaria released the fighters and listened.

'Dark Knight, Dark Knight, this is Starlight One, this is Starlight one, abort, abort, abort, return immediately to base, do you copy?'

'Dark Knight leader, I copy you Starlight One and please be informed for 14 seconds our entire wing was immobilised, please inspect our flight profiles.'

Within ten seconds, the wing could be seen descending back into the earth's atmosphere. 'Gregory, well done. I can't talk now I have a visitor. I will contact you shortly. Out.'

Miyuki returned her gaze to Olaria. She took a slow quiet breath 'Thank you,' she said.

It was Olaria's turn to smile.

You clearly are the person I need. Miyuki, when you read Sunstreamer's records, you will know that we have solved a substantial number of the survival problems that plague your planet. So, it may be, we will be able to assist you in resolving some of yours, although, of course, our differences are, in some ways, extreme. We do not have any of the population, climate or oceanic problems I have seen here, perhaps we may be able to assist you with some of these.

When you have examined the information from your crew, who have been sharing our life and ways for the five days they were with us, perhaps you will see some possibilities for using what we have learned. Perhaps just the fact that we seem to have none of your unresolved problems will make us a valuable partner for you.

I am uncertain as to how we are going to be able to use what we have learned, but we are hard at work figuring that out. Your existence and your technology are already causing huge disturbances in our world. Her mind, feverish but not unhappy.

When John has uploaded all the Sunstreamer data on Olar so you will understand us better. He will I am certain, also upload the entire crew recordings of their experiences on my world. These, I believe you will find to be of considerable interest, as per Zed's contract with you and our agreement of understanding with your crew. No personal data has been left on the files; however, no other alterations have been made. The recordings will offer you some gateways to solving some of the problems I have seen exist for your planet. What they have learned about our society, may also prove of some value to your world, I am less certain of this.

Olaria stopped speaking for a moment to assess how Miyuki was feeling about this entire disturbing situation. Realised she was handling it well, in the circumstances, and continued. Whilst they are with us, should you approve, I will undertake a journey with the Sunstreamer to a nearby galaxy where I have reason to believe, a world suitable for your purposes might exist. I will also help Tanzin complete your star maps for our solar system and a galaxy nearby.

Miyuki simply nodded, she was pretty much overloaded, but was coping! *If you are agreeable, I would be pleased to invite a small party of eight people to visit us in six months for, say, two weeks, to get a firsthand experience of our world. I believe you will need about that time to process all the data Sunstreamer presently holds. If you decide to take up this offer, the vessel must be similarly free of any armament, like Sunstreamer. I think you might find what we have learned very helpful. Your crew reports should assure you of this. What do you think?*

Miyuki was already planning to be one of the members of that visiting party. She was clear about the power and had some sense of the values of the Olarians and realised this might be a unique opportunity for Humanity to find another path.

During the following hours she communicated with every one of the key players involved in this drama, including a genuine spread of the top world media organisations. Using her position, her connection to the crew and Olaria, she created a non-negotiable deadline. Everyone who wishes to have contact with their intergalactic visitor will be in the World Council Meeting Centre in exactly twenty-four hours.

'There are to be absolutely no armed security in the entire building. No weapons of any kind.' Her instructions were explicit and non-negotiable. Anyone unwilling to abide by them will not be permitted to enter the building. The world press has been notified and selectively invited, they will broadcast the entire event live, that also is a non-negotiable item from our visitor.'

Miyuki asked Olaria if she would be willing to check the security arrangements to confirm Miyuki's instructions have been carried out. She agreed. Miyuki spent a not inconsiderable time during the period up to the time of the meeting dealing with a substantive number of truly angry and frustrated senior members of the world community.

In the end, she had her way. However, in the hour prior to the meeting Olaria saw someone interfering with the Media links to the outside world and she spoke to the Peta.

I need your technical help. It looks to me as though the output from the Council Chamber is being interfered with. However, I am unclear as to what exactly they are doing, and I will only know when the equipment is transmitting, and I can follow the power trail. Let me help you trace this process so you can show me how to remedy it.

Ten minutes passed before John, Peta and Gerard, using Olaria's images, located what they recognised as re-routing technology. With Olaria's help they disabled the rerouting network while Olaria, her partner Chand and Zed were then able to trace those responsible.

A team belonging to two of the world's largest global mining conglomerates were playing a remarkably high stakes game to deal with Olaria and any influence she might have. Four individuals who would be in the meeting, powerful and important players in the Council were identified and Olaria now knew who she had to manage.

No weapons were brought into the building. Olaria simply appeared on the chair on the podium from which she was to speak, in English this time, and arranged herself to be visible to the Holo recorders. She was warmly welcomed by the President of the World Council. She used the first second to destroy the bypass circuitry identified by the Sunstreamer crew.

Then she began. First naming the four men who had arranged to ensure the recordings of the meeting did not reach the outside world and informed the meeting that she had destroyed the entire bypass circuitry. She asked the four men to explain their intent. They lied about her accusations. She dismissed them saying; *I am already familiar with the patterns of lying, duplicity, dishonesty, dissimulation and the cunning twisting of meaning which you use to maintain your power base, wealth and position.*

She then immobilised them, in their seats. Those around were not aware of exactly what had happened. They all appeared normal and silent.

These patterns of behaviour do not exist on our planet. She continued. *Please understand, I am not attempting some silly racial or species competition here, the absurdly violent and insensitive killing that is carried on in the name of some deity or other on your planet, is not present on Olar, nor the acquisitive greed and interpersonal ignorance and insensitivities; it took us many discussions with your crew to understand them. I know you are not going to appreciate an alien being highly critical of your world, however, speaking the truth and what you refer to as, 'telling it how it is', are ordinary aspects of our world, so I probably need to apologise for being unusually blunt and your crew tell me, discourteous; by your standards.*

I have only spent three days observing your world, every continent and as many cities as I could. I have seen here appalling drug abuse and associated destructive behaviour and these also do not exist in our society. Please understand, I am not trying to create an invidious comparison.

She looked quickly into Miyuki and found what she was seeking, Miyuki approved of her approach.

The destruction of the upper atmosphere and the pollution of a great deal of the lower atmosphere and the rubbish and damage both on land and in the oceans are incredibly disturbing to me. The amount of interpersonal cruelty supported through what I understand to be a desperate search for power and status by many and things you call possessions are a phenomenon, almost impossible for me to understand as they have no counterpart on our world. I have had to rely on your Sunstreamer crew to be able to grasp an understanding of why these behaviours are permitted to occur and I again apologise for appearing as the crew keep explaining to me as, rude, insensitive and apparently, disturbing.

Again, she scanned Miyuki and again found support for what she was saying. She continued; *So, now I feel the need again to apologise to you for what I understand is a very negative image for a visitor to paint of another race's planet and behaviour. Yet, as I say these things I am also struck by the amazing achievements of your engineering and technology, far beyond anything on my world, the beauty of your arts, Architecture and the outstanding achievement in the solution of problems that are either unknown or not understood on our planet.*

Please do not take my observations as criticism, I am reporting to you what I have seen in my three days amongst you. Things that amaze me and which I have never seen before. And do not suppose that my planet is free of problems, we have an extraordinarily difficult problem with another race on our planet that we have carelessly failed to address and since your Spaceship visited us, we have realised that you may be able to help solve a problem about which we have the gravest concerns. No society is without flaws, it seems likely that we can finally be of some assistance to you and that you can be of some assistance to us. If, that is, you desire to have such a relationship.

The entire auditorium was still, not a sound, hardly any movement. It was as though the audience was in a trance. The request that I make here needs to be taken on trust as there is no way, in the time I am able to survive here, that I can give adequate proof of any of it. I am authorised to speak for the 6-700 million Olarians on my world. For a few moments I am going to put on Holomonitor a message from the Captain of the crew of your Sunstreamer Explorer Spacecraft. He and his crew have spent five days with us, and he asked to make a brief statement.

John Washington's image appeared on the Holomonitors; 'I am John Washington, presently Captain of the Explorer Spacecraft Sunstreamer, as Dr. Miyuki Khan will affirm for you, and I can attest to the absolute truth of all that Olaria has told you of her authority from Olar. I genuinely hope you will take this opportunity to begin to build the relationship she seeks. I should also tell you that the blunt and seemingly severe criticism the Olarians often give has taken us all of our five days with them to fully appreciate, and I can say as a human being, they often appear to be verbally abusive, however, they have never been anything but kind and supportive and helpful to us, although that is often not how they seem. Even saying this much breaches Space Fleet Command protocols, however, the value of our fortuitous discovery is truly fantastic.'

Olaria continued; *In 36 hours, I must leave here, and will shortly thereafter have crossed the first Wormhole and no longer be in contact with Earth. If you have agreed to allow your spacecraft and its crew to remain with us for the next year to assist us in dealing with our problem we will, I believe, each have an opportunity to solve some problems that so far have eluded each of our worlds.*

On the basis of your existence, we believe that probably other sentient life exists. If we could seek it out together, I think this would be amazing. My request is simple. You must, however, decide if you will agree to it. If you do, we will accept a visit from eight of your people in six months to learn more about us. In that six months you will have had the opportunity to learn everything that Sunstreamer and her crew have learned about us so far. At the conclusion of Sunstreamer's year, I believe our worlds will have had time to adjust to one another in some important ways and we will be able to learn co-operatively together things that may improve all of our lives. Also, I hope to learn some ways to speak with you that will seem less offensive than our natural ways of speech.

If you choose not to release your vessel to help us, we will recognise your right to do that and very sadly say goodbye to you for the present, believing, that at some time in the future, humanity may decide to contact us again. I would like to thank you for providing this opportunity to speak to your world and the several billions of you who have been watching and listening. I bid you for the moment, goodbye.

And she was gone. There was, for a moment, total and complete silence in the auditorium, not so on the surface of the planet nor on the moon.

The silence that followed Olaria's departure was absolute. No one moved, no one shuffled. Then almost as if someone had lifted their finger off the pause button, an almost uncontrollable babble broke out. There were those who thought Olaria arrogant, high-handed, disrespectful, unbelievable; and there were those, who did not.

'By what right did she imagine she could just borrow a billion-dollar spaceship and its crew for a year to solve the problems of an oh so perfect society?'

It was a loud and angry voice.

It seemed they were unaware of their guest being able to listen in! It was not as though Miyuki had not warned them, each and every one of Olaria's capabilities, it seemed perhaps they either did not remember or did not care.

Miyuki thought, *Olaria, are you there?*

Yes, and I feel as though I should apologise to you for making such a mess of that meeting. But what you call diplomacy is unfortunately anathema to us, and that is, it would appear, unfortunate for us.

Miyuki was less upset. *Be patient Olaria and watch how this kind of diplomatic gamesmanship is played out.*

At the President's request for silence the room settled down. He then called on Miyuki to speak; 'Your visitor, Dr. Khan!'

'Thank you, Mr. President. Members of this extraordinary assembly. We have a choice. You cannot have forgotten how difficult it has been for us to reach agreement on many matters, even ones connected to our survival on this planet. The person you just met, heard, is the leader of a society who have solved the problem of longevity, Olaria looks to be thirty-eight years old, but has been alive for fifteen hundred years. We have not been able to solve the problem of longevity. The Olarian society has solved the problems of lifelong health, we have not. They have solved these and a number of planetary survival issues, we have not. They are offering to work with us to help us with

211

problems, so entrenched, so resistant to solution on our world that we are trying to resolve them by taking them, unresolved, to other worlds.

Does anyone here seriously believe that the first contact with sentient life in the universe, life so close to our own that she could pretty well pass for one of us, should be allowed to slip away because of our unwillingness to help them, our inability to grasp an opportunity to possibly halt our own self-destruction?

Most of you were invited here because you have a global reputation for being able to play the long game. Olaria lives on a planet, in a galaxy previously unknown to us, quite probably thousands of light years away, one which we could not have visited twenty years ago. Yet, she spoke to you in perfect English, having been in contact with humans for eight days. Does anyone here imagine they could learn to speak fluent Olarian in that time? Even the world's top linguists, one of whom is a member of Sunstreamer's crew, believes it will take him at least two months to be able to converse at a basic level in either Olarian or Cretian the language of the other civilisation on Olar and he has only a very light smattering of Olarian at this time!

Twenty-three hours ago, at our request, to test our Captain's claims of her power, our visitor reduced twelve unarmed drones, launched simultaneously from every corner of the globe and the moon, to dust, in just five seconds; so, I think we are very fortunate that her people have not fought a war for approximately three thousand years. We on the other hand seem to be pressed to go three years without one.

The Captain of our Explorer vessel was sent to Olar seeking a new planet for human habitation, because, as you all know, we are not competent to manage co-operatively our population, our resources, nor our environment. He assures me he has the data on board Sunstreamer to prove conclusively, these people, these Olarians, do not only NOT have ANY of these problems, but have figured out how to fully reconstitute the toxic by-products of a toolmaking society such as ours.

So, unless we are so arrogant as to imagine we are the Creme de la Creme of sentient life in the universe, we should probably put away our sensitivities and excessive egos and figure out how we can work with these amazing people—people, because they carry an almost identical genetic footprint to our own!—to manage our world in a more intelligent and effective way whilst we have the chance, now it appears to have been put into our hands; not only by some illusive fate, but by our scientific efforts to explore the Cosmos.

One of our biggest fears has been, that we will populate other planets in other Solar Systems with people capable of creating planetary damage as good as ours, in less time than it has taken us.

Maybe, just maybe, the Olarians will help us build more safe, constructive, viable worlds than we so far have been able to manage.

Miyuki sat down.

There is a great deal that could be told of the following two hours. The outcome, however, with Miyuki's strong recommendation, was ultimately strongly in favour of building the Human-Olarian relationship. Miyuki got her agreement from the world to Allow Sunstreamer and her crew to spend the next year in Olar's Solar System. Olaria agreed to a meeting with twelve rather than eight representatives of Earth in six months and now the question of one day's leave for the Sunstreamer crew and reprovisioning Sunstreamer for a twelve-month mission needed to be arranged.

Olaria removed the cloaking and defensive energy screen around Sunstreamer, and Peta took the Sunstreamer into their standard moon orbit. The maintenance crews settled into their reprovisioning routine and only Raille and Zed chose not to take leave: Raille because there was no one he wanted to see for 24 hours and Zed likewise had no other close relationships on Earth.

CHAPTER 23

Zed & Sunstreamer depart for Olar

The Sunstreamer pulled easily from moon orbit, its powerful silent energy-distributing engines hauling it effortlessly from the blue planet and pouring it out into the blackness of space into what used to feel like dark soulless emptiness. It accelerated to near light speed. Tanzin had set the navigation system to take them to the first Instantaneous Travel Corridor (Wormhole). Almost a day ahead, Zed sat quietly beside Olaria and her companion, his attention focussed on Olaria.

Aboard the Sunstreamer there was an intense undercurrent of excitement.

The silver blue walls of the Sunstreamer glowed peacefully, but not for Olaria. She had witnessed so much collective behaviour which she had heard me describe as bureaucratic stupidity, regulatory rigidity and insensitivity, in her world an experience she had never imagined possible.

She had observed the total abnegation of responsibility for self by people in every walk of life. She had found several people of prestige, power and influence in religion, politics, business, the professions, nearly everywhere, incongruous, dishonest and corrupt, and she knew this was unfair and not completely accurate, but... There seemed no end to the litany of dysfunctions to which her psyche had been subjected but she had also been subjected to beauty, imaginative creativity, thinking about reality and the universe more sophisticated and deeper and complex than her people had ever been able to do! I had been following her and I was, in truth, finding it somewhat depressing. Then I thought about what she was recalling as she became aware of my presence and knew there was something I wanted to say to her.

She released herself from the traumatic review. I thought that what I wanted to say would change her perspective. I wanted to point out, what she had just seen and experienced was the possible future of the Cretians, might be their current situation. I felt the jolt and felt her mind clear. She quietly reviewed her entire experience of the Cretians, allowing me to observe. Interestingly, her experiences of them were extremely limited, she actually had no idea what they were like!

Finally, she turned and looked at me. Her eyes were troubled, but her mind was clear. She had managed to put the complexity of the last days away: some beautiful and brilliant and amazing and some awful and destructive, cruel and disgusting, and she realised, she lived in a society that had no experience of nor understanding of others who might be unlike themselves. The Cretians were as alien to her as the humans had been! A piece of her mind had become aware of how limited their experience of others actually was.

You will be able to help?

The unspoken but clearly formed question sat in my mind. Would we? In truth, in reality, could we? She believed I could. My yes was a given. We talked right up to the first Instantaneous Transit Zone. The tone of our conversation, optimistic and determined. Finally, Olaria turned to me and on her face a smile of real warmth which I felt simultaneously in my mind and through my entire being.

'What?'

The question slid out before I had even a moment to consider it.

I have a gift for you, she said. *It will, I believe, turn out to be perhaps the most astonishing and yet the most complexly disturbing gift anyone will ever give you. I have decided after much soul searching, to give it to you rather than let chance play its part, because, Zed, I find you to be a truly beautiful person, both Olarian and human to your very core. And, and I say this truly and utterly without duplicity, I have sought your help with a problem that you and Raille can perhaps manage between you on our behalf. The year you spend with us will enable me to maximise the likelihood that you will be able to make use of my gift in ways that would be otherwise impossible. I honestly, and without duplicity, but not without some self-interest, have brought you back to Olar for your sake, not alone for ours.*

By this stage my agitation was forcing me to concentrate very hard on simply remaining seated, but I knew Olaria well enough to both trust her and wait.

When I was on earth, I found six other Energy Telepaths, from our experience there should have been seven, but I could not find a seventh, they were like you genetically so far as I could ascertain, and, if I am correct, one of the women must have died! She paused a moment watching the information sink in. I was gobsmacked, Olaria smiled. I opened my mouth to speak, Olaria shook her head, and without more than an instant's hesitation I slid into her mind and asked the question she had known would be foremost in my mind.

'Why did you decide not to tell me whilst we were in Moon orbit?'

Zed, she murmured quietly into my disturbed mind. *I promise you it was not solely for my selfish purposes. We both know what the experience of the first Olarian Energy Telepaths was. I truly believe you will need all the help I can arrange for you during the next year to maximise your meeting and working together with these people to give you a chance at success. And, if you choose, and I would strongly recommend that you do, I will ensure that you learn how to manage longevity for you and your group on earth. Please think carefully on this. Remember our own early and disturbing history. I also need to tell you something my group finally understood about what you call your 'genetic makeup'.*

They finally completed their work the morning we left Olar. It is extraordinary. Your telepathic, telekinetic energy map is almost identical to my father's, to Jard's. It is exceptional. No single individual in our 3000 years of history has possessed so much potential power. There are some aspects of it none of us have ever seen before, ones which, when they compared with my father showed you have extended elements beyond those he possessed. You definitely possess, in addition. therefore, some significant but as yet unknown capabilities.

My mind was racing, I had more to think about now than I could grasp; but perhaps it would be true, the help Olaria and the Olarians could offer me might just allow me and the others to survive in what could conceivably become a very hostile world.

After my initial anger and frustration, I settled down to think about what all this might mean at the end of the year on Olar. I was pleased to be having this extraordinary opportunity and turned to Olaria and she did something she had never done in our time together. She drew me to her into a warm and gentle embrace. We looked at one another and with the entire crew looking on, she kissed me very gently on the lips.

The End. For now.

Phillip Boas

Shawline Publishing Group Pty Ltd
www.shawlinepublishing.com.au